# Say You'll Be There

Mia Denson

Mia Denson

ISBN 978-1-0690913-2-1



Original Illustration and Cover Design: Lisa Jager
Developmental Editor: Lisa Rivers
Typeset: Heili Paluoja

To our husbands, thank you for giving us the time and space over the past two years to embrace our "second job" with all its late nights and laughter-filled writing sessions.

*We love you.*

# One

# Oh Shit

There might be worse ways to spend a warm summer evening than at Trinity Common, but right now, I couldn't think of a single one. This was usually my happy place, but tonight, it was a social sinkhole I couldn't escape. Speed dating. The bar was packed, the crowd of twenty- and thirty-somethings already mingling around the gleaming wood tables decorated with small vases of white flowers and votive candles. Some people might call it romantic, but I wasn't one of them.

Jerry's boss, and the Trinity's new owner, Dan, had decided the best way to boost business was to "capitalize on people's fear of dying alone, but, you know, in a classy way," which meant an evening of awkward small talk and overpriced cocktails. And because Mel and I would do anything for Jerry, we were here – despite the million other things I should be doing.

Meeting a bunch of randoms when I had zero interest in dating didn't even crack the top twenty on my never-ending weekend to-do list. I still had to edit the photos from last weekend's dog wedding before their puppies arrived, finish prepping for the kids' photography class I ran at the YMCA, and deliver the prints for the Doyle-Alousis engagement shoot.

Most importantly, I had to finish my submission for the street photography exhibition at the Worth Gallery, due Monday. That was the one that kept me up at night, huddled over my laptop, sorting through photos that weren't quite ready, for a juried show that could change everything for me. If my submission were successful, I'd get to compete for a chance to win a month-long paid internship with my photography idol, Teo Castillo, in Panama City. It was the kind of opportunity that launched careers and would mean I could focus on creating art that made my soul sing, instead of taking on every job that came my way to make ends meet.

The sharp poke of Jerry's marker on my arm snapped me back to reality, and he slid a blank name tag across the bar. *Oh, right. Speed dating. Fun.*

"Fortify me, Jerry. Fruitiest and most alcoholic drink on the menu, please!" I said, forcing a smile as I grabbed the marker and scribbled out my alias. I handed him my two free drink tickets – the only perk of this hellscape of an evening – and dropped a stack of toonies into the tip jar with a solid plunk.

"You got it, Em." Jerry grinned, already prepping my favourite, a strawberry margarita, and Mel's usual, gin and tonic. "Thanks again for coming. It was tough to find enough women for tonight. I know this is the last place you want to be, so I'll make it a double."

Jerry was one of my favorite humans. He was sweet, funny, an excellent listener, and knew how to make all the best drinks.

"Thanks," I said. "I've got a ton to do when I get home so won't be here long."

The official "speed dating" part of the evening was only scheduled for an hour, so I'd be out of here in an hour and a half, tops.

Mel rolled her eyes and planted both hands firmly on my shoulders. Her smooth, flawless brown skin glowed, and her dark brown eyes sparkled behind thick, natural lashes.

"Emma, stop. You've brushed your teeth, done your hair, and put on makeup. That dress is cute as hell. You're twenty-six, for god's sake, and you deserve a night out. You've been cooped up in your little hobbit hole for the past month, obsessing over that portfolio – which is already amazing. A couple of hours here won't kill you. Meet a hot guy. Take one of these chuckleheads home with you, and I'll crash at Jer's."

I snorted. Mel and Jerry knew my stance on one-night stands – been there, done that, and generally, not worth the effort – and I definitely wasn't looking for a relationship. Nine months ago, after my last one had ended the way it always did – with Jason frustrated that I wouldn't open up, and me pretending I was too independent for needy guys – I'd called a moratorium on dating. With the singular exception of my dad, experience had taught me that men didn't stick around when things got real. I told myself I was too busy for a relationship, but deep down I knew I was just done putting myself in a position to be let down.

"I don't have time to pretend to be interested in some guy's fantasy football team or the startup he swears is about to take off."

Mel grinned and scanned the bar. "Lucky for you, there are options tonight." She nodded towards a guy in a bright orange high-visibility shirt with broad shoulders and thick arms balanced by a slight belly hanging over his belt. "I bet he could build you a sturdy bookshelf from scratch and then throw you up against it for a quickie before leaving for work in the morning."

"Hah, as tempting as that sounds, I think I'll stick to polite conversation and an Irish goodbye."

Jerry cleared his throat, wiped his hands on a towel, and gestured to the other end of the bar, where Anusha clicked on her microphone. She stepped out from behind the bar, her three-inch heels tapping on the wood floor as she addressed the crowd. "Alright, everyone, time for your first matches!"

"Unto the breach, dear friends!" I downed the rest of my margarita as Jerry slid me another.

Tucking my scorecard under my arm, I pinched the stem of my glass and toasted Jerry and Mel as I turned towards table fourteen. I wound my way through, careful not to spill my drink, as the rest of the bar's patrons swirled around me. The buzz of nervous chatter blended with the Arkells' cover of "Gimme! Gimme! Gimme!" as we found our seats.

I sat down and spotted Mel, getting settled at her table a few away from mine, and flashed her a subtle slash-across-the-throat gesture. She grinned, unfazed, and sent me an encouraging thumbs up.

As my first match sat down in front of me, I was stunned into silence. He looked like a young Cap'n Crunch – a live action remake that had just stepped off the box. A thick, swooping bleach-blond moustache took centre stage, curling slightly at the ends. His nose and chin were commanding – the kind that could lead a cereal-themed ship into battle, or at the very least, easily sniff out spoiled milk. Two small puffs of bleached curls peeked out from underneath a navy felt hat, trimmed with gold beading.

Bold choice. Kind of weird.

I didn't hate it.

A small grin started on my lips as I took in his…essence. Since I was here anyway, I might as well make the best of it.

"Hi! I'm Victoria!" I said, mustering some polite enthusiasm. "It's nice to meet you." I glanced down at his nametag, then back up to meet his wide blue eyes. "Galadon Wyldfyre? Is Galadon your real name?"

"No. Galadon Wyldfyre is my Dungeons and Dragons character," he said, a hint of pride creeping into his voice. "He's a Gnome Ranger and a master archer. He's also a skilled tracker, of both animals and humans, and has a majestic hawk called Thalos as his loyal animal companion." He lit up as he spoke. "Do you play D&D?" he asked.

"I don't, but maybe you could teach me sometime?" I was always up for learning something new when I wasn't bombarded with deadlines.

"No," Galadon sighed. "I'm looking for a partner. Not a project."

I laughed, taken aback by the Cap'n's blunt dismissal. Was this guy for real?

He scratched a sharp line through my name on his scorecard, flipped it over, and continued an elaborate doodle of a dragon. The artist in me admired the iridescent effect he'd created on the delicate wings and scales using nothing but his blue Bic pen. The woman in me thought he was an asshole.

"Great drawing," I offered after a beat of awkward silence. "I'm an artist. A photographer, but I draw and paint, too. Does your D&D character ride a dragon?"

"No." Galadon glared at me like any idiot would understand that his D&D character wouldn't ride a dragon. "A dragon is a formidable adversary. Our party has not yet formed an alliance with one." He scoffed, shook his head, and returned to his drawing.

I glanced at my watch – only two minutes in. *Fantastic.* Willing the three remaining minutes of our date to go faster, I counted eighty-seven beads on his hat. When Anusha's quacking duck timer went off, I breathed a sigh of relief as Galadon moved on to his next table. Godspeed, Galadon, on your quest for your "partner-not-a-project" D&D-playing woman.

Rupinder was my next match. He spent most of our time bragging that he was set to inherit his grandfather's ghost tour business – "The

6ixth Sense." I had a lot of questions for him: Do the ghosts give the tours? Do they have employee benefits or personal days? What's the proper etiquette for greeting a ghost? Do ghosts prefer foggy nights or is that a stereotype?

Rupinder blinked at me, then said, "Actually, fog's bad for business. Harder to see the apparitions."

He didn't have a lot of other answers for me, but he did give me a two-for-one coupon.

"Time's up!" Anusha called as her timer went off to signal the end of five minutes.

As Rupinder moved off, my attention was caught by the tall, lean Asian guy heading towards me. Beautiful dark hair, long enough to run my fingers through and thick enough to lose an earring in. His plaid button-down and well-worn jeans gave off a casual confidence. A slight buzz from the margaritas had me openly checking him out.

His gaze caught mine, and his lips quirked into a quick grin.

Ready to flirt for my life even though I had no plans to take it any further, I sent him my well-rehearsed soft smile, just as my elbow clipped the edge of the table, sending my margarita sloshing over the rim and splashing onto my hand. The bright pink liquid trickled past my wrist and threatened to drip onto my vintage white lace sundress. *Who did I think I was, wearing white? Have I met me?*

Panicking, I raised my arm to my mouth, dragging my tongue along my forearm to my hand. As I licked the side of the glass and tried to suck back as much as I could, I dipped my nose into my drink, making things a thousand times worse.

The dreamboat was still watching me, a wide smile stretched across his face. I dissolved into laughter, sputtering drops of margarita as he detoured to the bar and grabbed a couple of Wet Naps and a stack of napkins.

He arrived at my table, grinning as he handed them to me and sat down. "I'm Ryan."

"And I'm a complete disaster, thank you." I laughed as I cleaned and dried my face and hands. "I'm Victoria."

"Alright, V. We have five minutes to decide if we're soulmates. I've done a little research, and I have three important questions for you. Are you in?" Ryan's eyebrows quirked up as he pulled out a piece of paper.

He had a great smile and looked like he could build a bookshelf. *No! Bad Emma!*

"Absolutely," I said as I carefully clinked my glass with his, then took a sip and set it back on the table.

“First question: If you could have any superpower, but it could only be used for mundane tasks, what would it be?” He looked at me, pen at the ready to jot down my answers as if this were a police interrogation.

“Hmm. Super-speed. I’m a photographer so I’d love to take more pictures of that fleeting moment before someone has a chance to hide what they’re thinking or feeling. I live for that shot.”

The corner of his mouth ticked upwards as he nodded and scribbled something on his paper.

“You?” I leaned forward, tossing my long dark curls over one shoulder, before resting my chin on the back of my hand.

“Telekinesis. I would never have to leave the couch to get a snack or find the remote. I could open the toughest jars in the world without breaking a sweat and get all the groceries from the car to the kitchen in one trip.” It was clear he’d considered this.

“Sounds like you’re a bit lazy,” I said, grinning.

“Oh, I get plenty of exercise in other ways.” His playful smile returned along with a dimple in his right cheek.

A snicker popped out of my mouth as I considered the logistics of taking a body shot out of that dimple. *Do not lick the nice man’s face, Emma.*

“Next question.” I sipped my drink to cool off.

“If your life had a theme song that played whenever you walked into a room, what would it be?”

“Oooh, good one. Can everyone else hear it or is it only in my head?”

“Everyone, every room. Always.”

“‘Spice Up Your Life,’ by the Spice Girls, the greatest group of all time.”

“You’re spicy then, huh?” His eyes dipped briefly to my full “Rebel in Red” lips as he brought his beer to his, still grinning.

Was it getting a little warm in here? Maybe I should find Jerry and ask him to turn the heat down.

“What’s yours?”

“‘I Drove All Night,’” he said, as if this was the most obvious thing in the world.

I threw my head back and cackled at his proud grin. “The Celine Dion song? Why?”

He waved his hand dismissively as if this was the most ridiculous question I could ask. “We don’t have time for all that now. I’ll save it for our second date.” He paused. “I want someone worth the drive, V.”

“Right.” It sounded like Ryan was looking for something serious. Another reason to stick firm to my plan of not checking anyone off on my scorecard, no matter how interested I might be in taking him for a test drive.

"Question three–" Ryan started, but he was interrupted by the timer signaling the end of our date. He exhaled, shaking his head with an amused smile.

I frowned. "Wait, what's the question?"

He stood up. "I guess you'll have to find me later. Next margarita's on me." He tipped his paper towards me before getting up from the table.

"Sounds good. And Ryan? Thanks for trusting me with your secrets," I replied. "Especially Celine."

"Celine is no dirty little secret, V. She's a national treasure!" There was mock outrage on his face as he pushed in his chair.

I mentally awarded him ten bonus points for good manners. Maybe it was because my parents were teachers, but nothing screamed respect like pushing in a chair when you stood. I was today years old when I realized it was a kink of mine.

*Huh. Hot.*

As I watched him go, my eyes drifted towards a man standing at the bar, his back to me, ordering a beer.

*Damn – now that is a great ass.*

I forced myself to look away.

I was hopeful that Great Ass was on his way to table fourteen, as long as he didn't spend our precious five minutes making balloon animals or acting out scenes from his favourite soap opera. *Oh, who am I kidding, I would fucking love that.*

A little tipsy, my gaze crept back over and locked on his muscular legs as he turned around and approached my table, jeans snug around his powerful thighs.

I pressed my top teeth into my bottom lip, sympathizing with the blue Henley straining across his broad, chiseled chest and powerful arms, the buttons valiantly holding together against the strain of pure masculinity. I parted my lips and blew out an admiring breath. The things that those arms could do to me. A faint scrape of his chair against the floor pulled me back, and he stepped in front of it, ready to take his seat. *Keep your panties on, Emma. No more margaritas, you're cut off.*

As he sat in front of me, I raised my chin to meet his gaze, ready with a flirtatious quip. But then I met his eyes.

Familiar. Unmistakable.

My stomach dropped. My pulse kicked into overdrive.

*Oh, shit. I know those eyes.*

## Two
## August 27, 13 Years Ago

# Beam Me Up, Scotty

The first time I saw Jake Griffin was at my grade nine orientation.

The day had been a blur of awkward icebreakers, questionable cheese pizza, and a tour of my massive new high school – Roberta Bondar Collegiate Institute.

I'd been stressed about high school all summer. I'd heard horror stories about what it could be like here, especially for someone like me who doesn't sit back in a crowd. But despite the overwhelming size of the place, I was starting to get a teensy bit excited. It seemed to have everything I'd been dreaming about. Art clubs and classes, school dances, cute boys, and best of all, freedom. No more silent, single-file lines between classes or needing a note to go to Super Choi's for lunch. My stomach was buzzing, the kind of charged, nervous energy you get after chugging a Mountain Dew Code Red – like I was on the edge of something big.

My best friend Sarah and I exchanged a nervous glance, trying to look calm while mapping out every turn from the front door to our homeroom like we were prepping for an endless round of Subway Surfers. Right atthe library, left at the office, up the haunted stairwell, then past the suspiciously enthusiastic poster for chess club to D 32.

As we headed back to the auditorium, the school seemed to grow, a maze of identical hallways, thousands of aggressively teal lockers, and stairs twisting into unfamiliar wings. I had no clue how to get to my math class on "C and a half" and could already picture myself wandering into the wrong room, sitting down, and only realizing my mistake when the teacher started discussing advanced calculus.

But eventually we arrived back at the auditorium for a high-energy pep rally, the excitement for the new school year pulsing through the crowd.

When the Student Activity Council president called for volunteers to compete in a game of Freeze Dance – another way of humiliating the niners, I guess – for a chance to win a school swag bag with a Bondar gym shirt, water bottle, day planner and temporary tattoo, I did a quick risk versus reward calculation. Then I shot up my hand.

I was wearing my most comfortable DIY high-top Chucks (bedazzled with gold studs all over and spikes up the heel), a well-worn Spice Girls T-shirt, and dark wash skinny jeans. Participation was basically my brand, and I was all about living my best life. I also happened to need a day planner.

"Let's go," I said, grinning as I nodded towards the stage. "One of us is winning this."

I was confident. We hadn't played Freeze Dance for years, but we were pros after playing it at every highly official, two-person meeting of our One Direction fan club.

"No way," Sarah said as she shook her blonde head.

"Come on, please? You know there's nothing I love more than free stuff."

"So go by yourself. I'm trying not to be a loser this year." Sarah eyed the stage like it was a death sentence.

"Come on. You love to dance! Maybe this will get you noticed before the dance team has their tryouts." I pressed my hands together and tilted my head, eyes wide. She exhaled, fingers drumming against her leg.

"Fine," she rolled her eyes, but the corner of her mouth twitched. "I guess I could use another gym shirt."

Sarah always gave in to what she called my "Em-ventures," even if it took some convincing.

I clapped my hands together and she followed me, scooting into the middle aisle and heading for the stage, along with a handful of other brave niners.

As I climbed the stairs to the stage, his glance hit me like a lightning bolt, those gorgeous blue eyes locking onto mine. He'd been one of the group leaders all day and I'd checked him out a few times. And I may have snapped a covert photo to drool over with Sarah later.

Unable to look away, my toe caught the edge of the top stair and I stumbled onto the stage. Sarah grabbed my arm before I face-planted.

"Focus, dummy," she said. "It's about to start."

At first, everything was great. Sarah and I both made it through the first few freezes, and I busted out the Dougie, the Wobble, then threw it back to the Jerk. The crowd ate it up and I was in my element. When "Party Rock Anthem" kicked in, I went full Redfoo. Sarah and I had studied that choreography and practiced it in my bedroom approximately one bajillion times.

I glanced sideways at her as I shuffled my way to the front of the stage, smiling like the Cheshire Cat, and delivered Much Music Video Awards quality moves. After a few eight-counts, the music cut, and I froze – but Sarah still had one wobbly foot in the air. She shook her head as she was dismissed from the stage to loud jeers from the crowd.

It was down to me and one other competitor: a shorter blond guy who never lifted his feet, alternating between the Swim and the Shopping Cart like his life depended on it.

That swag bag was mine.

The crowd's cheers blurred in my ears as the wild, ridiculous dance battle unfolded – pride and free stuff on the line. Damp, chestnut curls clung to my neck while I switched to the Running Man, sneaking a glance at the hot older guy, grinning as he watched from below. I caught Sarah's howl of laughter from the side of the stage and turned to look at her – her eyes suddenly wide with surprise.

I hadn't realized how close to the edge of the stage I'd "run" until my left foot slipped over it. Time slowed as I lurched forward, hands flailing, reaching for anything to break my fall.

There was an audible gasp as I hit the floor, the bridge of the song echoing throughout the auditorium. Then, hysterical laughter and sympathetic groans rippled through the crowd. A few people held their phones out, recording every embarrassing second. *Welcome to high school, I guess.*

I was sprawled out, unruly brown curls everywhere. My ankle throbbed – sharp and insistent – another casualty of my frantic desire to "drive fast and take chances," as my mother always said.

I pulled myself into a sitting position, as Sarah peered over the edge of the stage, shaking her head and unable to control her laughter.

"Only you," she mouthed, capturing a photo before turning towards the stairs that led off the stage, hopefully, to come and rescue me, preferably with a working time machine.

I stared at my shoes and drew a steadying breath. This might be it. My TSN turning point. My high school life was over before it had even begun. I'd be the punchline of every joke for the next few years.

"Hey…Are you okay? That was…really…uh, something."

I looked up and found myself reflected in a pair of wide, concerned, crystal-blue eyes. They were the color of a flawless summer sky, framed by thick, dark eyelashes, a rogue spot of brown nestled in his left iris.

I was caught in his tractor beam, pulled towards him as if he were an alien spacecraft. People didn't look like this in real life. *Beam me up, Scotty.*

"Hmm, yeah." I nodded, as I forced myself to breathe. I scanned his face. Between those eyes was a straight nose and a beautiful mouth full of perfect white teeth. He was half smiling, unsure of my current state or what to make of me.

How many years of orthodontics and what kind of toothpaste did it take to create a smile like that? I blinked, refocusing as he held out his hand.

"Free stuff is my kryptonite. Can't believe I blew it." Heat tingled in my cheeks as I grinned and flicked my eyebrows up in that *I'm a klutz but also adorable and super fun and obviously your new best friend* kind of way.

I grabbed his warm hand and popped up too quickly in a feeble attempt to hide my injury, the top of my head clipping him hard under the chin. His head snapped back with a loud crack of his jaw. He grunted on impact and stumbled backward before sitting down, clutching his jaw, as I collapsed to the floor, my ankle definitely in need of medical attention.

I didn't know whether to laugh or cry.

Cry? Yes, definitely cry.

"Oh my god, I'm so sorry, are you okay?" I crawled over to him, panicked, as he shook his head, presumably shaking the little cartoon birdies away. He drew a breath as he blinked a couple of times before his eyes regained focus and landed on me.

"Uh, yeah, I think so. Phew. I'd help you up again but it's probably safer for the both of us down here."

"I'm so sorry, I'm a bit clumsy, as you and everyone else here have probably figured out by now. I'm basically a newborn baby giraffe, like all the time."

The corner of his mouth quirked up as he huffed out a laugh. "No worries. I'm sure I'll be fine. There's a poster on the door with concussion protocol so I'll grab a pic before I leave and monitor myself for symptoms." He glanced towards the large Rowan's Law poster.

"I'm Jake," he continued. "Welcome to Bondar. I hope the rest of your high school experience is less painful." He showed me his perfect teeth as his grin widened. His broad shoulders and lean, muscular arms made it clear that I was not in middle school anymore.

"Emma." I nodded, dazed that this hot older guy was still talking to me. Maybe it was his newly acquired head injury. "And thanks, I hope so too. Any tips?"

"I guess…" He looked back at me and tilted his head. "Be yourself and don't forget who you are, even if it is a newborn giraffe. I have a feeling you'll be fine."

I nodded, but I wasn't going to be fine. I was already picturing our prom (I was wearing pink, there were flowers), our wedding (I was wearing white, there were more flowers), and compiling a list of names for our future children.

My heart beat hard against my ribcage as I stood up and hopped over to the nearest table where I could sit down to check out my ankle as he continued to rub his jaw. I loosened the laces on my high top and tried to rotate my foot. A sharp twinge shot through my ankle, the kind of pain that made my stomach tighten.

"Great shoes," he said, tapping a finger on the toe of my sneaker. "But I think they're trying to kill you."

"Entirely possible." I grinned, the warmth of his attention eclipsing the stabbing pain in my ankle.

"Holy shit, Emma!" Sarah bubbled with laughter as she appeared beside us. "What was that?!" She shook her head before turning towards Jake. "Hey, I'm Sarah. Thanks for taking one for the team there." She scanned his face before nodding. "Glad to see your face still works."

Jake snickered as Sarah sat beside me and swiped through the pictures and videos she'd taken, describing the highlights as if she were on Sportsnet. Jake's warm, minty-fresh breath tickled my neck as he leaned in for a closer look and I couldn't focus on anything else.

At that moment, I knew that my initial mathematical calculations had been correct. The risk was worth the reward. Even if the reward was wearing a boot for the next six weeks and dragging crutches up and down four flights of stairs between classes, and to wherever the hell "C and a Half" was, it was also meeting him.

From that point on, I was officially living in my After I Met Jake era.

## Three

# Helium Balloons and an Explosion

A thousand thoughts whirled through my head as my mouth refused to form words. What was he doing here? The last thing I'd seen from my quarterly social media stalking was that he'd been in Waterloo during the pandemic with a live-in girlfriend named Krista.

"Emma?" Jake looked as stunned as I was. After a few quick blinks and a deep swallow, he glanced at my name tag. "Or should I say Victoria?" He huffed out a laugh. "Nice to see you've stuck with one of the Spice Girls."

"My friend Jerry made me pick a fake name because he was worried about stalkers. Personally, I don't think anyone here looks like one, although I've only met a few people. Galadon's definitely not – he doesn't seem interested in humans. What about you? Have you met anyone who seems like a stalker?" I cringed, horrified. I'd pictured seeing Jake Griffin again hundreds of times over the past ten years and I'd never imagined spending our first conversation since high school rambling about stalkers.

"Nope, no stalkers so far," Jake said, deadpan. "But who knows what the rest of the night holds." He leaned back in his chair and crossed his arms, his eyes flickering over my face.

As I searched my brain for something to say – anything resembling normal human conversation this time – I couldn't help but catalogue the differences between Jake from my memories and Jake now. The stubble covering his strong, chiselled jaw and the way his shoulders filled out his Henley made it clear that this was a man sitting in front of me, not the boy I remembered. His wavy chocolate brown hair was longer on top than it used to be. His crystalline blue eyes were the same – and just like in high school, I had to force myself to look away. I wouldn't let myself get lost in them again.

"Jake. Wow. It's been a long time. How are you?" I cleared my throat as a wave of confusion washed over me. Warmth crept up my back, tingling its way over my cheeks. I struggled to catch my breath. He smelled like cedar and citrus, making it hard to think.

"I'm good." Jake's voice sounded like it was coming from a long distance away. "Hey…are you feeling okay? You're looking a little pale."

He was so close to me, the faint line between his eyes telegraphing his concern. How many times had I seen that look before?

"Emma? Can I grab you a glass of water?"

"Yes, please," I said, dismayed that my voice was shaky. I hated that he was being so considerate, but hopefully, a brief reprieve from his overwhelming presence would help me pull my shit together.

"I'll be right back."

He wove through the tables with speed dating couples deep in conversation. He leaned across the bar towards Anusha, and I couldn't help but notice his jeans stretch across his taut ass. *Jesus, Emma, that isn't helping.*

I closed my eyes and pressed the heels of my palms against them as I set my elbows on the table. I focused on breathing in and out, trying with little success to ignore the snapshots of Jake that kept flashing across my mind: Jake, looking down in concern after I'd tumbled off the stage; Jake, beaming at me with his arms raised after he'd pitched a no-hitter against Bondar's biggest rivals; Jake, laughing as I wiped out on the bunny hill for the millionth time.

"Here you go."

A large glass of ice water landed with a clunk on the table, and he pushed it toward me, knocking me out of my memories. I grabbed the glass and lifted it with shaky hands, drinking half of it in one go. As I set it back down, I met his eyes again.

"Phew, I guess those margaritas hit me harder than I thought." More composed, I forced a laugh. Being the object of Jake's focused attention left me scattered like it always had.

"We've all been there," Jake said. "So, what are you up to these days?"

Anusha's quacking duck timer went off, saving me from further attempts at fumbling conversation. The sounds of overlapping chatter, laughter, and the clinking of glasses came back into focus. "Blame Brett" by the Beaches played over the speakers, and the men got up from their tables in preparation for moving on to their next date.

"Wow, five minutes goes by quickly. Can I find you at the end of the night? We should catch up."

"Sure," I said. *Not happening.* Thank god I'd already told Mel and Jerry I was leaving as soon as the official part of the evening was over.

"I'll see you later then…Victoria." Jake's gaze lingered on me as he moved off.

I blew out a shaky breath.

My god. Of all the people I could have run into at speed dating, it was Jake Griffin, who was somehow more attractive and compelling than I remembered. My right eye twitched, my trusty yet aggravating response to heightened emotion.

Luckily, I wasn't required to make conversation with my next date, the "drink-down-the-wrong-pipe" guy. He took one sip of his beer and then coughed for five minutes straight. His name tag sticker had curled at the edges, so all I could see was "ri" in the middle. Was it Brian? Enrique? Eric? I'd never know.

Aakash was so devastated by the recent death of his beloved parrot, Tango, that he spent the whole time swiping through pictures of the two of them. Nick, a door-to-door meat salesman and proud of his record as the most successful in his district, had come prepared with samples of his company's spicy Italian sausage in a thermos. He handed me two Dixie cups full before moving on to his next date.

Relief washed over me when Jerry dropped into the seat in front of me, sparing me from polite small talk with yet another random man, while a chaotic jumble of memories and emotions rattled around my brain.

"Oh Jerry, thank god." I shoved the Dixie meat cups into my purse before grabbing his hand.

"You met Nick, I see." Jerry flashed a grin. "Didn't your mother ever tell you never to take sausages from a stranger?" His smile faded when he noticed the stress on my face, and he squeezed my hand. "What's up? You look like you've seen a ghost."

I groaned as I covered my face. He wasn't far off. Jake had ghosted me ten years ago – and now he was back to haunt me.

"Pretty much. I can't get into it now, but I saw someone that, ideally, I never would have seen again."

I couldn't get into the complicated history of Jake Griffin and Emma Anderson in our remaining four and a half minutes, even if I wanted to. All I'd told Jerry and Mel about my disastrous high school experience was that I'd had to switch schools after grade eleven. I'd worked really hard to put it behind me and couldn't face revisiting it, even with my best friends. Time to stuff these memories back into the Rubbermaid container in my mind where they'd suffocate and die.

I dragged my focus away from my inner turmoil and onto Jerry. "How is your night going, Jer? Have you met anyone with potential yet?"

I couldn't understand why Jerry had never had a long-term relationship. He was adorable, with his tousled brown hair and crooked smile. I still called him my security blanket, much to his chagrin. "Emma, exactly *zero* girls want to hook up with someone another girl calls their security blanket, GOD," was a familiar refrain from university. But from what I could see, he had his pick of women – they were always flirting with him across the bar – but nothing ever seemed to make it beyond a few dates.

"Hah, no," Jerry said, before spending the next four minutes distracting me with stories from his previous dates. I learned that the sexy blonde a few tables over had been disconcertingly direct about her sexual preferences, and he'd deflected her by talking about the time he'd gotten athlete's foot from the change room at the Pan-Am Centre where he'd taken his adult swim lessons. As I laughed helplessly at Jerry's expression of mild horror, Anusha's timer went off.

"Okay, everyone! That wraps up the formal portion of our event tonight, although we hope you'll stick around and continue to mingle. Thank you so much for coming out and don't forget to hand in your match cards! We'll email you tomorrow morning with contact information for any pairs who both checked 'yes.' I hope you've made some beautiful connections tonight!"

Jerry draped his arm around my shoulders and guided me to the bar, where Mel had already ordered me another drink. I threw back half, determined to escape as soon as possible. I scanned the room. Jake was on the other side of the Trinity, deep in conversation with the sexy blonde. Hopefully, he'd find her sexual preferences so intriguing that I could leave before encountering him again.

Mel poked Jerry in the chest. "Gerald, where did you find these people? I have never encountered such an impressive assembly of time burglars in my entire life! Five minutes didn't seem like a long time until these wet socks held me hostage in a never-ending cycle of boredom. You should thank your lucky stars because if I didn't adore you, I'd have burned this entire establishment to a smouldering pile of rubble by now."

I laughed before glancing over at Jake to ensure he wasn't on the loose, accidentally catching his eye. *Shit.* I whirled back towards the bar, tossing back the rest of my drink, before peeking over my shoulder. Damnit, I'd lost him. I craned my neck, trying to spot him, ready to take evasive manoeuvres. At this very minute he could be making his way over here, and there was nothing I wanted to do less than catch up with Jake Griffin. It was time to pull the chute on this disaster of an evening.

"Emma?" Mel was looking at me with a penetrating expression. "Who is he?"

"What? Who?" I busied myself by stuffing my phone into my bag and slinging the strap over my shoulder.

"Umm, the tall drink of water who has you more discombobulated than that time you saw Neville Longbottom at the Brickworks. Do you know him, or did he give off an 'it rubs the lotion on its skin or else it gets the hose again' vibe?"

"I know him. Well, knew him." I peeked over my shoulder again as I slid off my barstool. Jake was nowhere in sight. "I promise, I'll fill you in later, but I've gotta go. Any chance you can create a distraction? Maybe something involving helium balloons and an explosion?"

Mel laughed. "Go. I'll distract and deflect if he comes looking for you."

"Thanks." I turned and came face to face with Ryan. I took a wobbly step back and he caught my elbows to steady me. Our flirty date seemed like it was hours ago.

"Whoa, careful there, Victoria! Already heading out?"

*Shit.* He seemed nice, and normally I'd be perfectly happy to flirt with a hot man for a few minutes, but panic was clawing at my throat.

"Yeah, unfortunately. I have a deadline on Monday, so I'm working through the weekend." Not the whole reason I was hunched over like a troll trying to edge my way out of the bar, but still true.

"I was hoping to chat with you about a project we're working on at the firehouse. We need a photographer and haven't found anyone yet. Do you do freelance work?"

"Yes, absolutely, sounds interesting." I fumbled in my bag to locate a business card, accidentally dumping the sausage cups inside. I groaned as I handed him my card, then started plucking out the pieces, one by one, dropping them onto a discarded nacho plate on the bartop.

"Is there a small German sausage factory in your purse?" Ryan said, delighted, as he handed me a napkin.

I laughed. "Feel free to email me and let me know more about the project," I said, as I wiped my hands and dropped the napkin on the plate.

I flinched when someone said my name from behind me; I'd recognize his voice anywhere. I closed my eyes and breathed, trying to calm my fluttering nerves. As I turned towards Jake, pasting a bright smile on my face, I caught Ryan looking at me quizzically before shifting his gaze to Jake.

"Jake, my man." He grinned. "Did you also have the pleasure of meeting Victoria? V – Jake works with my sister, and we play volleyball together. I dragged him here to help me find my soulmate."

Jake looked steadily at me. "We go way back, right *Victoria*?" he said, before winking at me.

The gall of this beautiful asshole! I resented how unaffected he seemed, while I was over here sweating and smelling like spicy Italian sausages.

"Yep," I said. "All the way back to high school."

I turned to Mel with a pleading expression. She abruptly stood up. "As fun as this has been, people, Emma and I are taking off." With that, she pulled me towards the door.

Jake stepped in front of me as I was manoeuvering my way around the bar stools and my next step brought me flush against his hard chest. Breath suspended, I tilted my head up to meet his gaze.

"Emma, it was good to see you," he said as he stepped back. "We need to catch up now that I'm back in the city." His eyes held mine with a hint of urgency.

"Umm, sure. Yes. Nice to see you too." I stammered as I managed to disengage myself. "Great meeting you, Ryan," I called backwards, as Mel steered me towards the door and into the humid night.

# Four
# September 18, 13 Years Ago

# Vote for Emma or She'll Give You a Concussion

"Remind me why I'm doing this again?" I glanced at Sarah, who was sitting at my desk. I flopped back onto my bed, tapping my pen on my notebook. We were struggling to come up with a catchy slogan and a couple of campaign posters since Sarah had gleefully nominated me for the grade nine representative position on the student council. All the other positions were decided last spring; it was me and one other person vying for this spot and elections were next Friday.

"Because you're nice, fun, creative, and dependable – and because you'd get to spend a lot more time with ol' blue eyes." Sarah popped a handful of Sour Patch Kids into her mouth. "Seriously, you were made for this kind of thing. You're so people-y. We just need a catchy slogan and we're golden."

I groaned. We were far from golden. Jake and his beautiful baby blues were out of my reach. In the three weeks since school had started I'd learned he was in grade ten, on the varsity baseball team in addition to student council, and had a way of making even the teachers feel like they were lucky to be talking to him. George, my opponent, didn't have a platform, but he'd done the Ice Bucket Challenge in the middle of the cafeteria at lunch today while the crowd chanted his name. He might be popular enough to have a shot at winning.

"Check it out, I'm done!" Sarah held up a poster with a sketch of me riding a unicorn, complete with the air cast I'd been wearing since I'd fractured my ankle at orientation, holding my crutches above my head in celebration. "Vote for Emma – She'll make all your wildest dreams come true!"

I laughed, sat up, and scooted back to lean against my headboard, eyeing my boot as I dragged it along my duvet. At least I didn't have to keep retelling the story of how I broke my ankle – everyone already knew. My little accident had made the rounds on social media, and now I was a minor celebrity at school. Sarah kept telling me there was no such thing as bad publicity, but I wasn't convinced.

I grabbed some Sour Patch Kids and threw one at her. It bounced off her forehead and landed on the carpet. "You're ridiculous."

Sarah picked up the candy and tossed it in her mouth. "How about, 'Vote for Anderson – she'll give you a handerson'?"

I threw back my head and laughed. "Oh my god, no!"

Sarah's eyebrows shot up as a burst of laughter escaped. "I meant you'll give them a hand with school junk, like cleaning their locker or helping with their homework. Not that you're giving out hand jobs… although that might get more votes."

"Yeah, right. Next idea." We were getting nowhere fast.

"Fine. How about 'Vote for Em, she's a Gem'?"

"Ugh, these are all terrible. Everyone already thinks I'm a dork. We need something cool." I exhaled as the weight of self-doubt pushed me sideways onto the bed, into the fetal position.

"Jake doesn't think you're a dork. He had stars in his eyes when I saw you two afterwards."

"Ha, probably because I gave him a concussion." I rubbed my hands on my forehead and rolled onto my stomach, pulling my notebook back in front of me.

"How about 'Vote for Emma or she'll give you a concussion?'" Sarah flashed a saccharine smile and got to work on the lettering as I scoffed.

"Wait, I've got it." Grinning, Sarah grabbed her phone, opened it, and flashed the photo of me, flat on my face after my fall. "We use this."

"And that will help me how?" I raised an eyebrow. A few kids were already calling me "Crash," and the last thing I wanted was to crash and burn in this election too.

"You know that saying – they aren't laughing *at* you if they're laughing *with* you, right? We can write that Confucius quote we talked about in English class last year underneath." She deepened her voice and continued, "'Our greatest glory is not in never falling, but in rising every time we fall.'" She got up from her chair and plopped onto the bed next to me. "Poetic and inspirational, just like you."

"That might work," I grinned, turning to face her. "Can we keep the unicorn one too?"

"It's basically your spirit animal. Of course it stays."

I was slightly more hopeful about my chances of winning this election.

Monday morning, Sarah and I went in early to the SAC advisor's office on C and a half and handed over our posters and flyers for approval. Mrs. Driscoll flipped through them, signing off in the bottom corner, until she stopped, pulled one out, and looked it up and down.

She turned to face me, her brows furrowed as she extended the poster to arm's length.

"What's this all about?"

It was the concussion poster, the goofy sketch I'd added in jest now coloured. Sarah must have smuggled it in. My mouth snapped shut and my wide eyes darted to meet Sarah's as hers lit up with delight. Mrs. Driscoll huffed as the poster was handed back to me due to its "threatening nature" and "moral tone." A nervous chuckle escaped as I reached for it and tried to explain it was a joke, but she waved me off and hurried through the last of them.

As Sarah headed towards the cafeteria carrying the large posters, I hobbled a step behind, slowed by my boot and crutches, with the flyers tucked under my arm. She stopped suddenly, nudged my side with her pointy little elbow, and nodded towards the water fountain at the end of the hallway.

"Look who's thirsty." She glanced at me, a smile playing on her lips. "And I don't mean you for once."

I rolled my eyes and followed her gaze to see Jake leaning over the water fountain as my heart threw a tiny party in my chest. Had I ever noticed a guy's butt before? I was definitely noticing now. And I kept noticing until I realized I was frozen in the busy hallway with my head cocked, mouth agape, giving off major creeper vibes.

I could have stayed that way all day but suddenly I was blindsided by what felt like a human freight train barrelling into me from the side, as some goliath jumped to catch a football. My stack of flyers flew through the air, coming down like confetti.

I crashed to the ground. My boot thudded against the tile as my crutches skittered away. The air whooshed out of me, leaving me gasping as the giant landed on top.

"Well, *hello* there!" he said, leering down my top. He smirked as he waved the football in my face to show he'd caught it, then jumped up and ran off.

I sat up and scooted backward until my back hit the wall, taking in a shaky breath. With a careful twist of my neck, I scanned my body for new injuries. Thankfully, nothing else seemed broken. I glanced towards the water fountain, hoping that Jake hadn't seen my latest catastrophe, and I couldn't see him anywhere. *Phew.*

I sat there for a moment as Sarah scrambled around the hallway, trying to collect the flyers before they were trampled, but I could see a few had already been stepped on, crumpled and torn. I rubbed my temples, trying to push back the wave of irritation. The thought of hauling my ass back up to C and a half to use the SAC copier again was enough to make me want to scream. I was so over this boot, these crutches, the constant clunkiness, but I had to deal with them for another four weeks.

"Hey, Emma." Jake's voice came from my left as he leaned my crutches against the wall before sitting beside me and putting his hand on my shoulder. He looked concerned as I turned to meet his gaze. "You okay? Murray's the worst." He shook his head as he handed me a few of my flyers. His hand slid down my arm and back to his side, leaving a trail of electricity behind. "So, you're running for SAC? That's awesome. It's a lot of fun."

"Yep." I made a mental note to never wash this shirt again. *Hmm. If I learned to sew, I could make it into a pillowcase to snuggle up with at night.*

Sarah had finished collecting the rest of the flyers scattered across the hallway and dropped them in my lap, putting the posters on top. "Jake, I have to get to class early for extra math help. Can you help Emma put these up?" She grinned at me before skipping off.

I was going to kill her. I turned to Jake. "Umm, it's really ok, you don't have to help. I can do it after class."

"It's no problem, I'm happy to help. We've still got fifteen minutes before first period." He tugged the stack off my lap. "What's this one?" He held up the concussion poster, which had been resting on top, his face splitting into a delighted grin.

"That – uh, Sarah made that. Well, I drew it but she coloured it. She thought it was funny," I stammered, feeling my cheeks flush. "But don't worry, Mrs. Driscoll isn't going to let us put it up, haha, not that we planned to." *Kill me now.*

"That's me." His lips came together, a sparkle in his eyes as he pointed to the poster.

I nodded. "Yep." I shifted my focus to the floor, begging it to swallow me whole.

"Can I keep it?"

I lifted my gaze in surprise.

"Uh, sure," I managed, wondering if we'd include this story in our wedding vows one day.

"Thanks." He beamed as he plucked it from the pile. "Come on, let's go put these up." He stood up and stretched his hand out toward me.

I hesitated, a flush of self-conscious heat creeping up my neck, cursing the everything bagel I'd had for breakfast. What if I had poppy seeds stuck in my teeth? I ran my tongue over them, my nerves kicking in before I grasped his hand.

"Thanks – you're a lifesaver. Twice now."

He chuckled as he pulled me up with ease and handed me my crutches. "Just doing my part. Besides, I enjoy the company." Jake shrugged, the kindness in his voice easing some of the tension from my shoulders. "Ready?"

I nodded, trying to ignore the flutter of my heart. "Lead the way."

## Five

# We Act Civil, and That's It

"Mom, we're here!"

Mel and I stepped inside my childhood home, the smell of my dad's coconut curry chicken making my mouth water. We kicked off our shoes, my beat-up white Converse slip-ons and Mel's black strappy sandals joining the jumble of shoes by the front door, before padding down the hallway towards the kitchen. The familiar sound of my parents chatting over the classical music that my dad played while cooking steadied me.

Monthly Sunday night dinners were a tradition at my parents' house, and usually a highlight of my month. My parents and I were close, and I often brought Mel, Jerry, or both. Tonight, I knew my mom would be digging for all the details about our night at speed dating. It was inevitable. No matter how many times I told her that I wasn't looking for a relationship right now, the hopeless romantic inside Michelle Anderson was always on the lookout for love – whether it was for me, Mel, Jerry, or the cashier at the No Frills where she did her weekly grocery shopping.

“Scotty, here’s the dessert I promised!” Mel deposited a white cake box on the kitchen island.

My dad’s eyes lit up as he saw the beige and white logo. “Hamblin’s? I knew there was a reason that you’re my favourite of Emma’s friends.” He crossed over to hug her before turning to wrap me in his arms and drop a kiss on top of my head.

Mel scoffed. “Scotty, you’ve told Jerry exactly the same thing when I’ve been standing beside him. Your favourite is whoever has most recently brought you cake.”

My mom laughed as she handed me the stack of plates to set the table. “Ding ding ding! She’s got you figured out, Scooter.”

My mom’s ridiculous nickname for my dad made me wistful. Together since high school, they’d never been anything other than rock solid. My mom was as artistic and quirky as I was, and my dad never seemed to want her to be anything other than who she was.

Over dinner, my parents caught up on everything happening in our lives. They were eager to hear about Mel’s summer school class and the Mathematics Specialist course she’d recently finished, and I updated them that my portfolio was just about ready for submission. It was due tomorrow, and I’d spent the entire day and last night trying to finalize everything, working until two, fueled by cortisol, caffeine, and Sour Patch Kids. I was exhausted.

“Are you happy with it?” my mom asked, eyeing me. “You look stressed.”

I sighed, pushing the last of my food around. “I don’t know. I keep tweaking things, but I’m probably just making it worse.”

Dad leaned in with a knowing smile. “Ah, the old ‘fix it one more time’ trap. Classic Emma. Sometimes it’s better just to call it.”

“Exactly,” Mel said.

“But what if–”

My mom cut me off gently. “Emmie, you’ve poured yourself into this. It’s about your vision, your voice. Art isn’t meant to be flawless; it’s raw, emotional, and subjective. Your perspective is what makes it meaningful. And that’s always enough.”

Mel gave me a little nudge. “Seriously, you’re overthinking it.”

My dad feigned surprise. “Emma? Overthink? Well, there’s a first time for everything.”

I rolled my eyes, but their reassurance grounded me. They believed in me, even when I couldn’t shake the self-doubt that had been dogging me since I’d started this project.

"It's ready. Trust yourself," he said, clearing our plates and heading to the kitchen. I sat for a moment, letting the warmth of their words sink in. My parents' confidence was a steady anchor against the pull of my insecurities. It was time to let go of the fear that it wasn't enough. My work was ready, even if I wasn't sure I was.

My dad brought dessert out, visibly salivating over the cake as he cut us each a large slice. Across the table, Mom's eyes sparkled with barely contained excitement. I wasn't getting out of this dinner unscathed. I braced myself.

"So, tell me everything about speed dating! I've been dying to hear how it went!" She wiggled happily in her seat as she filled four mugs from the teapot and passed around the milk and sugar.

With a glance across the table at me, Mel launched into a description of the amateur magician she'd almost slapped when he'd reached behind her ear to pull out a coin and the guy who had kept commenting on her perfect arches. Eager to avoid any mention of Jake, I jumped in with tales of Galadon and his dragon art and the door-to-door meat salesman.

"Aww, it sounds like you had something in common with Galadon." My mom was a sucker for weirdos since she was something of one herself.

"Sure, but he was kind of a jerk."

"So, no one with potential?"

"Nope, definitely not," I said firmly and stuffed a forkful of cake in my mouth. Crisis averted. Time for a subject change. "Anyway, I saw this post on Reddit – apparently cereal is a soup. What do you–"

Mel cut me off, eyes gleaming over the rim of her mug. "What about that hot guy from your high school?" She took a slow, obnoxious slurp of tea. "Spill."

*Very funny.*

I'd have to be selective in what I revealed to my mom, especially in front of Mel. After she'd rescued me at speed dating and let me disassociate on the walk home, I'd put off the inevitable interrogation by getting back to work on my portfolio. Luckily, she'd left early Saturday morning to visit her dad for the weekend.

"Oooh high school? Who was it?!" My mom clapped her hands, practically vibrating with excitement as she looked between us.

Shooting Mel an irritated look, I turned to my mom, trying to figure out how to downplay this. My mom and I had always been close, and when everything blew up in high school, she was right there supporting me, familiar with all the players on the stage of Emma's High School Disaster.™

"It was Jake Griffin," I said, unable to figure out a way to dissemble.

My mom's eyes widened. She dropped her fork to her plate with a clatter, sending a little blob of icing onto the tablecloth. Her look of concern made my heart squeeze in my chest. Mel looked between my mom and me, her brow furrowed, seeming puzzled by the intensity of my mom's reaction.

"Jake? That must have been a surprise," she said slowly, with a sidelong glance at my dad, who appeared as stunned as she was. "How was it, seeing him again?" She blinked a few times as she sipped her tea.

"It was fine, honestly, Mom." I tried to sound indifferent. "We chatted for a few minutes. It's no big deal. Honestly. Really, it's totally fine. It was a long time ago." I winced; I could tell I was protesting too much.

There was a brief pause.

"Well, that's good. I'm glad." My mom used her fork to scrape the icing off the tablecloth and brought it to her lips. "I didn't realize he was back in town – Julia didn't mention anything."

"Julia?" I asked. *As in, Jake's mom?*

"Jake's mom."

"I know who she is, Mom."

"Remember I told you about the book club that Sue Vine started up last year?" my mom said, referencing one of her neighbourhood mom friends in a confusing conversational left-turn.

"Wine club," my dad said, through a mouthful of cake, making Mel and I laugh. We all knew that book club was an excuse for my mom to get together with her friends to drink wine and chat.

"Yes, Mom – I know about book-slash-wine club." I tried to tamp down my impatience. "Julia goes?" My hungry urge to find out everything I could about Jake surprised me.

"Well, she came for the first time last week. We didn't get to chat too much, but she mentioned she'd moved back to the neighbourhood."

"Oh." As I cast around for a new topic, desperate to move on, Mel gave me one last pointed look that said we were going to replay this conversation in detail on the way home before turning to my dad and asking him what classes he had been assigned for the upcoming school year. My mom's gaze lingered on me, her concern like a weight pressing against my ribs. I wasn't ready to unpack her thoughts – or mine. So I cut another mammoth slice of cake and ate my feelings.

"Thanks for a great night as usual, Andersons!" Mel called back to my parents as we traipsed down the sidewalk towards the Uber my dad had called. I busied myself getting settled in the silver sedan, buckling my seatbelt, and saying hi to our driver, Mohamed. I was dreading the conversation Mel and I were about to have, like I was in the dentist's chair and Dr. O'Grady was getting ready to do a root canal. Mel waited beside me with her metaphorical drill and a look that said "Open wide."

It was weird that I hadn't told Mel the full story. She and Jerry had been my closest friends since our first year of university at Toronto Metropolitan. We'd met at a Halloween costume contest at the on-campus pub. I'd dressed up as Baby Spice – I was her namesake, after all – wearing a blond wig in pigtails, blue contacts to cover my hazel eyes, a pink slip dress, and platform sneakers. I'd been on my own, but as I'd surveyed the crowd, a pair had caught my eye: A guy wearing a Union Jack minidress and a bright red wig talking to a girl wearing a cheetah-print bra top. Nerves spiking, I'd steeled myself before striding over and planting myself in front of them.

"So, tell me what you want, what you really really want!" I'd sung in their faces, using my index finger as a microphone.

After a beat of unbearable silence, the guy dressed as Ginger Spice had quirked a smile and sung back – in a terrible baritone – "I wanna, I wanna, I wanna, I wanna, I wanna really, really, really wanna zig-a-zig ah!"

And from that moment forward, Mel (cheetah-print bra top, a.k.a. Scary Spice), Jerry (Ginger "Mel made me dress up like this" Spice), and I had been inseparable. They were close friends from high school, and I would be forever grateful that they'd folded me into their little group. First-year exams, bad dates, epic Thursday nights out at Lee's Palace, more epic hangovers, terrible summer jobs, Mel's inappropriate relationship with her super-hot chemistry TA, tiny shared apartments without air conditioning, Jerry's existential crisis about what to do after graduation – we'd experienced the highs and lows of university together and they were the friends I'd call if I needed a stunt double for one of my overly dramatic life story reenactments.

But still, I hadn't shared the most painful part of my past with them. And I didn't really want to revisit it now. It was in the past, I was over it, and the last thing I wanted to do was dwell on what had happened ten years ago.

Mel tapped her nails on the armrest, waiting.

Eventually, I stopped fussing with my seat belt and turned to her with a bright smile. "Well, you made Scotty's night with the cake!"

"Emma."

Oh god, she was using her concerned best friend voice. A lump formed in my throat. How many times had Mel propped me up after a shitty breakup, a harsh review of my art, or any of the other times I'd needed support in the eight years we'd been friends?

"Tell me what's going on with Jake. All you told me on Friday night was that you knew him in high school, but your mom seemed shocked when you brought him up." Her eyes widened. "Oh my god. Was *he* the reason you had to switch schools?" A militant tone came into her voice, ready to ride or die for me the way she always was.

"No, no. Not at all." Not quite the truth, but I wasn't prepared to tell her the whole story. "I knew Jake before I switched. I haven't mentioned anything about it because it's super embarrassing."

"Come on, I've watched you fall out of a bus straight into a mud puddle, then puke all over yourself while you lay in the mud. Why would you care about sharing another humiliating story with me?" Mel grinned, remembering that rainy night after the bar in our first year of university. "Come on, hit me with it, so we can laugh about it."

I had to tell her something.

"Ok, fine. Jake was a grade ahead of me at school. I met him when I fell off the stage at grade nine orientation, which is super on-brand for me. He helped me up and I fell madly, hopelessly, and deliriously in love with him in the way that only high school girls can. We were on student council together and I spent the next three years in the friend zone. I finally worked up the nerve to make a move, after which he ghosted me." Semi-true, but definitely not the reason I hadn't been able to sleep the past two nights.

"That's it?" Mel said, incredulous. "Everyone has a painfully embarrassing crush as a teenager that makes them do stupid things. Hasn't Jerry told you about the time he had a crush on the captain of our high school Field Hockey team and sent himself a Valentine-Gram as if it was from her? She found out about it and forced him to print a retraction in the school paper."

"No!" I gasped, sputtering with laughter. "Poor Jerry."

"And Jake does not see you as an awkward teenager with a crush now." Mel shook her head, grinning. "On Friday, he looked at you the way your dad looks at the delicious cakes from Hamblin's."

"Mel, stop. He did not."

"I promise you, he did. But just say the word, and I'll punch him in the balls for rejecting adorable high school Emma. Or maybe you need me to wingwoman you while you convince him that you're all grown up now?" Mel's grin was wicked.

"Ugh, stop," I laughed. "You sound like a pervy old man. Neither of those. If we happen to run into him again – unlikely – we act civil and that's it."

"Boring," she said, "but if that's what you want, that's what we'll do."

As Mel and I moved on, with her unearthing more stories about high school Jerry that made me snort, I was relieved that she'd let it go. Yes, I'd had an all-consuming crush on Jake Griffin in high school that made me cringe looking back.

But our story was more complicated than that.

# Six
## December 11, 13 Years Ago

# Sparkles and Public Humiliation

I bounced on the balls of my feet while I waited in the wings, palms slick and nerves fizzing, more with excitement than dread. This rent-a-friend auction was exactly the kind of event I loved – chaos with a cause, and just enough embarrassment to lock it in as a core memory. The hum from the crowd barely registered over the quick beat of my heart and the opening pulse of "Spice Up Your Life." My cue.

We had the afternoon free from class. The entire student body had been squirreling away their money in preparation to purchase their friends or enemies and unleash a Friday of embarrassment, complete with outrageous costumes, hairstyles, and god knows what else.

I wasn't worried. I'd slipped Sarah some cash earlier, just enough to make sure I wouldn't be standing up there like an idiot with no bids. It was obvious that most of my fellow participants were part of the popular crowd, but the SAC members had been encouraged to participate, so here I was.

I'd volunteered to kick things off, even if it meant setting the bar for donations comically low. Better that than following up a generous bidder by bringing in ten dollars, Viola Desmond's sympathetic half-smile on the purple bill expressing her sincere condolences. Few things were more damaging to your self-esteem than learning your exact dollar value and doing so in front of hundreds of your fellow students.

My gaze skimmed the crowd, catching Sarah poised to bid, and then landing on Jake in the front row with the rest of the volunteers. He wasn't cheering like everyone else. His arms were crossed, brow faintly furrowed. His eyes darted around as he leaned to his right, half listening to the person next to him – like he was trying to enjoy himself, but something was distracting him. Maybe he was stressing about his turn coming up.

Over the past few months, Jake and I had been spending a lot of time together on the SAC. Since we'd both been on the planning committee for this event, we'd even added each other on Facebook to join the same group chat.

"First up, we have Emma!" Mrs. Driscoll's voice boomed through the mic, stretching every word as if she were hosting a glitzy award show instead of a cringe-worthy high school auction. "She's not only our grade nine rep; she's the guru of groove and the Vivaldi of vintage chic. Emma's the kind of friend who'll serenade you with a Spice Girls song while upcycling old magazines into coasters. Need fashion tips, sick dance moves, or a locker transformation? Emma might just be your perfect rent-a-friend! Bidding starts at ten dollars, and remember, all proceeds go to the Scarborough food bank, so don't hold back! Do I have ten?"

"Do the Running Man!" a voice erupted from the back, sending ripples of laughter through the crowd. I shuddered dramatically before obliging, though in the safety of the centre of the stage this time. Mrs. Driscoll pointed here and there to raised hands in the crowd, finally reaching Sarah at thirty dollars. "Going once…Going twice…"

Thank goodness that was over. I could finally sit next to Jake, catch my breath, and gossip about the rest of the bidding and who got the best bang for their buck. I bowed theatrically, then turned, but before I could leave the stage, Mrs. Driscoll spoke again.

"Forty! To the gentleman in the white hoodie…"

My head snapped toward the other side of the auditorium to where Mrs. Driscoll pointed at the white-hoodie-wearing, football-playing behemoth, Murray Fraser, with his hand raised and a smirk on his stupid football-shaped face.

That guy was pure sleaze – almost every girl I knew had a story about an "accidental" ass grab or a time he'd managed to brush his hand over their chest. *Please, no.*

"Do I hear fifty?" Mrs. Driscoll lit up, thinking only of the food bank and not about what this perv would make me wear next Friday, the day before winter break when the rent-a-friend event was happening.

"Fifty!" Sarah piped up, her eyes wide with shock. She looked at me and panic-shrugged.

She didn't have fifty dollars to save my ass, but I was thankful she was trying. Hopefully, Mrs. Driscoll would let us bring the cash tomorrow. I could ask my parents for an advance on my allowance or try to sell a kidney on the black market tonight.

I glanced back at Murray as he snatched a couple of bills from a friend, cupping his grubby hands around his mouth and bellowing, "Eighty!" with a lewd smirk.

My skin crawled at the idea of spending a day with him.

"One hundred!" Sarah yelled, leaping out of her chair. A couple of Murray's friends checked their pockets, and one held out a five-dollar bill, but he looked up towards Mrs. Driscoll, scoffed, and sat down. I waited, holding my breath.

"Going once, going twice…SOLD, for one hundred dollars to the girl in the pink sweater. Thank you so much for your generous donation!" Mrs. Driscoll beamed.

The blood rushed in my ears as a huge exhale poured out of me. Sarah walked towards Mrs. Driscoll and handed over a wad of cash that must have fallen out of the sky. I'd have to ask her about that later, but for now, I was thankful to keep all my vital organs.

I collapsed into the seat beside Jake, giving him a shaky smile. He put out his hand for a high-five and I reached for it – a perfect smack. I lingered on his palm to savor that precious zing that jolted through my fingertips whenever I touched him.

"That's big bucks, Anderson. Hopefully, Sarah will go easy on you and stick to the sick dance moves." He smiled, running his hand through his hair as he exhaled.

"Yeah, let's hope so. I'm pretty sure she robbed the cafeteria lady to have that cash handy, but I'd rather do whatever she wants than anything for Murray Fucking Fraser." I shuddered.

"Thanks for my amazing intro, too," I said. "Wait 'til you hear what I wrote for yours." I snickered as I nudged his shoulder. Zing! Yep, still worked.

"Ha. Driscoll made me take out the word *adorkable* but that doesn't mean it doesn't apply."

I shifted slightly in my seat to create another gentle brush against his shoulder. I smiled as I settled in, feeling a little lighter now that the auction was behind me. Jake's presence beside me was a steady buzz of good energy.

"Kind of wild this whole circus is for the food bank," I said, as the next auction round kicked off. The guy on stage tossed a fistfull of glitter as he burst from the curtains and did a front tuck into the splits. "Nothing like sparkles and public humiliation to solve food insecurity."

Jake huffed out a laugh. "Right? Weirdly effective, though. Last year we made nearly three thousand dollars, and that much money goes a long way with their suppliers."

"How do you know so much about it?" I said, turning to him.

"I volunteer on Fridays," he said. "I started last year in food service for the hot meal program, but after one rogue lasagna, I looked like a murder suspect and they moved me to produce."

I laughed, "No way."

"Yes way. Total carnage." He gave me a half smile that made my heart skip. "Produce is safer."

"It's cool you volunteer there," I said. Hot, funny, and he volunteers for a good cause? Could he be any more perfect?

"It's great. You should come. Do you have your community service hours figured out? If not, I can send you the link to sign up."

Hubba-wha!? Jake was asking me to hang out with him, in a way that made a difference? I blinked, my insides melting like a Dairy Queen Blizzard on my walk home from school in June. Heat crept up my neck, the warmth spreading across my cheeks.

"I'm in," I blurted out, way too quickly. "I've been meaning to get started on those. We need, what – a hundred hours before we graduate?"

"A hundred and twenty-five."

"Yikes. Thanks for thinking of me."

"Of course. If I'm there, I can make sure no one gives you a hard time on your first day." He reached up and tugged on one of my curls, then turned back to face the stage, grinning.

The electricity from his touch lingered in my hair. I ran my fingers through it, collecting the static he'd left behind, feeling it pop and tingle in my fingertips and all the way down my arm.

Violet, the SAC president, tapped Jake's shoulder and gestured towards the steps to the stage, where the next group of people being rented was already waiting.

"Showtime," he said, grimacing as he stood up. "Wish me luck."

"Break a leg," I said, turning his comment over in my mind. Would he forever see me as someone who needed looking after – or was this his way of saying he liked me?

# Seven

# Fucking Henry Cavill

I pulled open the door to the Moonbean Café, my shoulders easing as I joined the short line in front of my favourite barista, Luca, ready to order my usual: a blended caramel cappuccino shake and a spinach and feta boreka. My morning work sessions at Moonbean usually brought a sense of calm but today was going to be hectic. Since I'd spent so much time on my portfolio over the past few weeks, I was behind on processing images from a couple of recent shoots, and my inbox was a total disaster. It certainly didn't help that thoughts of Jake kept buzzing around my brain like an annoying fly that couldn't be shooed away, especially after hearing his mom was back in our old neighbourhood.

*Why was he back?*

The rich aroma enveloped me, a warm reminder of how much I loved this place. It was cozy and the owner had been kind enough to exhibit my work. A few of my pieces had sold here, and one was hanging above the corner table where I usually worked. It featured a wide shot of Kensington's iconic Garden Car from the north side of Oxford Street, overflowing with wild greenery and bright flowers. The graffiti-covered walls behind it added a riot of color, while a blur of shoppers and street musicians gave the scene its restless energy. It was vibrant and a little chaotic – exactly like me.

"So? How's Bella settling in?" I asked. Luca was in the trenches of puppy parenthood. He'd adopted a Labrador from the humane society last week and there had been a pretty steep learning curve.

With a sigh, he stepped around the side of the counter to show me his Boulder Boots, the toes punctured by small tooth marks, hot pink socks peeking through the holes.

"Noo…" I groaned as I tapped my phone to pay, adding a generous tip towards the new boot fund.

"She's lucky she's cute." He handed me my order, shaking his head.

I climbed the two stairs to my usual table and plunked my bag down next to my chair. I exhaled, pushing aside the lingering haze of Jake and the frustration simmering beneath it. I didn't have time to be distracted. I opened my laptop, ignoring the unread emails piling up, and clicked into my drafts folder, where my submission to the Worth Gallery was ready to go. I re-read it for typos, then checked the link to my portfolio. I hadn't sent it when I'd finally stopped fiddling with it after midnight last night, just in case I'd accidentally signed off with "love you" or attached one of the procrastination memes I'd been sending to Mel and Jerry for the past week.

I breathed a huge sigh of relief once I clicked send, my shoulders relaxing down from where they'd been hovering around my ears. Even though there was no guarantee I'd be accepted to exhibit – let alone have a chance at winning – I was proud of what I'd put together. I spent the next fifteen minutes texting celebratory gifs back and forth in my group chat with Mel and Jerry and chatting with my mom, before turning my attention back to my laptop.

I grimaced at the dog wedding folder staring back at me. Overdressed poodles, a three-tier kibble cake, and a couple who'd spent more on their dogs' vows than most people did on their own. It wasn't exactly the kind of work that set my creative soul on fire, but it paid the bills.

Within the hour, I uploaded the last ridiculous proof into Dropbox and stretched my arms overhead. Sipping my shake, I opened Lightroom to finalize another set of proofs from a cake smash I'd shot a couple of weeks ago. Shot after shot revealed little Arjun pounding his tiny hands into the vanilla buttercream and pulling handfuls towards his mouth. That one had been fun. And messy.

I clicked back to my email, sent out the Dropbox links, and then noticed a new email from Ryan Li.

**from:** Ryan Li <not.that.ryan.li@gmail.com>
**to:** ea.photography.to@gmail.com
**date:** August 13, 2025, 11:28AM
**subject:** Not a love connection… But maybe a business one?

Hey V,

Turns out we aren't soulmates after all - I noticed you weren't on my list, but I have to tell you that no one else came close to your level of appreciation for Celine.

Anyway, keeping things professional, I checked out your website and think you'd be perfect for the project we're putting together at the firehouse. It's a fun piece for a good cause, and I think you'd enjoy it.

Would love to grab lunch to fill you in, throw around some ideas, and talk about rates. Let me know if you're interested!

Ryan

Ryan seemed fun and easy-going, and I'd never turn down an opportunity to photograph some hot firefighters. I hit reply as the bell on the door to the cafe jingled.

I glanced towards the door in time to see Jake stepping over the threshold. I gasped – how was it possible that he and his Great Ass were invading my favourite coffee-slash-people-watching-slash-work spot, after already desecrating the Trinity on Friday?!

I scooted my chair backwards a few inches and ducked lower, using my laptop screen as a shield, hoping that he would be in and out without seeing me. My breathing increased as I hunched over like a turtle, pressing my nose to my keyboard.

"Shit," I muttered, as the man next to me cleared his throat. I turned to face him. He was staring at me, one arched brow and then both popping up towards his hairline. He opened his mouth to say something, but I was faster.

"Shhh!" I hissed, pressing one finger to my lips. I discreetly flashed the "okay" sign to accompany my tight grin before he returned to his work. I leaned down, re-tied both my sneakers, and then fiddled with items in my bag to buy myself some time. I was definitely doing something extremely important, and not hiding from the hot man ordering a mocha frap at the counter.

I risked another peek around the side of my laptop screen. Because Luca was a master of his craft, the line had moved quickly, and Jake was now paying. Another big donation to the new boot fund would be coming Luca's way tomorrow morning.

As casually as my shaking hands would allow, I dug out my charging cable and jammed it into the nearby socket. *Why does he still have this effect on me?* I breathed deeply to steady myself before tossing the cord over to the other side of my computer where the input was, but in the process, it came up under the lens of my glasses, catapulting the frames off my face. They skidded down the two steps, landing right in front of Jake.

As his right foot stepped forward, I winced at the unmistakable crunch. One of the arms bent awkwardly to the side. Jake lifted his foot as he looked down, and I noticed the arm had come clean off, the pesky loose screw on the right side having met its final challenge.

A groan escaped my lips. I folded my arms on the table and laid down my head in resignation. *If I stay still, he'll go away.*

His footsteps got louder, each step drawing nearer until his crisp, white Adidas stopped next to my table.

"Emma?" he asked. "Are these yours?"

"Yep." I sighed, as my eye twitch reignited double time. I glanced up but still didn't lift my head from my arms. "Just drop them on the table and go on your way. Great to see you again." My last words were muffled as I buried my face back into the crook of my elbow. I cursed the far-sightedness that forced me to wear glasses whenever I used my computer.

"Seeing each other twice in a week, after all these years. Maybe it's fate or something."

"Ha," I huffed. "Or something." Was this karma from the time I'd assured my mom that cutting micro-bangs was a good idea? Micro-bangs were *never* a good idea.

I picked up my one-armed glasses and turned them over in my hands. It wasn't that bad – the screw was gone and there was a small scratch across the top of the left lens, but at least they weren't broken. I put them on my face, where they drooped pathetically to one side. I picked up the other arm and tossed it in my bag.

"All good!" I chirped, like an over-caffeinated lunatic. "See? They still work. Have a great day, enjoy your coffee!" I turned towards my computer again.

"Em."

I inhaled sharply at the ease with which he still said my name.

"I'm so sorry. I can fix them. My practice is down the street. Do you have twenty minutes or so?"

"Your practice? What even are you?" I eyeballed him, my glasses wobbling sideways, drawn to his large, capable hands. Maybe a masseuse or a chiropractor, someone who would have to put those hands all over my body, pressing and kneading, stretching out all the sore muscles I had from the stress of seeing him again. Preferably with his shirt off, body oil, and some relaxing mood music. I'm not sure how that would fix my glasses, but I'd give it a try.

A wide smile spread across Jake's face, and his eyes twinkled. My god, they fucking twinkled.

"I'm an optometrist. I'm working at a friend's practice down the street. I can replace the screw in no time."

"Well, I'm pretty busy right now, as you can see." I shuffled around on my trackpad, clicking wildly between open tabs on my screen, careful to avoid the Instagram tab where I'd left his profile open after creeping last night. "I'll make an appointment for laser eye surgery; I've been meaning to do it anyway. Good day to you, fine sir!" I cringed as the word vomit kept spewing and my cheeks started to burn. Sweet baby Jesus, what was I saying?

"It's good to see you haven't changed, Emma." Jake chuckled. "You can come with me, or I'll take them and be back in twenty. We didn't get to chat much on Friday." He looked at me earnestly, his eyebrows raised in a question. "Please?"

I squinted at him, considering the quickest way to get out of this situation, while also getting my glasses repaired. It made more sense for me to go with him rather than stay here, on edge and unable to work while I waited for him to return. And a small part of me was the teensiest bit curious about what he'd been up to in the ten years since I'd last seen him.

"Fine." I slammed my laptop closed and shoved it in my bag, tugging the cord out of the wall and throwing it on top. I pulled off the one-armed glasses and added them to the bag. "But only because you asked nicely and it's your fault I can't see my screen."

I stood, taking a bite of my forgotten boreka, pastry crumbs exploding all over my face and down my vintage Britney T-shirt. I brushed the crumbs off with a greasy hand, hitched my bag over my shoulder, and gestured in front of me. "Lead the way."

"Thank you." Jake tipped his head with a grin, heading out and holding the door open for me.

"Luca!" I called back towards the counter. "If I'm not back in half an hour, call the police and check Find My Friends." I shared my location with him as Jake ran a hand through his thick brown hair, an amused glint in his eye.

"You got it, but text me if you need a little longer." Luca winked after blatantly looking Jake up and down with an appreciative smirk.

I rolled my eyes before stepping through the door. We moved in silence while my thoughts buzzed louder than the crowd outside on Kensington Avenue. I couldn't believe I was side by side with him again. The last time we'd done this was when he'd walked me home after our first kiss, a moment I'd replayed a thousand times.

"So. Why Kensington?" I asked, staring at our feet perfectly in sync on the sidewalk.

"I'm working in a practice on Dundas. It feels like a long time since I've been home for longer than a weekend and it's nice being closer to my mom."

"How's your mom doing?"

"She's great," Jake sent me a quick smile. "She and her fiancé are getting married at the end of September."

"Oh, wow," I said, my mind whirling. So much had changed since we were kids. I didn't even know where to start. "That's exciting."

Jake nodded as we turned right onto Dundas Street and then reached into his pocket for his keys.

"This is it." He slid the key into the lock and turned it with a click as his shoulder brushed mine.

The heat from his touch sparked throughout my body as if I'd stuck my finger in an electrical socket. I was a nervous teenager again. I stepped back to put some space between us as he opened the door.

"After you," he said, gesturing inside.

"Oh, no, you go ahead." I reached to hold the door for myself, careful not to make any physical contact with him as I threw my back flat against it and considered pushing him through.

*Who did he think he was, acting all gentlemanly?*

"Go on," I said. "I don't have all day."

He shook his head and laughed, stepping over the threshold, wafting cedar and citrus in his wake. As he passed, I noticed the subtle creases that had formed around the sides of his eyes since high school, and I was instantly nostalgic for everything in his life that I'd missed in the ten years since he'd disappeared. I wondered if he'd played baseball in university and if he'd ever thought of me when he saw a ridiculous sign at a game.

*What the actual fuck, Emma.*

Jake led me past the displays of glasses and diagnostic machines and into a small office at the end of the hall. He flicked on the light, sat on a worn leather chair behind a large wooden desk, and gestured for me to sit across from him. A large, framed photo of an Asian couple smiling in front of the clinic's entrance hung on the back wall, in between two certificates from the College of Optometrists of Ontario. The desk was neatly organized, with a stack of frame catalogues on one side, a small lensometer and pupillometer resting on top, and a frame warmer on the other.

"Let's see the victim," he said, as I dug the pieces out of my bag. "And I'm sorry again. If I had known that it was you when I walked in, I would have been more alert to the possibility of projectile glasses hurtling across the room." One side of his mouth ticked up as he took the glasses from my hand.

An unwilling laugh slipped out as I jerked my fingers away, feeling that familiar spark of chemistry between us. He blew out a quick breath as he turned his attention to his desk drawer and pulled out a plastic case filled with tiny screws, hinges, screwdrivers, and microfiber cloths.

My eyes were glued to his large hands as Jake deftly replaced the tiny screw and tightened it. He picked up one of the microfiber cloths and wiped down the lenses before standing up and reaching across the table to put my glasses on my face.

"How does this feel?" His hands lingered at the sides of my face, his thumb grazing my temple and smoothing the hair behind my ear, making my breath hitch. I nodded slowly. His jaw tightened and his gaze dropped down to my lips.

Now, I'd been to several optometrists in my life, and this wasn't the first time one had put glasses on my face, but it was the first time I'd wanted to climb over the table and rip the optometrist's clothes off.

Yeah, it was time for me to get the hell out of here.

I planted my feet on the ground and shoved my chair backwards, rolling into a lamp tucked into the corner beside me. I jumped to steady the lamp, then scrambled to gather my things as Jake put his hands down on his desk. He leaned towards me, drawing my attention to the muscular forearms revealed by his rolled-up sleeves, with their perfect dusting of hair.

*Is it weird to want to lick someone's forearms? Asking for a friend.*

I forced myself to focus, to remember the state I'd been in when he'd left – when my life had blown up. It had taken years of therapy to rebuild the best parts of myself, to feel whole again. I wasn't about to let that fall apart just because he showed up looking like fucking Henry Cavill and acting like I still mattered to him.

He exhaled a long breath. "Emma," he said softly, looking up at me, "we really need to talk about how we left things."

I froze for half a second before throwing my bag over my shoulder.

"How *we* left things?" My voice was tight. He must be *fucking kidding me* with this bullshit. "You abandoned me."

"Seriously?" he said, standing now. "Do you honestly think it was all my fault?"

"You're not going to take any responsibility?" I gripped the strap of my bag like it was the only thing holding me together. Angry tears sprang to my eyes, but there was no fucking way I was going to cry over this asshole again.

His mouth opened like he had more to say, but I didn't wait to hear whatever excuses he was about to offer. No matter what he said, it couldn't change what had happened. I turned on my heel and walked out before the past could pull me under.

# Eight
## December 18, 13 Years Ago

## A Hardy Girls' Mystery

I scratched the itchy green paint on my face, eager to shower and activate Lazy Christmas Mode. Today had been a pretty fun day for the most part, carrying Sarah's books to her class, buying her lunch, and cleaning her locker – easy stuff. The hardest part had been her request for me to speak in Seuss-like rhymes all day. If I never heard one again, it'd be too soon. The Grinch onesie was cozy though and I was planning to keep it. Five stars, 100% would recommend.

After my shower, I snuggled back into the onesie and pulled the hood over my damp hair. I opened Facebook and headed straight to the SAC page to check out the flood of costume pics from today. Abbie had fully committed to being Emo Elsa – floor length ice-blue gown, combat boots, fishnet gloves, black lipstick, smudged eyeliner and a glittery snowflake choker. She glared into the camera. Her caption: "Frozen heart, frozen soul." I snorted.

I paused on Frankie, dressed as Buddy the Elf, who had reportedly eaten nothing but spaghetti with syrup and marshmallows all day. Her mission: tape a candy cane on every locker, shouting, "The best way to spread Christmas cheer is candy canes taped far and near!" every ten seconds like a holiday siren. She'd ambushed unsuspecting students, flinging her arms around them and screaming, "SANTA! I know him!" at the top of her lungs.

And then there was me – Sarah had just posted it. I was sitting in the hallway, leaning against my locker in full Grinch mode, arms crossed, lip curled in a sneer like I was about to bite someone. Classic. I saved it immediately and made it my profile picture.

But I wasn't here to relive my own fuzzy green humiliation. I was here for one reason: to see if someone had posted a picture of *him*. I scrolled with purpose now, scanning group shots and blurry selfies until – yes.

Jake.

In a full butler outfit: crisp white gloves, black bow tie, a cheesy drawn-on mustache curling at the tips. He held a silver tray, smirking at the camera like he'd been born to serve overpriced mocktails to teenage royalty. His charming smile and bright eyes filled my screen, forcing a groan from my lips.

Of course, the photo had been posted by Annika – the grade eleven girl who'd rented him for a ridiculous $225, pooled with her entourage of equally perfect friends. With her glossy black hair and that effortless Queen Bee confidence, I both despised her and wanted to be her in equal parts.

While Jake had been charming Annika and her giggling girl gang all day, I'd been grinching around the building, scowling at the hand I'd been dealt in life: an awkward fourteen-year-old born a year too late.

I saved his picture in my creeper file (inconspicuously titled "Really Important Assignment"). There were already a few gems in there – one from the Halloween dance where he'd been dressed as Emmet from *The Lego Movie*, rocking a bright orange vest, a wide, goofy grin, and perfectly coiffed hair. Another was the photo of him from the school baseball team – in full uniform, staring down the camera like it had just tried to steal home. His hair stuck out under his cap, and there was just the faintest hint of a smirk, like he already knew he was going to strike you out. And my personal favourite, a selfie he'd photobombed during lunch, his face suddenly popping into the frame just as I was fixing my hair. I'd started the folder back in October, mostly as a joke. But now? The next two weeks were going to seem endless without my daily Jake fix.

We'd been orbiting closer lately – little conversations by our lockers, the way he'd wait half a second to walk with me if we were heading in the same direction down the hall, stuff like that. I'd finished my foodbank training last week, and after the break, I was going to start volunteering with him. The idea of losing that momentum – of pressing pause on something that felt like it was maybe, possibly, actually becoming something – made me irrationally grumpy about the holidays. Grinchy, even.

As I was about to head downstairs, that telltale two-note trill announced a new Facebook message. I sat down at my desk and clicked to open it, prepared to tell Sarah she would have to kill me and drag my cold dead body from this onesie if she ever wanted it back.

I stared at my screen for approximately ten years.

It was Jake.

Jake messages me now? Wait, was this the SAC group chat?

**Jake:**
So, how are things up on Mount Crumpit?

**Jake:**
Did you take your costume and dump it?

**Jake:**
Also...How did you talk like this all day?

This was not the group chat. This was not the group chat, people. *Okay Emma, be cool, be cool. Think.*

**Emma:**
I do not want to take it off.
I do not know what rhymes with off.
I would not, could not change my clothes.
I could not, would not, if it snows.

*That was not cool. Oh my GOD, my brain is broken.*

**Jake:**
Ha. It did look warm and comfy.

**Emma:**
The coziest thing ever and it's never coming off. How about you, Alfred? Still rocking that bow tie?

*The bow tie was hot.*

**Jake:**
Sadly, I had to give it back. Keeping the mustache though, it suits me.

**Emma:**
LOL. My heart grew three sizes when I saw it.

**Jake:**
Ha. Happy to be of service.

**Emma:**
I noticed – you sure were busy today.

**Jake:**
All in the name of foodbanks and fun. Gotta go, Owen's back from Uni and my dad's not working for once so my mom wants to take us tree chopping. Family fun time, my favourite.

*Did he not like spending time with his family? I didn't know, but I really wanted to.*

**Emma:**
Well, I hope it goes well. Just stick with the Blue Spruce and don't forget to leave the Truffula Trees for the Brown Bar-ba-loots. 😉

**Jake:**
😆 Will do. Talk to you soon, Grinch.

**Emma:**
Later, Alfred.

Soon? He wanted to talk to me *soon*? Holy crap. When exactly was "soon" anyway? Tonight? Tomorrow? I unplugged my laptop, gathered it in my arms and ran toward the stairs.

"Mom! What does this mean?!" I slipped on the last step as I rushed to the kitchen, then dropped my laptop on the table.

"What does what mean? Oh, you're back in the suit. Is that green face paint on the hood? Come here, let me wipe it off." She picked up a cloth and ran it under the tap.

"Never mind that – Jake wrote to me. Just me. Not in the group chat. Read this and tell me if he loves me," I demanded as my mom stifled a laugh. "Okay, maybe I'm overreacting a bit, but this feels like an important break in *The Case of the Blue-Eyed Charmer: A Hardy Girls' Mystery*."

My mom laughed out loud and turned the computer towards herself. "You're ridiculous." She furrowed her brows as she scanned our chat. "Hmm…interesting."

"What?!" I slapped my hands down on the table. "What does it mean?"

"It means you read too much Dr. Seuss."

"Mom. Please. Come on! Help a Hardy Girl out here, I'm dying," I begged, but she just wiped the green face paint off my hood before enveloping me in a warm hug.

"Bar-ba-loots, Emma?" She chuckled, squeezing me tightly.

"I know!" I groaned. "Could I be less cool?"

My mom's eyes sparkled as she broke our hug and held me at arm's length. "Love you, Baby Spice. You're the coolest."

"It doesn't count when your mom says it."

"Let's make cookies. Cookies always help." She started pulling ingredients onto the counter. "Dad's picking up sushi on the way home and we can relax and watch A Christmas Story tonight."

I sighed, opening the cupboard and taking out the stand mixer. My rational side seemed to have taken a Christmas vacation. I needed to report this new development in the case to Sarah, my fellow Hardy Girl, or the next two weeks would be spent obsessing over every clue.

# Nine

# This Lauren Woman

Rushing up to Taco Taco a few minutes late, I scanned the patio for Ryan, hoping he had been delayed so I'd have a minute to get myself together. My hair was likely doing something unfortunate after the brisk, ten-minute walk in the August humidity, and since we were going to discuss a possible job, I wanted to look halfway presentable. If I also saw this meeting as a chance to get some intel on Jake – well hey, I could multitask.

Before I could escape inside to the bathroom to tame the frizz, I spotted Ryan at a table for two under a crisp white umbrella.

"V – great to see you again," he said with a broad smile, standing as I approached the table. Intricate lines of black ink decorating his upper arm peeked out from beneath the sleeve of his fitted white T-shirt. Objectively, Ryan was even hotter than I'd remembered. If only there'd been a spark between us, I might not have spent the last few days with my brain on the Jake train, my stop nowhere in sight.

"I feel like you can call me Emma at this point," I said with a laugh.

"Nope – can't think of you as anything but Victoria now, sorry." Ryan gave me a cheeky grin.

The waiter dropped menus and water on the table and took our drink order, a virgin watermelon margarita for me and a pint of Hawaiian ale for Ryan. We chatted as we waited for the drinks to arrive, one part of my mind brainstorming ways to bring Jake into the conversation naturally.

"Cheers," Ryan said, once our drinks had arrived, clinking his pint glass with mine.

"So, what's the project you're working on?" I asked.

"It's a calendar for the Humane Society. We're scrambling because we're scheduled to shoot this Sunday and the photographer we usually use just got a last-minute job doing portraits on a cruise ship. He's on his way to the Mediterranean as we speak."

"Ah, so shirtless firefighters snuggling kittens and puppies?" I grinned as a parade of hot firefighters danced through my imagination. "I might be able to squeeze that in. It's for a good cause, after all."

Ryan laughed.

"Did you have a location in mind?"

"There's a bit of green space over on River Street; and the mural along Queen Street might work. But obviously, it would be up to you if you want the job."

"I'd be happy to do it." I wasn't in the business of turning down work, especially a job that promised to be as fun as this one. And I'd had a cancellation for this upcoming Sunday, so the day was wide open. "Send me the contract and we can finalize the details."

"Deal."

Conversation flowed between Ryan and me while we ate. I learned that he'd been a firefighter for ten years, was born and raised in the Beach, lived on his own in a one-bedroom apartment in Little Italy, played about a million different sports, and loved the chipotle chicken burrito and the street corn at Taco Taco.

When he described the antics of his parents' aging male Schnauzer, who was inexplicably named Nancy, I laughed so hard I snorted margarita through my nose. But even as I enjoyed our conversation, my mind churned away at the Jake problem. This was my best opportunity to find out why Jake was here and whether he was back for good. Maybe if I circled back to speed dating, I could bring him up. Super casually, of course.

"Alright, Ryan. You need to tell me about Celine. You can't go around acting like the president of her fan club and not explain why." I picked up my fork to wrestle all the toppings that had fallen off my loaded nachos into my mouth.

He grinned. “My younger sister, Lauren, was a huge fan of *Titanic* when we were growing up. She played it constantly and would make me ‘Titanic’ her at the edge of the couch.” He sipped his beer.

“I’m sorry, what? ‘Titanic’ her?”

“You know, that scene where Jack stands behind Rose at the bow of the ship and they hold their arms out and she’s all ‘I’m flying, Jack!’ She was little and I’d do anything for her, so yeah.” He shrugged. “And she played ‘My Heart Will Go On’ all the time. I have a wicked falsetto, but nothing like Celine. She’s unreal, V.”

“You’re not wrong,” I said. *Now’s my chance.*

“So, Lauren works with Jake?” I struggled to sound nonchalant when in actuality I was super chalant. It was risky, digging for information about him, when I wasn’t ready to answer questions that Ryan might ask. But I’d been replaying the look on Jake’s face since I’d bolted from his practice the other day, unable to stop wondering what he’d been about to say.

“Yeah, they went to school together and now they’re working at my parents’ practice. Lauren’s officially joined the team but Jake’s just here for the summer, filling in for my dad while he recovers from rotator cuff surgery. Thirty years of weekend golf finally caught up to him.”

“Oh, sorry to hear about your dad’s surgery. It’s nice that Jake’s filling in.” So, he’d be leaving again. That tracked. But wait – he came here for her? Were they partners, not just in optometry, but in life? My mind immediately conjured up a picture of adult Jake “Titanic-ing” this Lauren woman.

Ryan had said he’d dragged him to speed dating. *Great.* Jake had already been occupying far too much of my mental space – rent-free, my brain the last piece of affordable real estate in Toronto – and now I could add this to my list of Jake-related questions to obsess over.

“Yeah, Jake’s a good guy. He and Lauren have been tight since their first year.” He paused. “The vibe between you two the other night was… intense. You know him from high school?”

“Yep.” My heart jumped to my throat before beginning to beat double-time.

“Were you guys close?” he asked.

My face flushed like an Instant-Pot, no preheating necessary. I took a long sip of my water, buying time as I searched for the right words. “We were friends. But I haven’t seen him in forever.”

“Why did you lose touch?”

My shoulders tensed. “He was a year ahead of me, and we stopped hanging out when he went away to university,” I said, leaving out the part where he'd disappeared overnight, like he'd fallen into a black hole, taking half of me with him.

I needed to steer this conversation elsewhere – fast. I flipped through my mental Rolodex of weird conversation starters, before landing on something I'd been curious about since speed dating.

"Before I forget – I was wondering – I know we aren't soulmates, but what was the third question you never got to ask?"

"My deal breaker." Ryan grinned. "Thoughts on cats?"

"I'm allergic. Do you have one?" I exhaled like a balloon deflating, grateful Ryan had allowed the conversation to move on.

"Hell, no. Cats freak me out. Purring? Bumpy tongues? They're sneaky and you never know which way they're gonna go." He shook his head until he snapped out of it, a trace of sweat evident on his forehead, then checked his watch.

"Woah, I have to get going." He smiled and waved to the waiter for the bill. "We have a volleyball game at Central Tech tonight, and I need to start stretching early to make sure I don't pull a hammy. Dan's promised us half-price wings at the bar if we win."

"Dan's pretty stingy, how'd you manage that?"

"He sponsored our team."

I snorted. "He sponsored a men's recreational volleyball team? That's a thing?"

"Oh yeah, it's a goldmine. We get a Trinity T-shirt, draw massive crowds, and then all six of us hit the bar after the game. Eight when the subs show up." He was trying to keep a straight face.

So Jake's appearance at my favourite hangout wasn't a one-time-only thing? *Super*.

"Speaking of Dan, I'm putting together a team for trivia night at the bar next weekend. Jake, Lauren and I are in, but we need a fourth. Any interest?"

*A thousand percent no*. But Mel would kill me if I backed out of trivia altogether. "Mel's already recruited me." I said. "She's been quizzing us for weeks, so you better find someone who knows their stuff."

"Shots fired! See you there."

I laughed. "Good luck tonight. Try to stay off the injured list."

The sun pressed down on me as I headed home after lunch, my thoughts about Jake burning hotter than the pavement, twisting and sparking like a wildfire. I'd spent years keeping the door to my complicated feelings about him sealed, but ever since he'd cracked it back open, something restless had been clawing at the edges, making it difficult to sleep. I'd been on edge since he'd ambushed me at Moonbean on Sunday, worried that he was going to pop out like a Jack-in-the-Box when I least expected him, and I hadn't stopped wondering what he'd been about to say before I'd noped out of our conversation.

And now that he was coming to freaking trivia night, I was on a crash course with another awkward and uncomfortable interaction with him if I didn't deal with this. It would be best to have this conversation on my terms and get Jake's explanation for what he'd done back then out of the way.

Before I knew it, I was outside his office.

*Was I really going to do this?*

A list of cons popped up. I might cry, I might throw things at him, or – if he showed me his forearms again – I might accidentally kiss him. But the pros were compelling. Dr. Kuri would be proud of me and convincing my therapist I was thriving was basically my part-time job. And getting some sort of closure might stop the 24/7 Jake show that had taken up residence in my brain.

I pushed the door open before I lost my nerve, the cool air inside offering relief from the oppressive heat. A woman with long, silky black hair and flawless skin sat at the desk, looking over some paperwork. The plastic name tag pinned on her shirt said "Dr. Li." She glanced up as I entered.

This must be Lauren. She was as perfect as I'd expected her to be.

"Hi, can I help you?" she asked.

"Hi – I was wondering if Jake was working today?" I tried to keep my voice steady.

Lauren smiled, picked up a stack of papers, and stapled them together. "Jake's with a patient right now. He should be out in a few minutes." She gave me an appraising look. "Feel free to take a seat if you'd like to wait."

"Great, thank you." I sank into a chair in the waiting area and grabbed an old copy of Chatelaine magazine, flipping through the pages without paying attention.

Dammit, I should have written out what I wanted to say. Now that I was here, with the weight of Lauren's gaze on me, I was second-guessing my impulse to come. I already knew what Jake would say – he'd make some excuse – and what? I'd forgive him? Unlikely. So, what was I really hoping to accomplish here?

I stood up, resolving to back out of trivia with a fake cough and hole up in my apartment like I was avoiding the zombie apocalypse in *The Last of Us* until Jake left again. Then his low chuckle echoed down the hallway, followed by a child's giggle. Jake appeared in the waiting room with a little boy who was no more than eight, with big glasses that nearly swallowed his face. The kid peeled a sticky wall-crawler out of its packaging, his toothless grin stretching wide as Jake crouched down beside him.

"Take care of those glasses, buddy. No more headers in soccer practice." His voice was light and teasing, filled with that familiar warmth I remembered. He glanced up, and his eyes locked on mine with a flash of surprise.

"Thank you so much for fitting us in, Dr. Griffin," the boy's mother said, following them into the waiting room. "What would we have done without you?"

"I'm sure Dr. Li would have taken good care of you," Jake replied, polite and professional.

She stepped closer to him, a playful glint in her eye. "Well, I think you deserve a reward for saving us. How about dinner on Friday?"

Jake chuckled. His gaze flicked briefly to mine, his cheeks flushing pink. "I think I'll have to pass on that one, but thank you for the offer."

"Well, if you change your mind, you know how to find me." She winked before heading towards the door. "Take care, Dr. Griffin."

As the door closed, Lauren said, "Jesus, Jake. Can't get through one shift without a divorced cougar trying to make you a stepdaddy."

Jake rolled his eyes and turned to face me.

"Hey, Em." His voice was tentative. "Nice to see you. This is Lauren."

I barely heard him, still focused on her teasing comment. The easy banter between them, the way she looked at him and checked me out. Were they just friends, or was there something more?

*Ugh, Emma, it doesn't matter*. I was here to clear the air and exorcise Jake from my system, not to dig into his relationship status.

"Nice to meet you," I said, offering her a small smile as she grinned back at me.

"Likewise," she said.

I forced myself to focus on Jake's face. "I'm sorry to bother you at work. I was in the neighbourhood and I was hoping we could find time to talk."

As I spoke, Lauren glanced between Jake and me, her curiosity bouncing back and forth like a tennis rally. She didn't bother to hide it; her attention was laser-focused on our exchange.

Jake's mouth ticked up into that half-smile I remembered so well, and his eyes did that warm twinkling thing that had always made me melt back in high school.

"For sure. I don't have another patient for a half hour." He glanced over at Lauren. "You're good, right?"

She arched an eyebrow. "I'm sure I can manage. Grab me a coffee from Fika while you're out?"

"Of course," he said, opening the door for me and gesturing in front of him.

We stepped out onto the bustling street, narrowly dodging a food delivery person on an e-bike who was zipping onto the sidewalk to avoid traffic. We turned up Kensington Avenue towards Fika, walking as the hum of Dundas faded behind us. I didn't really know how to start this conversation.

I took a deep breath. "Jake, I–"

"Before you say anything, I owe you an apology. I've been thinking a lot since I saw you again. I'm so sorry about how I left things back then. It wasn't fair." He glanced at me, and I read genuine regret in the lines on his face.

That wasn't what I'd been expecting. I had been preparing myself to hear excuses and wondering if I'd have the guts to tell him just how much his behaviour had hurt me.

"You're right, it wasn't fair." I blinked furiously to relieve the sudden stinging at the back of my eyes.

"I should have handled it differently. I'm sorry I wasn't there."

His simple and heartfelt apology hit me right in the gut and left me floundering. I hadn't realized how much I'd needed to hear it. "It was a long time ago – we were kids." The lump in my throat grew as I turned away from his steady gaze. I didn't want to hear any more.

Part of me wanted to cling to the anger because it was safer, more predictable. But another part, one I'd tried to bury, had always missed him. I was tired of carrying it. I'd brought it into every relationship I'd been in, whether I wanted to admit it or not.

"Yeah, we were kids. But you were also my best friend." His voice was quiet but sure.

I stopped beside the Dala horse in front of Fika and turned to face him, the back of my hand brushing his. "We're both adults now. Honestly, it's forgotten." The last thing I wanted was to do a detailed post-mortem on our high school relationship.

Jake curled his finger around mine, and I froze, struck by how close we were.

"All of it?" Jake's eyes flickered over my face.

"What?" I was breathless, my brain no longer braining.

"Have you forgotten all of it?" His voice was low and husky.

My mind was overrun with memories of the boy I'd known. The late-night conversations, the easy laughter, the way I'd trusted him more than anyone. And the way it had all spectacularly gone up in flames. Holding his gaze, I shook my head slightly.

"Good."

After a pause during which I could almost see my memories reflected in his eyes, he blinked twice and stepped back, disengaging his hand from mine and bringing it up to rub the back of his neck.

"Right. Well. I'm glad we're okay."

"We're good, Jake. I accept your apology." My voice was quiet as inwardly I reeled from the intensity of my attraction to him. My fingers tingled where he'd touched them. I couldn't believe he still had this effect on me.

"Thanks," Jake said with a sigh of relief. "It's been surreal seeing you again."

"You're telling me." I cleared my throat. "I hear that you'll be at trivia night next week?" I forced a small smile, trying to dispel the lingering tension.

"Did Ryan invite you?"

I laughed. "Unfortunately for you, I'm already on a team." There was something about being around Jake that yanked me back into our old rhythm – the easy back-and-forth that was once second nature.

"Well, I'll see you there." Jake grinned. "I better grab that coffee for Lauren and head back to the office. She gets angry when she's under-caffeinated."

Lauren. Right.

"Sounds good," I said, taking a few steps back.

"I'm really glad you came to see me." Jake held my gaze before turning and heading up the wooden steps to Fika.

As he disappeared into the café, I tried to ignore the small flicker of hope that maybe things between us weren't completely finished.

## Ten
## January 20, 12 Years Ago

# Where Were the Sinkholes When You Needed Them?

The gravel crunched under our tires as my mom pulled into the parking lot at the Scarborough food bank. I'd completed my training earlier this month, and this was the first time I was meeting Jake to volunteer. We'd been messaging regularly on Facebook since the holiday, but we'd never hung out outside of school before. I hoped I didn't do anything stupid.

I spotted Jake striding towards a beige Toyota Camry a few spots down, where an elderly woman stood beside her open trunk. The sharp January wind pushed the hood of his bright blue puffer jacket down, ruffling his dark hair. He flashed the woman a quick grin before reaching into the trunk and heaving two bags of donations onto a trolley.

"My shift ends at seven, but don't come until I call you. I'm gonna see if Jake wants to grab a bubble tea when we're done." The thought of being alone with him detonated a glitter bomb of nerves.

"Mmm-hmm," My mom looked at me with a knowing grin and her eyes dancing.

"Ugh, Mom, stop. I'm nervous enough already!"

Jake glanced towards us, smiling and waving as our eyes met. His smile was knee-melting from a distance and even more lethal up close. I wasn't sure I'd be able to keep it together while we worked side-by-side for the next few hours. I stifled a groan, making my mom laugh.

"Well, I hope you have a good shift, Emmie. Don't forget the bags in the back," she said.

I climbed out of the car, my heart beating a little faster. I leaned into the back seat to grab the bags of clothing and book donations I'd collected, just as Jake arrived at our car with the trolley.

"Hi, Mrs. Anderson," Jake said, bending down and waving. "Thanks for the donations. These are great – we never have enough books or warm clothes."

"Nice to meet you, Jake." My mom nodded at the bags. "That's all Emma."

A blush crept over my cheeks as I piled them on the trolley. Every kid that visited the food bank got a free book, and he'd told me they were running low.

"Of course," he said. "We should get inside."

"Bye, Mom," I said, hastily closing the car door before following him towards the entrance.

When Jake pushed the trolley over the threshold, he was immediately surrounded by people who opened the donation bags and started sorting the food onto the shelves. Jake grabbed the bag of books and dropped it in front of a tall brown shelf before coming back to pick up the bag of clothing and gesturing for me to come with him towards the clothing rack. He opened the bag, and we started putting things on hangers.

"Jacob, this must be your girlfriend!" An elderly Asian man beamed as he approached Jake and me. "It's so good to meet you!"

"Uh, no…I…" I crossed my arms, shrugged my shoulders, then planted my hands on my hips, trying to act completely natural. I wasn't Jake's girlfriend…unless you counted my dreams.

Jake's guffaw cut me off. "No, Rick, this is Emma. We're on the student council together. I'm helping her get some community service hours."

*Did he have to laugh like it was the most ridiculous thing in the world that someone thought I was his girlfriend?*

I forced a smile, trying to shake off the pinprick of hurt.

Rick was unfazed, his grin widening. "Emma! How's the foot? Jake told us all about your fall." He looked down at my feet. "Doing okay now?"

*Oh goodie, I was hoping we'd bring that up again.*

"Yep, great," I said, with far too much enthusiasm. I even danced a little jig to prove everything was in working order. Oh yes, Riverdancing in the middle of the food bank was definitely going to convince Jake to go on a date with me. I glanced around, searching for a rock I could crawl under.

Rick laughed. "Well, good to meet you! When you're done with the clothes, can I get some help moving potatoes and onions?"

"Of course," I said, giving a final tippity tap and bow.

Jake grinned as he hung up the last of my dad's donated cardigans, then squeezed the empty garbage bag into a ball. "Let's go, Anderson, I'll show you how it's done."

Jake and Rick explained how everything worked, which crates of food were reserved for our shift, and how much to give to each person. Rick mentioned it was a good day; there had been a big donation of garlic and melons, which was rare, and there were so many potatoes that we were allowed to give out extra. With a few minutes to go before customers came in, Jake and I busied ourselves filling the shelves, and Rick moved off to make sure that the bookshelves were organized.

Now was the perfect opportunity to ask Jake if he wanted to grab bubble tea once our shift was done. My stomach tightened. *How do words work again?* I fumbled a melon with clumsy hands, just saving it from dropping.

"Hey, I was wondering–" I started, a quaver in my voice, just as the bell above the door tinkled and the volume in the food bank abruptly intensified with the influx of people.

Jake turned and smiled. "Here we go!"

Saved by the bell, I was unsure whether to be frustrated or grateful that he hadn't heard me.

Over the next three hours, I met so many kind people, shared laughs with customers, complimented a couple of great outfits I saw, and doled out extra food when I could. I loved every minute, completely swept up in the welcoming energy. And it was only made better because I was with Jake. I was struck by how many people he knew by name. It was clear he had built relationships with them, asking about their families and recommending certain books that he thought their kids might like. Now and then, we'd catch each other's eye or brush shoulders reaching into the bins, and I'd feel that spark of excitement. Being in Jake's orbit made everything brighter. And I was pretty sure he felt it too.

Before I knew it, it was nearly seven o'clock, the last customer was leaving, and our shift was over. I was tired and my feet were sore, but I was filled with a warm sense of accomplishment. We'd been so busy that I hadn't had a chance to ask Jake what he was doing after our shift. As we got our coats from our lockers and pushed open the door into the cold January evening, I gave myself a pep talk. *He wouldn't have asked me to volunteer with him if he didn't like me.*

"You're a natural, Anderson," Jake said. "I knew you'd be perfect for this."

I grinned as Jake's compliment hit me right in the heart. "Thanks! I loved it." *Now or never, Emma, just do it.*

"Hey, do you–" I started to ask, but I was cut off by a voice calling Jake's name from behind me. He glanced over my shoulder, and a smile spread across his face. I turned around to see Annika making her way towards us.

"Hey, you," Jake said, his voice softening as Annika reached him. A white martial arts uniform and a red belt peeked out from under her coat as she stood on tiptoe to kiss him.

*Record scratch.*

I turned away, but the arrow still found its mark, sharp and unforgiving in my chest.

"Hey, Emma. How was your first shift at the food bank?"

Annika had a genuine smile, and I had a sudden urge to stick my fist in it. But if the red belt was any indication, I wouldn't get very far.

"It was great!" I said, forcing a smile. When had *that* started – Jake and Annika? And why hadn't the high school rumour mill done its job and clued me in?

"Nice of Jake to help you out with your hours. They're a real bitch to finish if you start late." She ran her hand down his chest and looked up adoringly at him. Jake grabbed her hand as she slid it off him and held it tight.

*Barf.* This was not how I'd pictured the evening ending. It was so far from the ending I'd hoped for that I had whiplash.

Thank god I hadn't actually asked him out.

My blood ran cold just imagining the terrifying awkwardness I'd have inflicted on both of us if I'd gotten the words out.

"We're going to grab a bubble tea next door. Do you want to join us?" Jake asked, but his tone made it clear he was just being polite.

"Yeah, we can wait with you until your mom or dad picks you up,"

Annika said, making me feel about ten years old. "I'd give you a ride, but we're meeting some friends at the mall after I change."

"Oh, no, you kids go ahead," I said, morphing into a forty-year-old mom. "I need to swing by…" I cast my eyes desperately around the plaza to find somewhere I might conceivably need to go. "…Pet Valu. To pick something up for my…pet." I winced. I didn't have a pet.

"I didn't know you had a pet," Jake said. "What kind?"

They looked at me, waiting.

"Uh…" I blinked, struggling to come up with something. My brain had short-circuited. "A, um, soft one."

Jake raised an eyebrow. "A soft one?" he repeated, a hint of amusement in his voice.

"A fish," I blurted, the only thing that came to mind besides the glow-in-the-dark alien on my T-shirt. I was in deep now. There was no turning back. *For fuck's sake, Emma.*

"A fish is definitely soft…I guess." Annika exchanged a glance with Jake, both trying not to crack up. "What's its name?"

"Fluffy," I said, the word slipping out before I could stop it. I could feel my face burning like I'd just opened an oven door, heat spreading from my cheeks to my ears. I looked at the ground. Where were the sinkholes when you needed them?

Jake laughed, shaking his head. "Why am I not surprised?"

Of course, he wasn't surprised. I was always like this around him – awkward, fumbling, and constantly putting my foot in my mouth. I couldn't even answer a simple question without embarrassing myself. The total opposite of cool, confident Annika.

"Welp, will you look at the time?" I spouted, my forty-year-old alter ego making a reappearance. I needed to get to Pet Valu, stat. Fluffy needed her fish pellets, and I needed to escape the weight of Jake's sympathetic gaze.

"Okay – text me when your mom gets here so we know you're safe," Jake said. His voice was gentle but firm, like I was the little sister he had to take care of.

"Yes, sir!" I called, giving a half-salute as I turned around, cringing as I power-walked to Pet Valu and threw the door open, the harsh fluorescents buzzing and flickering overhead as if they were annoyed with me, too.

I texted my mom that I was ready to be picked up before stomping towards the fish aisle, dashing away tears of embarrassment and disappointment.

Jake had a girlfriend. I should have known that he was hopelessly out of my reach, but my stupid heart had been stupidly hoping that the zings of excitement and connection I'd felt whenever we'd spent time together or texted late at night weren't one-sided. Sarah was right; it was never going to happen. And I needed to accept it and stop acting like an idiot around him before I embarrassed myself more and ruined the possibility of friendship between us.

Eight minutes later, my mom's car rolled into the parking lot. I texted Jake to let him know, and he sent a thumbs-up reaction in reply. As the car stopped, I climbed in, cradling a bag of water with a fan-tail goldfish inside, along with a plastic fishbowl, some gravel, and a container of fish pellets. Since I'd hallucinated Fluffy, my soft pet fish, into existence, I'd needed to make her a reality. Better that than having to pretend that she'd died and faking a heartfelt flushing ceremony on Facebook. I'd always kind of wanted a fish anyway.

I slammed the door shut with more force than I'd intended, and my mom gave a soft, knowing laugh.

"Don't ask," I muttered, not sure if I was more embarrassed by what I'd done or that she wasn't even surprised. I stared at Fluffy – her bulging eyes wide with judgement – and wondered if even a fish could sense how hopeless I was. One thing was for sure – I was about to have a lot more time for my art, now that I wouldn't be obsessing over Jake or fine-tuning my "Emma + Jake 4Eva (Vol. 2)" iTunes playlist.

# Eleven

# Will They or Won't They

As Anusha gave everyone a few minutes to get their answer sheets and pencils, my attention drifted to the table next to ours, where Jake and Ryan were chatting with Lauren and her friend Zoe. My mind immediately went to work, trying to decipher what was happening between Jake and Lauren. I kept trying to tell myself I didn't care, but even I wasn't buying that anymore.

Now, as I watched, I went full Enola Holmes. His hand was on the table, just a couple of centimetres from Lauren's, but not quite close enough to confirm anything. He leaned in eagerly when she spoke, his whole body angling towards her like she was recruiting him for an MLM pyramid scheme. God, he would be selling fucking Scentsy before the night was over. Was he just an attentive listener, or was he about to propose?

Anusha clicked on her microphone.

"Welcome to Trivia at the Trinity, everyone! Here's how things are going to work. There will be three rounds, with ten questions each. You'll have one minute to write each answer on the paper provided. After each round, you'll pass your paper to the next table, and we'll take up the answers. Good luck! First question: Which pop star is the godmother of both of Elton John's sons?"

"Let's go, people, we got this!" Mel reached kitty-corner across the table and snatched the trivia answer sheet out of Jerry's hand. "I'm writing."

"Chill, Mel." Jerry grimaced. "This is supposed to be fun." He turned to face his friend Raymond, who rounded out our team. "She didn't talk to me for a week the one time my team beat hers at Cranium."

Raymond laughed.

I glanced back at Jake's table as he pulled out a pair of dark brown rimmed glasses, transforming from Superman to Clark Kent as he reached for their answer page.

"Oh, for fuck's sake," I said, pressing my nails into Mel's arm as I jerked my head towards Jake's table. Mel turned to look. Hot guys in glasses were my kryptonite, and I had the opposite of a poker face. Mel had once called it my "resting enthusiastic face." I was doomed.

"Oh, snapdragons, you're screwed." She turned back to me. "I promise, we'll circle back to that, but focus! Elton John!"

I shook my head like a wet dog, trying to fling away the attraction as my team rattled off guesses – Madonna, Cher, Adele.

"It's Lady Gaga," I whispered.

Mel scribbled down the answer as Anusha called out the next question.

"Which pop star accidentally set fire to her home gym with candles?"

We all looked at each other and said, "Britney."

Jerry whispered, "Leave Britney Alone," and I burst into laughter, catching Jake watching me with a wistful smile. And suddenly I was back in front of Fika – his voice low, his eyes searching mine.

*Have you forgotten everything?*

As if I ever could.

In the last week and a half, we'd crossed paths a couple of times at the bar, and it had started to feel like he'd never left. He'd shared the story of how we'd first met with Mel – me, face-down on the gym floor – and told her he'd befriended me to protect me from myself. Her sparkling eyes had met mine; she'd been charmed.

And it wasn't just her. I felt it too, but I was trying not to get drawn back in, despite how much I liked being around him.

He was leaving in a month. He might be dating Lauren. And none of that mattered anyway – given our history, he was the last person I should want to start a relationship with.

I turned back towards Jake and Lauren, ignoring Anusha's next question and squinting as I stared. Did his finger twitch? Were their knees touching? Jake laughed – rich and full – the kind he used to give me. I wanted to slap myself for the way it made my chest tighten.

*Get a grip, Emma. It doesn't matter.*

After the tenth question, Mel handed me the answer sheet and nodded towards his table.

"Trade ya," I said, as I approached.

"How'd you do?" Jake's fingers brushed mine as he gently slid the scorecard out of my hand, that familiar warmth spreading through my arm to the rest of my body. "That was right up your alley."

"Pretty sure we crushed it. I'm afraid to think what Mel would do if we didn't."

"Yeah, she's making me nervous," Ryan snickered, glancing towards her as she gave Jerry a spirited pep talk.

"She's always like this with trivia. Her dad told me she broke their TV as a kid when she got a question wrong in 'Twilight: Scene It.'"

Jake chuckled as Anusha flicked her mic back on to let everyone know it was time to take up the answers.

I sat down at my table and glanced at him, just as his eyes dipped down to my lips and lingered for a moment, sucking the air from my lungs. I was caught, unable to look away as his eyes traveled slowly back up to meet mine. He quirked his lips in a small, private smile.

"Jesus, Emma, this is not the time!" Mel's voice yanked me out of the moment, her eyes darting between Jake and me as Anusha read the correct answers. "Save the eye-boning for after round three. Pay attention!"

Right on cue, his eyes – those damn perfect blue eyes – shifted to land on Lauren as she said something that made him laugh.

I tried to swallow the bitter lump in my throat.

Was she really that interesting? She was an optometrist, for god's sake – how interesting could she be?

But why did I care?

I didn't care!

"Sports?!" Mel cried after Anusha announced the topic for the second round. "Jerry, didn't you have any pull with these? Why couldn't it be video games, cocktail recipes, counting toonies, or something else you're good at? You know I love you, but you're dead weight!"

"We got a perfect score in the first round, so we have a little room for error," Jerry said. "Plus, I know a bit about golf."

"Golf is *barely* a sport." Mel was frantic. "I want that gift card. Do you have any idea how much money Em and I spend here? I need to sub you out."

"Gladly," Jerry said, as Raymond belly-laughed.

Mel stood and turned, wagging her finger between Jake and Ryan. "Which one of you turkeys knows more about sports?"

"Not it!" Ryan touched his forefinger to his nose like we were a group of kids playing hide-and-seek.

Mel turned to stare directly at Jake. "Pretty boy. You're in. Jer's out. Trade spots."

Jake glanced at his silent teammates for support. Ryan grinned triumphantly.

"What, are your legs painted on? Get up." Her teacher's voice activated. "Now!"

Holy hell, Mel was terrifying.

"Yes, ma'am." Jake did what he was told, as Jerry picked up his beer and shuffled over to their table.

I tried to gauge Lauren's reaction. She was laughing at something Zoe had said, her attention elsewhere, leaving me with nothing to go on. Maybe they were so secure in their relationship that it didn't matter where Jake sat, or maybe they were just friends, and I was overthinking everything. But damn, I hated how badly I wanted to figure it out.

Through his thin grey tee, Jake's solid shoulder grazed my bare arm when he sat down next to me, sending a current through my body. I shifted my chair slightly away from his, trying to quell the sudden rush.

"Okay, everyone, after round one, we have two teams tied for first with ten points: 'Trivia Rodrigo' and 'If You Wanna Push My Buzzer,'" Anusha called.

Mel hooted and banged on the table when our team was mentioned.

"Round two, first question: Which five NFL teams are named after birds?" Anusha asked.

Mel groaned. Resigned, she slid the paper and pencil towards Jake. He grinned as he picked up the pencil, jotting down the correct teams, before sliding the paper back to Mel.

"Keep it," Mel said, "I'm useless this round – now I know what it feels like to be Jerry." She downed her gin and tonic as Jerry laughed with his new team and wondered aloud if a "49er" was a bird.

I tried to focus on the game, but being close to Jake consumed me. Every shift of his body had me on edge, torn between dreading and desperately hoping for any chance of him making contact with me. It was maddening, this tension between wanting to stay distant, to protect myself, and the overwhelming pull that had me craving his touch.

"Last question for this round: Who are the most decorated figure skaters in Olympic history? I'll give you a clue – it's a tie," Anusha said, before reminding us to switch our papers with another table once we were finished.

*Easy.*

Raymond and Mel threw out the names of a few American skaters while Jake dove into the intense "Battle of the Brians" from Calgary in 1988.

"Are you guys for real right now? Hello? Tessa Virtue and Scott Moir, the greatest love story that never was? They each have five medals."

My face flushed as I remembered their spectacular "Goose" lift from 2010, the breathtaking "Moulin Rouge" routine in PyeongChang, but most importantly, the heart-stopping kiss they shared during the free dance warm-up at the Sochi Olympics in 2014. I'd watched that YouTube clip hundreds of times while digging deep into a "will they or won't they/ did they or didn't they" Tessa and Scott rabbit hole.

"They were so hot together. I hope they did it at least once." I sipped my cocktail and fanned myself with my napkin before looking over to find Jake's eyes intense on me. I imagined us reenacting their risqué "cunninglift." I was confident it would be a gold medal performance.

"Of course!" Mel said as she wrote their names down gleefully before glancing between Jake and me. "Raymond, let's go trade cards with Jer, and grab more food."

She hopped out of her chair, throwing a wink back at me. Raymond followed her, leaving me alone with Jake. I silently cursed Tessa and Scott's obscene sexual chemistry, which was spinning in my head and making it harder to sit next to him.

"This is fun," Jake said, leaning in so I could hear him over the din in the bar. "I've missed hanging out with you."

I wasn't prepared for the way his words filled the space between us, warm and familiar, like a song I hadn't heard in years but still knew by heart. My grip tightened around my drink as I forced myself to meet his eyes.

"Me too," I said.

His cedar and citrus scent wrapped around me, stirring something reckless. I had the sudden, unhinged urge to lick his neck, just to see if he tasted as good as he smelled.

*Nope and nope.*

"And Lauren and Zoe are really hitting it off." He nodded towards their table, where Lauren was laughing with her hand on Zoe's shoulder. "She was nervous about bringing her here for a first date."

First date?

*Oh.*

*Ohhhhh.*

The realization cracked through me like a lightning strike – sudden and bright. He wasn't with Lauren.

Jake was single.

My libido sat up like a puppy begging for a treat.

"Yeah. Zoe could have turned out like Mel." I gave a wobbly grin, hoping he couldn't see how much that revelation had rattled me.

Mel dropped a basket of sweet potato fries between us. "We're in the lead after the last round, but I'm still worried about Trivia Rodrigo, so let's focus, people." She snapped her fingers and sent a pointed look in my direction.

I barely registered the questions about TV and movies – something about a *Friends* spinoff and a Tarantino cameo – as it all blurred into background noise. Mel and Raymond had it covered, and Jake and I slipped into a parallel timeline where it was just the two of us.

We reminisced about high school – like the time Priya Patel had done a full-blown emotional performance of "Since U Been Gone" at the talent show. She'd had backup dancers. A wind machine. She'd ripped open a feather pillow and kicked over a chair.

We laughed, but then our eyes locked and the air thickened between us. His knee brushed mine under the table, and I didn't move. At the heat of his touch, the pulse of something familiar and tempting swirled between us.

Before I could fully process the moment, Anusha's voice broke through, sharp and decisive.

"And the winners are…'If You Wanna Push My Buzzer!'"

Mel whooped, and the rest of the teams clapped politely as she jumped up from the table to collect our gift card. I turned back to Jake, trying to reset.

"Thank god. Mel would have been pissed for days if we'd lost." I offered my hand for a high five, hoping to discharge the electricity building between us. His hand connected, then lingered for a moment before he gave mine a gentle squeeze.

"Alright, team, we all deserve a celebratory drink for that stellar performance, and Anusha said we can use the gift card right away. What does everyone want?" Mel asked.

"I have to head out," I said. "I have an afternoon wedding to shoot tomorrow, so the bride needs me by eight. One-quarter of that gift card is mine, though!"

I was glad to have an excuse to leave early. I was struggling to ignore my attraction to Jake. There were a million reasons not to start something with him, but they were becoming harder to remember.

As I pushed my chair back from the table, Mel jumped in.

"You shouldn't go by yourself. Kensington gets a little sketchy at night."

"I can walk with you," Jake said.

Yes!

No!

*Shit.*

"It's really not necessary," I said. "It's less than ten minutes."

"Come on, Anderson. I'll feel better if I know you've gotten home safely."

A small, traitorous part of me did a little happy dance, anticipating being alone with him. I rolled my eyes, trying to mask my nervous excitement. "Whatever helps you sleep at night."

We walked the few blocks to my apartment, and the humid summer night wrapped itself around me, a slight breeze fluttering the short skirt of my sundress. The street was packed with beautiful people, their laughter and voices echoing off the graffitied brick around us.

The easy rhythm of my conversation with Jake reminded me of high school and why I'd fallen so hard and fast for this guy. It was effortless, but the undercurrent of awareness between us made this walk that I'd done a hundred times before feel dangerous.

"So, tell me more about your photography," he asked, clearing his throat. "You're doing what you always said you would. That's amazing."

"I'm getting closer," I said, shrugging. "I've been doing lots of family stuff – weddings and portraits – but street photography is my real passion. I want to know peoples' stories – like what decisions this person made, and what they went through to become who they are at this exact moment in time. There's nothing more fascinating to me," I said. "Does that make sense?"

"It makes perfect sense," Jake said, his gaze steady on mine.

"I just submitted my portfolio for a street photography exhibition at the Worth Gallery. It's part of a juried competition across the city, and two of the exhibitors will be chosen for a paid internship with Teo Castillo in Panama City for a month. I've idolized him since I was a kid, so it's a pretty big deal to me. I could learn so much from him."

"That's awesome. I'd love to see your exhibit when it's up."

"Well, I don't know if I've been accepted yet – I should hear in the next week or two."

"You will. You were so talented in high school, I can only imagine you've gotten better."

"Thanks. The waiting's hard." I looked up at Jake with a half-smile. "I need to do another night shoot around the city next week, in case I get in. I want to capture how the city shifts after dark – those contrasts between stillness and chaos. Big, glowing cityscapes mixed with small, raw moments on the street."

Jake nodded. "That sounds incredible. Cinematic."

I laughed. "Yeah, well, hopefully less blurry than my last one."

Jake chuckled. "I hear it gets pretty sketchy at night, so let me know if you need an assistant. I'll hold all your bags and protect you from potholes and drunks."

"It's fine, I've done it a hundred times," I said, brushing it off.

"Seriously, let me give you my number." He held out his palm. "I'd love to help."

I hesitated. His eyes were warm and sincere. Unsure whether I was making a terrible decision, I unlocked my phone and dropped it into his hand, reasoning that I didn't need to call him. He entered his number and handed it back to me. I could feel my resolve to keep him at a distance cracking.

"Well, this is me." I glanced up at my apartment, then rummaged in my purse to find my keys. "Oh score! I forgot I had these in here!" I pulled a half-empty bag of Sour Patch Kids out of my purse.

"Still your favourite, huh?" Jake's warm smile beamed down at me. "Well, don't be stingy, Anderson, give it here." He held out his hand expectantly.

As he took a handful, my mind tripped over the fact that after ten years, he still remembered my favourite candy.

"Remember movie night?" Jake snickered, popping the candy into his mouth.

"Oh my god, the hair!" I snorted.

Jake grinned. "I still can't believe he didn't notice."

Chewing on the candy, I busied myself putting the bag back in my purse. I could feel Jake looking steadily at me, the air between us thickening like honey. I was suspended in the moment, memories of the boy I'd loved intertwining with my undeniable attraction to the man standing in front of me.

As the silence between us stretched, he stepped closer and reached out to brush the corner of my mouth with his thumb, the soft contact sending tingles down to my core. He smelled like summer and every bad decision I suddenly wanted to make.

"Sugar." His voice was gravelly.

My entire focus was on Jake's thumb brushing back and forth. His gaze dropped to my lips and my thoughts scattered. Slowly, his head dipped down and he pressed his lips softly to mine. He felt achingly familiar yet the scratch of his stubble was new. His head lifted, his mouth a hair's breadth away. As our breath mingled, his eyes searched mine, asking whether this was okay, if this was something I wanted.

This flash of the Jake I remembered made my heart thump painfully in my chest before I reached up and looped my hands around his neck. At my touch, Jake breathed my name before capturing my lips again and dropping his hands to my hips, gripping tightly. Feverish now, I gasped and Jake's tongue slid smoothly against mine, the tang of the candy we'd eaten heightening the delicious taste of his mouth.

"Get a room, love!"

The shout was like a spray of cold water from a garden hose and I jerked away. A pair of old men across the street were cackling as they walked away. My cheeks flamed as I became conscious of how close I was to Jake.

My body was all in – ready to yank his head back down and feast on his perfect mouth – but my brain was issuing a red alert, still rational enough to know that this could only end badly. I'd never fallen for someone the way I'd fallen for Jake, and picking up the pieces of a freshly broken heart was not on my agenda for my mid-twenties.

*Abort.*

"I better get inside," I blurted in a bright, cheery voice as I stepped back and plunged my hand into my purse again, desperately feeling around for my key. "The bride's expecting me early tomorrow."

I pulled out my key, and shoved it in the lock. "Thanks so much for the walk home, have a great night!" I said over my shoulder, tripping over the doorstep into my building.

I chanced one look back at him – he sighed as he ran his right hand through his rumpled hair – before I slammed the door. I leaned against it from the inside, breathing heavily, my entire body buzzing.

*I am so screwed.*

# Twelve
## April 13, 12 Years Ago

# The Movie's About to Start

"Jake, help please!" I called, trying to wrestle life-size cutouts of Scott and Ramona through the auditorium door at the same time – not my best idea, as I kept getting stuck no matter which angle I tried and didn't want to break the neck on Scott's guitar.

"Whoa, you made these, Em?" Jake bent sideways to look at the Scott cutout. "They're so much bigger than I expected."

He took Ramona from me and manoeuvred her through the doorway without issue. He set it up across from the popcorn stand near the entrance to the school and stood for a moment, considering it.

I held my breath – too big? Too much? I'd spent a huge amount of time on them. Turns out, not spending all my brain power thinking about Jake had freed up a surprising amount of space for my art. And it felt like it was paying off. I knew they were good, but I was still nervous. Jake had never seen my work before, and I still really cared what he thought.

"These are amazing." He shifted his attention to the Scott cutout I was setting up on the other side of the doors, before turning towards me with a look of admiration.

I exhaled, his praise like adrenaline injected into my veins.

"How many of these did you make?" he called back to me as he strode into the auditorium and retrieved the Katayanagi twins.

"Nine all together. Scott, Ramona, and the seven Evil Exes." I flipped him a mischievous grin. "What can I say? The students of Roberta Bondar High School deserve to have their red-carpet fantasies fulfilled."

Tonight was movie night at the school to fundraise for the arts programs at Bondar, and we were showing one of my favourite movies, *Scott Pilgrim vs. The World*, in the auditorium at seven o'clock.

After we set the cutouts up at strategic points around the lobby and took a couple of selfies with them – Jake doing Lucas Lee's cocky-stare-with-furrowed-brow, making me gulp audibly – he slowly turned in a circle, considering the display with a low whistle.

"How long did these take you?"

"I may or may not have spent the past couple of weekends taking over the art room. And maybe I also convinced Ms. Goldsbie to let me work on them during art class."

"Ha. I had no idea you were such a good artist. When you mentioned making cutouts, I was picturing you printing out pictures of the characters and sticking them to popsicle sticks."

I gasped. "Never!"

"You should consider running for arts rep next month."

"Oh. Yeah, maybe," I said with a noncommittal smile, as if I hadn't already planned out my entire campaign. These cutouts were step one in convincing the student body that I was the best option for arts rep. A little squee of excitement coursed through me that Jake wanted me to be part of the SAC again. We'd spent a lot of time together since January – working side-by-side in the produce section at the food bank and texting constantly as we worked on various school initiatives. I'd given up on him ever seeing me romantically, but we were friends. He and Annika were still going strong. She wasn't here tonight because she had an important recital to prepare for her grade eight piano exam.

"Come on. Let's go grab some of the pizza Mrs. Driscoll ordered before we're on popcorn duty," Jake said, slinging his arm around my shoulders and steering me back towards the SAC office.

The lobby was packed with students, buzzing with excitement. My cutouts were a hit – people were lining up to take selfies with them, striking silly poses or pretending to high-five the cardboard versions of the characters. After the first rush of students got their popcorn and stocked up on candy and drinks, Jake and I fell into a rhythm. We chatted while we worked, scooping and handing out popcorn bags like we were seasoned movie theatre employees.

"So, what are you up to this weekend?" I asked as I handed a bag of popcorn to Dev, one of my grade nine art club buddies.

"Well, it's our first exhibition game this weekend, and I'm pitching. My mom isn't on shift, and Owen is coming home from Mac for the weekend, so they're going to come to heckle me."

He rolled his eyes, although I could tell he was pleased they'd be there. Over the past few months, I'd gotten to know a bit about Jake's family, hoarding every crumb of information he dropped about his life like a squirrel preparing for a long winter. His mom was an ER nurse at Centenary Hospital, and his brother was in his third year in the Health Sciences program at McMaster University in Hamilton, with plans to go to med school.

"What about your dad?"

Jake's face shuttered. He rarely mentioned his dad, and when he did, there was always an edge of tension in his expression.

"Nope. Travelling for work again." Jake's jaw tightened. After a pause, during which I panicked that I'd put my foot in my mouth, he shifted his focus to me. "What about you? Any more ridiculously elaborate art projects in the works?" He grinned as he scooped more popcorn into a bag.

"My mom and I are heading to the Museum of Contemporary Art this weekend. It's my happy place – my parents have been taking me since I was little. I'm super excited because there's a Teo Castillo photography exhibition on right now that I've been dying to see."

"Photography?" Jake said, a questioning look in my direction.

"I'm obsessed with photography." I was thrilled to be talking about my favourite subject with him. "I can't wait to join yearbook next year. My parents got me my first Nikon when I was five. My dream is to go to school for photography, but I haven't decided where yet. Probably somewhere in Toronto to be close to my parents – maybe Toronto Metropolitan or OCAD," I said.

I stood up after bending down to grab another stack of popcorn bags to find Jake's eyes on me, considering.

"What?" I was self-conscious as I looked down to make sure I hadn't spilled something on myself. Oh my god, I hoped I didn't have a booger.

"I had no idea you were so passionate about art. Not many minor niners know what they want to do at university. I sure don't. It's impressive." He looked steadily at me, a serious expression on his face as he nudged my waist with his elbow.

I hesitated in confusion. Our relationship so far had consisted of me being ridiculous and him tolerating my out-there-ness with mild good humour.

*This. Was. Different.*

A warm glow of pleasure coursed through me at the thought that Jake was impressed by something about me. As I bit my lip to stop a goofy smile spreading across my face, I noticed his gaze dip to my lips.

*WTAF.*

Before I could respond, my phone buzzed in my pocket. I turned away slightly to hide the burn in my cheeks, then pulled it out and glanced at the screen.

**Kevin:**
Looks like you've found yourself a hot date. Hope you're still free on Sat.

I grinned. He was replying to the Scott Pilgrim selfie I'd sent him earlier. He'd sent a selfie back, in front of his TV with the movie playing in the background. Only Bondar students were allowed to attend tonight, so it was sweet he was watching at home so we could talk about it later.

**Emma:**
Still can't believe you've never seen it. I'll quiz you then!

**Kevin:**
I'm taking notes.

I added a heart reaction on Kevin's text and pocketed my phone. Kevin had been endearingly excited when I'd told him about my project in our Saturday art class at Cedar Ridge Creative Centre. A couple of weeks ago, he'd asked me out for lunch after class – my first ever date, since I didn't count the time Brandon Jones gave me a scratch and sniff sticker and asked me to be his partner for our Seasonal Changes inquiry project in grade one.

I glanced up at Jake, still studying me with that curious expression.

"What's that smile about?" he asked. "Did Sarah send you another photo of Grumpy Cat?"

I hesitated. I hadn't planned to bring it up. I hadn't even wanted to. But now that the moment was here, pretending I didn't have a boyfriend would be hiding something, and that was worse. Still, the word was clumsy in my mouth, like it didn't belong there yet.

"It's from my boyfriend, Kevin," I said, blushing. Kevin and I had been texting and hanging out a lot, and last week, he'd asked me to be his girlfriend. I really liked him…and a teensy part of me hoped that going out with someone else would douse any remaining embers of my crush on Jake.

Jake raised an eyebrow. "Oh. I didn't know you had one."

"It's new," I said, quickly. My voice was higher than usual. I shrugged, trying to act casual. I liked Kevin. Ugh, why was this so awkward?!

Jake's gaze lingered longer than usual, his eyes narrowing slightly. A flicker of something unreadable passed over his face before he cleared his throat and nodded.

"Well, he's a lucky guy."

"Yo, Jake! Bro! Stop checking out the grade nines, douchebag. A bunch of us still need our popcorn."

Murray Fucking Fraser, his braying voice breaking the fragile thread of awareness that had spun between Jake and me. As Jake laughed good-naturedly and handed out popcorn, unfazed, I turned away and occupied myself by pouring a new batch of kernels into the machine. I filed the moment away to obsess over it later, under "WTF was that?!?" Had Jake been flirting with me? He couldn't have been – he was with Annika and I was with Kevin, and everything was exactly how it was supposed to be. Right?

"Alright, kids, the movie's about to start," Mrs. Driscoll called across the lobby. "Go grab your seats and enjoy yourselves after all your hard work!"

After Jake and I shut down the popcorn machine, we entered the auditorium with the rest of the students who'd been working in the lobby. Murray and his group of jerky jocks were throwing popcorn at each other; their obnoxious cackles audible over the chatter and laughter of the rest of the students.

I scanned the auditorium for Sarah and the empty seat she'd promised to save for me, hoping she'd found one close to the screen for maximum viewing pleasure (we were both of the firm opinion that movies were best enjoyed as close to the screen as possible, the better to immerse yourself in the experience). Once I located her in a prime spot, I headed towards her before faltering in confusion, that icky feeling of dread creeping up my body. The seats to either side of her were already filled. She turned around, saw me, and shrugged.

"Sorry! You're late, and Jess couldn't find a seat!"

I looked around – yes, it was busy, but the auditorium still had empty seats here and there. I was pretty sure Jess could have found another place to sit.

"No worries," I called back, stung that Sarah hadn't waited for me. Suddenly warm and itchy, I stood there – out of place in the middle of the crowded auditorium. We'd been doing our own thing more lately. She'd been hanging out a lot with Jess and her new friends from the dance team, and I'd been busy with the SAC. But we'd seen this movie in the theatre together, and I'd been looking forward to reliving that epic experience with her. As I turned around to look for a different seat, hoping that some of my art club buddies might have an extra nearby, I registered Jake's eyes on me.

*Perfect, now he's seen me get rejected by my best friend.*

"Em, over here! You can sit with us," he called.

I clocked the two guys sitting to his left as Rohan and Weston, friends from the baseball team. Grateful and a little shocked that he'd invited me to sit with his friends, I headed in his direction.

"Thanks," I said as I sat down, a little breathless, right as the lights dimmed.

After a brief swell of noise, the crowd settled down as the movie began to roll. As I settled in with my popcorn, Jake shifted in his seat, his broad shoulder nudging mine, sending that familiar zing of electricity down my arm. He tilted his open bag of Sour Patch Kids towards me, offering them up.

"Ooo, yes, my favourite, thank you!" I grabbed a handful and sprinkled them into my bag of popcorn. "They're the best this way," I said.

"Weird, Anderson, but I'll test your theory." He threw a couple of candies and pieces of popcorn into his mouth at once. He chewed, his brow furrowing as a hint of surprise flickered across his face. "Not bad." He grinned at me before dumping the rest of the candy into his popcorn and turning back to the screen.

My awareness of Jake was a low hum throughout the movie, tugging at my attention and making me feel guilty that I was still so drawn to him even though I was dating someone else. It distracted me from Scott Pilgrim's quest to defeat Ramona's evil exes – until Roxy crashed through the skylight in a shower of glass and knocked Scott flat on his back.

I jumped, letting out a screech as I simultaneously stepped on Jake's toe and my popcorn flew up and forward, most of it landing in the long hair of the guy sitting in front of me.

Clutching my chest as I wheezed from shock, I caught Jake's incredulous glance and dissolved into giggles. Jake winced as he rotated his foot, the side of his mouth I could see ticking upwards, which only made me laugh harder as I strangled out a whispered "sorry" before another wave of suppressed giggles came over me.

Jake's shoulders shook, and I was delighted to hear a muffled snort from his direction, making us laugh harder. When Jake gestured at the guy's hair in front of us, adorned with at least twenty pieces of popcorn and one orange Sour Patch Kid that he hadn't seemed to notice, I clapped my hand over my mouth to contain my shout of laughter, tears streaming down my face.

Eventually, we pulled ourselves together, although I had to keep swallowing stray giggles during the rest of the movie, especially whenever the guy in front of us moved his head and dislodged a piece or two of popcorn.

As the credits rolled and Mrs. Driscoll turned on the auditorium lights, I blinked in the harsh fluorescents. I turned to Jake, ready to apologize again for stepping on his foot, and found him grinning at me.

"I had no idea you were such an entertaining movie companion."

I really liked Kevin. But the way Jake looked at me sometimes made everything a little less certain.

"I guess I'm full of surprises."

## Thirteen

# A Good Old-Fashioned Sexorcism

I plopped onto the couch, handed Mel her grapefruit Bubly, and situated the bowl of popcorn between us, before tying my damp hair back in a scrunchie and pulling a thick grey fleece blanket over my legs. Most of the time, movie night was an excuse to catch up and gossip, and *13 Going on 30*, one of our favourites, seemed like the perfect backdrop to get Mel's advice about Jake. My attempts to suppress the attraction that had reignited between us weren't working, and I wasn't sure if I could keep ignoring it.

"So," Mel said through a mouthful of popcorn, once we'd settled in with the movie playing in the background. "How good a kisser is he, on a scale from one to Michael B. Jordan?" She shot me a devious grin.

I pulled the blanket up to my chin as my cheeks flamed. "Too good. But it's never happening again." I'd been thinking about nothing else since Jake kissed me. I'd spent years convincing myself I'd moved on, and he was just a stupid blip from high school. But now it was like he'd walked back in and flipped every light switch I'd spent years turning off.

Mel looked deeply skeptical.

"I know you've always been picky, but if someone who looks like Jake had looked at me the way he looks at you – like he wants to make all of your hot librarian fantasies come true – I'd have laid right down on the bar top and invited him to do me right then and there."

I laughed reluctantly, but my chest tightened.

"And despite the 'we're just going to be civil' bullshit that you gave me a couple of weeks ago at your parents' house, it's clear you're attracted to him. What's the hesitation? For real this time." She scooped up another handful of popcorn.

I groaned and yanked the blanket over my head, so I didn't have to face Mel's gaze. I couldn't describe the jumble of emotions tangled up inside my brain. Yes, in a perfect world, Jake and I would be tearing each other's clothes off. Bad-Decisions Emma – the one who dove headfirst into things, driven by optimism and impulse – was urging me to pursue this flirtation with him to its natural end. But Cautious Emma – the one I trusted to make responsible relationship decisions and remembered the mess of the last time – had a red flag in one hand and a megaphone in the other.

"Em. I know there's some awkward history with him, but you can't tell me there's nothing there. And don't even try me with a random ick."

The blanket was yanked off my head, static crackling as my hair lifted with it. I blinked up at Mel, staring at me like a smug little truth fairy.

"Unless he talks about himself in the third person, or ends every sentence with 'hashtag blessed,' I'm not buying it. He's basically perfect for you."

I groaned and reached for my Bubly as I considered what to say to her. "He was this perfect boy–" I took a long sip. "And then he ghosted me. It was humiliating."

What had happened in high school had rewired something in me. Since then, every one of my relationships had followed the same pattern. Me, keeping my distance. Them, getting tired of knocking on a locked door. Trust was expensive, and no guy had ever proved he was worth the price. And now Jake, of all people, was the one stirring something in me that I hadn't felt in years. I took a deep breath.

"Oh, babe," Mel said, her eyes widening. "Now your whole 'I'm just super picky' thing makes sense. You're not picky…you're scared."

"I let him in once and got burned." My fingers tightened around my can as I glanced up at the ceiling.

"Sounds like he was a dumb kid in high school. But weren't we all? People change."

"Not that much," I muttered. "I need to shut it down."

"Nope. Uh-uh. You need the exact opposite. If you're not interested in something serious, the only way to get him off your mind is to bone him out of your system."

A sharp laugh burst out of me, and I gave her a look.
"What? Seriously?"

She shrugged, innocently. "I'm just saying – get under him to get over him. Sometimes closure looks a lot like very hot, very responsible sex." Mel pointed a finger at me. "And he's only here for a month. Perfect timing. No pressure, no strings – just a good old-fashioned sexorcism!"

I shook my head, laughing. "You're the worst."

"I know." She grinned. "But I'm also the best. Trust me, it works."

Heat surged up my neck. The thought of Jake's solid frame pressing me into my mattress and the slow drag of his mouth along my skin made my breath hitch. My fingers twitched, already itching to map the firm lines of his chest, to sink into the muscle of his back, to grab a handful of that perfect ass. Maybe it wasn't a terrible idea.

"My portfolio is in, work's calm, and it's been so long since I've had good sex. You know Jason always kept his black crew socks on."

Mel snickered. "You deserve a little fun, Grandma. You think Jake'll keep the glasses on? I knew you were a goner as soon as I saw them."

"Oh my god, Mel," I groaned. "He's already unfairly hot, with his large hands, superhero chest, and a jawline that could cut glass. But then he puts on freaking square-rimmed glasses? Jesus."

Flopping back on the couch and stretching out my legs, I fanned myself with the edge of the blanket and settled it over me.

"Get it, girl." Mel picked up my phone from the table and tossed it to me before turning back to the movie, where Matt and Jenna were searching for Razzles.

Could Mel be right? Could a fling with Jake Griffin help me finally close the door on that shitty chapter in my life? Could I go through with it and not get hurt if it all went sideways?

Cautious Emma fired up the megaphone again, blasting worst-case scenarios like Aesop's Fables. But I wasn't that naive girl from high school anymore. This was my chance to rewrite the ending to our story. My therapist would definitely approve of a little cognitive reframing. Besides, Jake was so ridiculously hot it almost felt like a crime not to indulge. I knew exactly what I was walking into, and I was not going to get attached this time.

I started typing before I could talk myself out of it.

**Emma:**
Hey. It's Emma.

I tossed my phone down and tried to refocus on the movie, wondering if I would hear from him tonight. Immediately, my phone buzzed with an incoming text. I grabbed it, fumbling as I swiped it open and tapped into my messages.

**Jake:**
Hey. It's great to hear from you. How was the wedding?

**Emma:**
It was beautiful. Sunday afternoon weddings are my favourite. Relaxed, low-key, and I'm home and in bed by nine. 🙌

**Jake:**
Are you in bed now?

I blushed and stole a glance at Mel, who was engrossed in her Instagram feed.

**Jake:**
Sorry, did I send that out loud? 😬 I meant because it's 9:30, not because I'm picturing you in bed.

**Jake:**
Great, now I'm picturing you in bed. Put me out of my misery.

I laughed out loud this time, my stomach fizzing, as Mel "tsk'd" me without looking up from her phone.

**Jake:**
Well, it was nice knowing you. Packing my bags and booking a one-way ticket to Saskatoon as we speak.

**Emma:**
Lol, no, please stay. I'm watching a movie with Mel. On the couch.

**Jake:**
Ok, cancelling the flight and putting my socks back in my drawer. That was close.

**Emma:**
Too close. 😉 How was your day?

**Jake:**
A pretty standard Sunday, but looking up now. Last night was fun. We should do it again.

Here was my opening.

**Emma:**
We should. I was wondering if you might want to come along on my night shoot later this week. Having someone to carry my bag sounds great.

**Jake:**
Absolutely. I'd love to. It'll be like the old days when you had me hauling your tripod and backdrops around all the time.

**Emma:**
😆 That's right. I forgot that I've already trained you.

**Jake:**
Oh, I'm sure there are some new things you could teach me.

Heat crept up my body, onto my neck, and spread through my cheeks. I pulled off the fleece blanket and glanced at Mel.

"Getting hot in here?" She raised her eyebrows. "What's he saying?"

I groaned as I tossed my phone over to her.

She smirked as she scrolled to the beginning of the texts, reading through them before looking back at me.

"Oh damn, he is up for this. I told you. Just pump and dump, baby!"

"Ugh, gross, Mel." I rolled my eyes and caught my phone as she tossed it back to me, just as another text popped up.

**Jake:**
About photography, I mean. Obviously.

**Emma:**
Obviously. Don't forget your glasses, I'm sure they're helpful in low-light conditions. 😉

**Jake:**
Got it. Thanks for the tip. 🤓

I snickered as I tapped the little red magnifying glass and chose one of my favourite Michael Scott gifs, from the "Dinner Party" episode of *The Office*, where he yells "That's what she said!" from the dinner table, raising his open hands to exaggerate his point.

My phone sprang to life in my hand, vibrating as Jake's name flashed on the screen. I smiled as I swiped it open and brought it to my ear, as Mel shook her head at me and grinned.

"You're ridiculous," he said, his rough laugh rumbling from my ear, down through to my chest. "Remember the bloopers?"

"Of course." I giggled, picturing Michael Scott adjusting his tiny flat-screen TV.

"We must have watched them a thousand times," Jake said as his laugh subsided.

The air in the room thickened as I listened to him breathe for a moment.

*How do people talk on phones again? Should I comment on the weather?*

"So where are you planning to shoot?" he asked, before I had a chance to ask him what he thought about the cold front coming in on Tuesday.

"Probably Sankofa Square. It's amazing at night. I was thinking Wednesday, as long as the weather cooperates. Does that work for you?"

"Great," Jake said, the warmth of his smile evident in his voice. "I'm looking forward to it."

"Me too," I said, as another thick pause settled between us.

"I should let you get back to your movie."

“Sure. Matty and Jenna are about to kiss under the swings, the best part.”

“*13 Going on 30*?”

“Yep. It’s a classic!”

He chuckled. “Goodnight, Em.” His deep voice cascaded down my neck as I remembered the feel of his soft lips, warm breath, and the teasing scrape of stubble along my jawline.

“Night, Jake…nice talking to you.” I switched the phone to my other ear, closed my eyes, and rubbed the sensation of him off my neck.

“Always,” he murmured before ending the call.

I sat there for a moment, his words lingering, sending a spark through my body.

Pulling the blanket over me, I curled up on the couch, but the rest of the movie barely registered. My mind kept drifting to him, wondering how things would play out on Wednesday. I couldn’t wait to find out.

## Fourteen

# Absurd Emotional Science Project

I tucked a couple of extra batteries into my camera bag and slung it over Jake's solid shoulder. Seeing his large body in the cramped front hallway of our apartment, his hip brushing the wicker table holding the jade plant I'd miraculously kept alive, was doing funny things to my insides. He was wearing his glasses and eyeing my photographs with quiet interest.

I was two seconds away from skipping the fieldwork and climbing him like a tree, and I needed to get him out of the apartment before "please ruin me" slipped out of my mouth. That could wait – at least until I had my shots. Like an absurd emotional science project Mel had assigned me, tonight I was planning to test the theory that sex with Jake might actually help me move on.

I double checked that I'd tossed my chunky cardigan into my backpack and tied my hair back into the bun I used during shoots. Slipping on my Converse, I led the way out of the apartment, Jake trailing behind.

We hopped off the streetcar at the southwest corner of Sankofa Square, the centre of Toronto. The sun had set, the sky to the west full of purples and pinks with deep blue encroaching from the east. The night was beautiful with a hint of coolness in the air, suggesting the end of summer approaching.

The Square was heaving with activity, with late-night shoppers emerging from the Eaton Centre loaded down with bags, a long-haired guy on a drum kit playing along to Queen blasting out of the speaker behind him, tourists spilling off the bright red hop-on hop-off sightseeing bus, and the giant billboards surrounding the square casting everything in an electronic glow. Absorbing the energy of the hundreds of people milling around me and eager to start, I grabbed Jake's hand and guided him north across Dundas Street. I turned to him and unzipped the camera bag he was carrying.

"Tell me more about how you work. You don't have as much equipment as you used to."

Right as Jake finished his sentence, "BELIEVE!" was shouted from directly behind him, impossibly loud and with an explosive sound on the beginning B. Jake startled so hard he almost dropped my camera bag, taking a panicked step forward and almost knocking me over. I grabbed for him to keep from falling on my ass, hands full of his biceps through his soft green henley. Jake whipped his head around to see everyone's favourite Toronto uncle in his white T-shirt with a serene smile, his preaching a staple on the northwest corner of Sankofa Square for decades, according to his five-star Yelp reviews.

Jake turned back to me with an incredulous look as I started giggling, enjoying the feel of his strong arms as I steadied myself. I popped my head around him.

"Hey, Sarko. Nice to see you!" I said, trying to suppress the giggles. "This is my friend, Jake. Do you have time for a photo today?"

At Sarko's nod, I manoeuvred a still recovering Jake beside him, grabbed my camera, and looped it around my neck.

"Smile!" I said, taking a couple of snaps of the two of them before scooting Jake out of the picture so I could take a few photos of the beaming Sarko alone. I thanked him before steering Jake east across Yonge Street.

"Well, that took about ten years off my life," Jake said, with a disgruntled look. "How were you so chill?"

"It's a Toronto rite of passage to be startled by Sarko," I said, with a cheeky grin. "After spending four years downtown during university, I'm immune, but the first time he did it to me, I screamed and spilled a half-full Venti frap all over Jerry."

"That sounds more like you." Jake laughed. "Sorry, I almost took you out back there."

"It was worth it to see the look on your face," I said, smirking. "Flustered Jake is pretty adorable."

"Adorable, huh?" His grin was rueful.

"Jake Griffin, are you blushing?" I teased, delighted to see two flags of colour high on his cheekbones. "Look at you, getting more adorable by the second," I said, bringing my camera up to capture Jake's sheepish expression. In truth, the juxtaposition between Jake's boyish bashfulness and his extremely grown-up physique was only making him sexier.

"Focus, Em. We're here to work. This is serious," Jake said, making me laugh. "But for real, explain to me how you do this so I can be helpful tonight." He seemed genuinely interested in my work.

"Well, you were asking why I don't have much equipment. Street photography is about being as unobtrusive as possible, so it's usually just me and my Nikon."

"Is that why you're dressed like a jewel thief?" Jake grinned, gesturing to my faded black jeans with a rip at the right knee and slim-fitting cropped black T-shirt.

"Exactly!" I said, impressed. "I try not to be noticed."

"I can't imagine you blending into the background, no matter what you're wearing," he said, his voice low and warm, as he reached out to tuck an escaped curl behind my ear.

Now it was my turn to blush. Tingles radiated outwards from his warm fingertips.

"Trust me, if I'm doing my job well, no one is paying attention to me," I said, lightly. "Anyway, tonight, I'll be looking for unique characters and interesting contrasts – moments where the city's energy collides with stillness. Sometimes I capture people as they go about their business, but if I'm captivated by someone, I'll ask if I can take a few photos and ask them a few questions."

Jake continued asking questions as we walked around the Square, although he seemed to know instinctively when to stop talking so that I could focus. I could feel him nearby, but he was keeping a low profile. I became absorbed in my work as I always did, experimenting with different angles and perspectives. The varied backgrounds of Sankofa Square provided context and texture for the stories of the people I was capturing.

Occasionally, I explained to Jake what I was doing and showed him certain photos I'd taken, reminding me of our seamless teamwork on the SAC from years ago.

Finally satisfied that I had some good material – I was particularly excited by the shots I'd taken of an elderly couple sitting in the centre of the square, framed by the faint blur of passing strangers, their motion a soft smear of color that captured the fast-paced rhythm of the city – I stretched my arms above my head, then checked the time on my Apple Watch. It was after eleven.

"Holy shit, I didn't realize it was getting so late!" I said.

Three hours of near silence, aside from the odd explanation or answer to a question. Jake must have been bored. But maybe that was safer – less talking, less accidentally-on-purpose brushing up against him meant I'd been able to focus on my work instead of falling into fantasies of his mouth on my neck or his hand sliding over the curve of my hip and into my jeans.

But now that the shoot was over, he had my full attention, and the nerves I'd been suppressing all night kicked off a party in my stomach. My confidence that I could handle any sort of relationship with Jake Griffin had waned. I was seriously rethinking Mel's "achieve closure through fucking" plan.

I turned to put my camera back in my case, and had to stifle a groan as my back twinged.

"Hey, come here," Jake said, tugging me gently towards him. "No worries at all. I was fascinated by your work and happy to help out tonight." He turned me so my back was against his chest, then dropped his large hands onto my shoulders and began to knead.

A half-moan escaped my lips at the warmth and pressure of his hands. My eyes closed, and my head fell forward as I swayed back towards him.

"Oh god, that feels good," I breathed. "I'm taking you along on all my shoots from now on, as my own personal masseuse. Don't stop."

He chuckled softly behind me, his breath sending shivers over the back of my neck, the sensation crawling down my arms and setting my skin on fire. His thumbs slowly worked their way down either side of my spine, his hands splayed out around my ribcage, then paused at my waist. His fingers brushed the strip of exposed skin just above the waistband of my jeans.

"Better?" he murmured.

"Mmm-hmmm," I sighed, the noises of the busiest intersection in

Toronto and every single one of my doubts silenced by the feel of Jake's hands on my bare skin.

"I can't stop thinking about you," Jake whispered in my ear before turning me to face him, his hands sliding around my waist, my body obeying his touch without conscious thought.

He ducked his head, the soft touch of his forehead resting against mine in sharp contrast to the taut muscles of his chest under my hands. He stared intently at me through his slutty little glasses.

"I'm not sure I ever have." His stubble scraped gently across my cheek as he leaned down to whisper in my ear, his voice unsteady and rough as sandpaper.

I caught my breath at his honesty, but quickly reminded myself – this was just about sex, scratching my decade-old Jake itch, nothing more. I wasn't about to catch feelings. Our time was limited, and the time was now. Mel was visiting her dad for the night, and the apartment was all ours.

"Take me home," I said.

I pulled Jake across the sidewalk and up the three steps to the front door of my building, desperate to get him inside before I changed my mind. After a brief fumble for my keys, we made it in, and I tugged him up the three flights of stairs to my apartment. Abruptly, Jake spun me around and pressed me up against the front door, pulling my hips against his so he was tight between my legs, his muscular chest pressing against my breasts, the size of him overwhelming me. He crushed his lips against mine, my mouth opening eagerly under his as he thrust his tongue inside. My mind blanked as his mouth slanted over mine again and again. His kiss was different from the last time – rougher, desperate, more urgent. A reminder of what we were about to do.

Part of me knew how big this was, how much this meant – Jake had been my first love, after all – and a small voice in the back of my head cautioned that maybe it wasn't a good idea to cross this line, that it would mean more with Jake than it had with anyone else. But the heat between us was all-consuming, drowning out every rational thought, leaving only my raw hunger for him. There was no time to dwell on the significance of it, and I didn't want to.

I fit my key in the lock, and my apartment door opened behind me, making me stumble backwards, dragging Jake with me.

Jake stepped inside, kicked the door shut, dropped my bags, and gripped my hips to bring me flush against him again. He crowded me up against the inside of the door. His head dipped to my neck, my head falling back to allow him better access, and he reached down and hooked his hands under my ass. He lifted me effortlessly, my legs wrapped around his waist, as his tongue did its best to make me forget my name. We both groaned as his hips pushed forward, his cock rubbing right where I needed him.

The clatter of something hitting the floor, followed by Mel hissing, "Shit!" penetrated the fog of my acute desire. Jake and I weren't alone. My head snapped forward from where it had been lolling against the door.

To my horror, Mel was scrambling off the couch across the room, frantically grabbing tissues to mop up her spilled cereal, her spoon and bowl overturned and abandoned on the floor in front of her. Her hair was protected with one of the silk bonnets she wore to bed, and an "I am SO sorry" grimace twisted across her face, illuminated by the light from the television.

"Jake," I hissed, swatting at his shoulder.

"Emma," he murmured from down at my neck, entirely oblivious, his tongue dragging a hot, wet line up to my ear.

"Jake!" I said again, louder this time, pushing his head off me as I started to laugh. He raised his head, his eyes dazed, glasses askew, not understanding why we were stopping.

"Hey, Jake. Welcome to our home," Mel said, hurrying past us into the kitchen with her spoon in one hand and her bowl full of soggy tissues in the other. "Glad I made my presence known before your pants came off. Sorry, Em – my uncle surprised my dad with Jays tickets, so I didn't end up staying over. Gausman's pitching."

"Oh, hey Mel," Jake blurted, his cheeks flaming red. His lips were swollen, and his chest heaved as he glanced at her, and then back at me.

I was still pinned up against the door, his hands full of my ass and my legs wrapped around him.

"I forgot you lived here," he added, as Mel cackled from the kitchen. His mouth twitched into a sheepish smile as he set me down on the floor, straightened his glasses, and ran a hand through his hair.

"Don't mind me, I'm heading to bed now anyway. You two do your thing!" Mel stuffed her bowl in the dishwasher and scurried to her bedroom, closing the door behind her.

Laughter bubbled out of me, a mixture of embarrassment and leftover desire lending it a hysterical edge. The mood was shot. We'd have to pick this up another time.

"Tonight was fun," I said. I ran my hands over his chest. "What are you up to this weekend?"

"Seeing you, hopefully. Can I take you out for your birthday?"

"You remembered?" I bit my bottom lip to contain my glowing smile.

"Of course," he said, his voice warm.

"Mel, Jerry, and I are going dancing on Friday. Wanna come? We could see if Ryan and Lauren are are free too."

"Wouldn't miss it. Text me the details."

His smile held a promise that Friday night was going to be fantastic.

I turned towards the mirror on the wall beside the front door, assessing the redness on my neck as Jake ran his hands over my hips and stepped up close behind me. I gasped as he spun me around and dipped his head to nip my lower lip, before giving me the slowest, most erotic kiss of my life.

"Night, Emma." Jake stepped out of the door and closed it with a gentle click.

I floated over to the couch, dropping my exhausted body onto it.

"So that happened," Mel said, coming out of her room, grinning at me.

"Holy shit, Mel," I said as I pulled the fleece blanket over my head.

*I could not wait until Friday.*

# Fifteen
## December 15, 12 Years Ago

## Dead to Me

Winterfest at Canada's Wonderland was a magical delight, and I didn't care if Kevin thought it was cheesy. Tonight was going to be amazing. The amusement park was aglow with twinkling white lights strung through every tree, including the hundreds of towering Christmas trees that they brought in every year to decorate. The waterfall under Wonder Mountain was brightly lit, and the skating rink below was awash in pinks, blues, and purples. The crisp air was filled with the smells of pine, hot chocolate, and burnt sugar funnel cakes, making my anticipation spike.

"I still can't believe you've never been to Winterfest," I said as we hustled towards Thunder Run. "I guarantee you're going to be won over by the impeccable Christmas vibes by the end of the night. Plus, roller coasters."

Kevin laughed. "If you say so. I'm sure it'll be a great time… despite the over-the-top Christmas-on-crack aura," he said, pointing out a Canada's Wonderland employee dressed as Mrs. Claus zooming by on roller skates.

"Embrace the whimsy!" I ordered, making Kevin laugh again as we approached my friends.

Spending an evening with my SAC buddies at Winterfest was an awesome way to celebrate our recent successful toy drive for Sick Kids Hospital. Shirantha, our president, had suggested we all get together at Winterfest to celebrate collecting almost twice as many toys as the year prior.

Jake was standing with his arm around Annika, smiling down at her as she gestured with her hands. Shirantha stood beside them on tiptoes, looking over the small group, then pointing at us as we approached.

"Em, glad you guys finally made it," Jake said. "We've been waiting forever!"

"Shut up, Jake, we have not." Annika whacked him in the stomach. "We got here less than five minutes ago, Emma, don't worry."

I sent Annika a quick smile before rolling my eyes at Jake, taking off my mitten and shooting up my middle finger, making him grin. Jake teasing me and Annika coming to my defence had become a weirdly familiar routine. Now that I'd gotten over my crush and realized that I didn't have to hate her by default, I'd gotten to know Annika better. She was okay.

I was relieved that Jake and I were friends now, my ridiculous crush of last year forgotten (hopefully by everyone). Sure, now and then, I would catch myself noticing how physically perfect he was, usually when he did something casually athletic on the baseball field or smiled down at me with those unfairly blue eyes.

But my crush was dead and buried.

Gone.

"Alright, let's get in line, people," Shirantha called.

The group obediently followed him into the lineup. It was shorter than I'd been expecting. The park had been pretty packed on our way in, a mix of families with little kids staring wide-eyed at the Christmas magic surrounding them, groups of teens like ours, and even some older couples strolling around the lanes. It was still shortly after opening, so maybe most people hadn't made their way to the rides yet.

I squeezed Kevin's hand in excitement. "I know Thunder Run is really the lamest roller coaster here, but I still love it. When I was too short for the big ones, my dad would take me on this as many times as I wanted. One summer, I made him ride it seven times in a row."

Kevin grimaced. "Seven times? That man deserves a medal."

"Don't worry, once is enough for today. There's lots of other stuff to do."

He grinned. "Thank god. I actually hate roller coasters. I peed my pants on the Ghoster Coaster when I was six and have never recovered."

I snorted. "The Ghoster Coaster? That thing's barely taller than a jungle gym."

"Well, to six-year-old me, it was a near-death experience."

I bumped my shoulder against his. "Thunder Run is as wild as it gets during Winterfest – no big hills – so you're safe."

When we reached the front of the line, we piled into the four-person car, designed to look like an old-timey train, the excitement reaching a fever pitch. Kevin and I slid into the front seat together, the cold metal bar locking across our laps. I glanced over to see him gripping the sides like he was bracing for liftoff.

"You good?" I asked, grinning.

"Define good," he muttered. "Just remember this the next time I say no to karaoke. This is how you know I love you."

The train jerked forward, Kevin let out a loud, chicken-like "bwak!" – and I burst into laughter. We shot into the tunnel, and I scream-laughed my way through the familiar dips and turns of the roller coaster. As we zoomed past the dragon's glowing red eyes, Kevin let out a startled yell that dissolved into laughter, his eyes wide, hair blown back, and knuckles white on the bar.

When we pulled back onto the platform, I was breathless, cheeks aching from smiling. Kevin shook his head, dazed.

"That," he said, exhaling as he helped me out of the train car, "was way more intense than I expected." He adjusted my toque, which had almost flown off at one point during the ride, and I wound my arms around his neck and planted a big smack on his lips.

"Thank you for not peeing your pants." I laughed and kissed him again.

"Alright, kids, move it along," Jake said, his voice tight as he gestured for us to go ahead. I gave him a saucy grin before grabbing Kevin's hand and pulling him down the pathway.

"Kev, bro, I didn't know you were going to be here!"

Kevin and I turned at the familiar voice.

"Sam, Reid - what's up? Yeah, Emma and I are here with some of her friends."

As Kevin began chatting, I turned back to the group, who were bickering about where to go next.

"Hey, Em," Kevin said as he touched my elbow from behind. "Sam and Reid are meeting up with Karthik – he just got back from his trip a couple of days ago, and I haven't had a chance to see him yet. Would you be okay if I went to say hi and catch up for a bit, and joined you guys later?"

"Oh! Of course," I said, suppressing a flicker of disappointment. Kevin hadn't spent a lot of time with my friends, and I'd been looking forward to him getting to know them better. But Karthik was one of his closest friends, and he'd been gone for a month, so I understood. "Just text me and I'll let you know where to meet us."

"You sure it's ok? I promise, I'll be back soon."

"Totally fine!" I reached up and kissed his cheek. "See you in a bit."

As Kevin hugged me, I caught Jake staring at us, his jaw set, before he turned away.

My friends and I spent the next hour and a half on the rides, eating funnel cakes, and soaking up the magic of Winterfest. The only person who didn't seem to be having much fun was Jake. I wasn't sure what was going on with him – he'd seemed grumpy since we'd arrived and hadn't even laughed when Monica had asked the surprisingly sexy Santa if she could go for a ride on his sleigh. I was having so much fun that I didn't even notice that Kevin had been gone for a while until I checked my phone and saw that it was already almost nine. I fired off a quick text asking where he was, then hopped off the bench where I'd been sitting.

"I need a refill on my hot chocolate. Anyone else?" I asked.

"I'll come," Jake said. "I think there's a station not far from here."

While everyone else huddled around the map to plan the rest of our route, Jake and I fell into step beside each other, heading towards the hot chocolate stand.

"So, when's Kevin coming back?" His tone was casual, but there was an edge beneath it.

"Uh, not sure." I checked my phone. "I know they were meeting up with another friend. Maybe he was late. He'll text when he's done."

"Huh."

That "huh" was thick with judgment.

"Why?"

"I just wouldn't have expected him to ditch you for his friends after coming here with you." His fingers tightened around his mug. "Seems kind of shitty."

Irritation flared in my chest. He wasn't wrong – now that I'd realized how long Kevin had been gone, I was annoyed – but I didn't want Jake to know that.

"What's the big deal?" I said, keeping my voice light. "I'm not some needy girlfriend who needs to be glued to her boyfriend's side all the time."

We passed our refillable mugs to the booth attendant.

Jake exhaled sharply. "Em, come on. It's not about being needy." His voice was low, controlled. "A guy who respects you wouldn't abandon you for nearly two hours."

*Okay, moving right past annoyed to full-on pissed.*

His paternalistic tone made it clear that he thought I was a wide-eyed innocent, and it was his job to teach me what a good relationship was all about.

*Please.*

I folded my arms. "You're not my big brother, and I don't need you lecturing me." My pulse kicked up, fueled by a mix of embarrassment and frustration. "Just because you and Annika are joined at the hip doesn't mean that's what every couple wants."

Jake turned back to grab our mugs of hot chocolate from the attendant and shoved one towards me. "Leave her out of this," he said, his voice sharp as he stepped closer.

I blinked up at him.

"Excuse me? You felt free to tell me exactly what you thought about my boyfriend, and I can't say anything? I wasn't even criticizing you!"

"I'm not criticizing you. He's the fucking problem here!" Jake ground out, his voice rough as he raked his hand through his hair. "You deserve better than a guy who treats you like an afterthought."

"What are you talking about? He just went to meet some friends!"

"It's not just tonight, Emma. Where was he at your birthday party?"

"My birthday party?! He was out of town."

"Ok, then, what about the arts night that you spent a month organizing? He couldn't even bother to show up for you then?"

It had kind of sucked that Kevin hadn't been able to switch his shift to come, but I didn't understand why Jake was keeping score and making it his business – he didn't get a vote. Especially if he was going to be a condescending asshole about it.

I swallowed hard. "You need to back off." I jabbed a finger at his chest. "Kevin is a good guy. I'm happy with him."

Jake let out a short, disbelieving laugh. "Well, you shouldn't be."

His words hit me like a punch in the gut.

"Why do you care so much?"

Jake stepped closer, the air crackling in the small space between us.

"He's not good enough for you," Jake said, his voice nearly a growl.

I sucked in a breath, my heart hammering as I met his stormy blue eyes. His jaw tensed, like he was holding back a tirade of words.

"So who is, Jake?" I asked, daring him to say it out loud.

His mouth opened slightly – but nothing came out. He exhaled sharply with a puff of steam, one hand curled into a fist at his side, the other squeezing his mug. His throat worked, like he was swallowing the words he wanted to say.

"I just…you deserve someone who sees you. All of you." His voice was rough, almost breaking. "Someone who can't imagine being anywhere else but here. With you." His gaze dipped to my lips.

For one wild, reckless second, I thought he might actually do it. And I ached for it. All the dreams I'd tried to kill for the past year sprang back to life, running riot through my senses. I held his eyes, daring him, begging him to kiss me.

The moment stretched, an elastic band pulled to his limit. His hand twitched as if he had to stop himself from reaching for me. Then Jake stepped back with a slight shake of his head and a ragged exhale, eyes pleading for me to understand.

*Snap.*

"That's what I thought." I shook my head with a bitter laugh. "You asshole."

Of course he would stop after making me question everything about the relationship I'd been happy in.

"Em…" Jake's voice hummed with suppressed emotion. He reached out, his fingers grazing my cheek.

"Don't fucking touch me!" I jerked my hand up to push him away just as my phone buzzed with an incoming text.

I stepped back and pulled my phone out of my pocket.

**Kevin:**
I'm so sorry. Karthik was late, and then we got stuck in the longest line for Klockwerks. Tell me where to meet you, coming now.

I typed with trembling fingers.

**Emma:**
Just getting hot chocolate but I'll meet you by the games.

Jake stared at me, his blue eyes impossible to read.

"It's Kev. He's heading back."

I stalked back towards the games area, Jake calling my name from behind me. I couldn't get away from him fast enough.

"Wait, Em, please," he said, as he wrapped his hand around my upper arm. "I'm sorry, you're right, I–"

I spun out of his reach and turned to face him, fuming.

"Leave me alone." I wiped my eyes and took a few deep breaths, willing myself to get it together before we got back to the group.

"I'm just looking out for you. I'm trying to be a good friend."

"Fuck you, Jake. I don't need a friend like you."

My words hit him like a slap, and he flinched, stumbling back as if I'd physically pushed him. I pictured jabbing a finger into his forehead and watching him tip like a cut tree, crashing to the ground in a puff of dust.

I took one last steadying breath before turning to make my way back towards our group. As I turned down the path, I spotted Kevin, surrounded by my friends, laughing. He glanced over my shoulder at Jake as we approached, his eyes narrowing slightly as he registered the tension between us.

I went straight to him and pulled him into a long kiss. His lips were warm and familiar in the cold night air, and when we finally pulled apart, his face was soft and apologetic.

"I'm sorry for disappearing like that," he murmured, pressing his forehead against mine. "Everything okay?"

"It's fine," I said. "I'm glad you're here now." I wanted to focus on Kevin, but Jake's words kept swimming to the surface.

How dare he make me question my relationship? Before tonight, he'd made it abundantly clear that he didn't see me as anything other than a friend. And he was with Annika! Why would he crack open the door just enough to make me think there could be something more for us, if he had no intention of walking through it?

And to dismiss it all, as if he was just trying to be a good friend.

*Please.*

Fuck this guy. He was dead to me.

# Sixteen

# I Love This Journey For You

I adjusted the hem of my short red dress, the fabric smooth beneath my fingertips, as Mel and I sat in the backseat of the Uber. Jerry sat up front, making conversation with our driver. We were minutes away from pulling up to The Six for throwback night to celebrate my birthday, and I couldn't wait for the night to begin. Everyone had chipped in for bottle service, earning us a pair of couches and a couple of bottles of vodka and rum to share. The pulsating energy of a dark nightclub with Jake beside me on the couch, or grinding up against me on the dance floor, was exactly what I wanted for my birthday. *TGIF*.

We'd been texting nonstop since my photo shoot, and my vibrator had been getting a serious workout. I needed to talk to him, just to make sure we weren't walking into something with different expectations, but I had high hopes for where I'd be waking up tomorrow morning.

My phone buzzed, snapping me out of my lusty haze. I looked down to see an email titled "Competition Results – Worth Gallery." *Oh shit*. My night was about to get exponentially better or exponentially worse.

“Guys,” I said, my voice strangling in my throat. “The results of the Worth Gallery competition are in.”

Mel squealed, and Jerry whipped his head around, his conversation with the Uber driver cutting off.

“Open it,” Mel said, her voice ringing with confidence. “You’ve got this.”

“I don’t know if I can.” My voice trembled and tears sprang to my eyes. “Oh fuck, what if I didn’t get it?”

Jerry leaned over and grabbed my hand. “Mel’s right. Your work is too good. There’s no way they turned you down. Just open it so we have another reason to celebrate.”

I took a steadying breath before swiping open my phone and clicking on the email, clutching Jerry’s hand in a death grip. I scanned the email, my eyes tripping over themselves in an attempt to absorb what I was seeing.

“Well?” Mel demanded.

“I think…I’m in!” I was light-headed.

Jerry whooped and Mel screamed before snaking her arms around my neck and squeezing. I laughed, my face smooshed into Mel’s shoulder.

The Uber pulled up in front of the club and we tumbled out. Jerry picked me up and gave me a bear hug before setting me back down on the ground.

“I’m so fucking proud of you,” he said, before pressing a kiss to my temple.

Mel slid her arm around my waist on the other side and squeezed. “This is it. Your career is taking off. You’re almost at the final boss!”

I caught my breath. It didn’t seem real yet that I had a shot to win this competition and get to work with my idol, Teo Castillo. “This is officially the best birthday ever.”

“Damn right it is. Now let’s go celebrate!” Mel crowed as she steered us towards the line.

We bypassed it, a perk of bottle service, but not before Mel pointed out a guy in skinny ankle-length dress pants, no socks, and loafers doing a standing backflip, attempting to prove his sobriety to the bouncer to get in. The crowd erupted in cheers as he stuck the landing, and the security guard held the door open for him with a slight grin. I loved my city.

Once inside, the hostess led us through the crowded club to a set of white leather couches. “Say You’ll Be There” by the Spice Girls blasted through the speakers. I was on a high, drunk off the anticipation of a great night out and the promise of sex with Jake. And beneath it, the pride and thrill of knowing my work was good enough to compete with the best in the city was making me giddy.

Mel and I sang along and danced in front of the couches, doing our best impressions, pulling a reluctant Jerry up to dance with us until the hostess returned with the bottles, mixers, glasses, and ice. Jerry sat down and began mixing drinks for the three of us while Mel and I kept dancing, waiting for the others to arrive.

"Happy birthday," Jerry said, handing us our drinks as we sat down. We clinked our glasses together.

"I love you guys," I said, sucking back half of my cranberry vodka. "Thanks for putting this together. It feels like forever since we've been out dancing."

"Love you too, babe. We're going to dance our faces off," Mel said, as she clinked my glass again. Her gaze shifted to look behind me. "They're here!"

I turned to see Jake, Ryan, and Lauren following the hostess to our table. My eyes were all over Jake like greedy hands. He wore fitted dark jeans and a crisp white button-up. His sleeves were meticulously folded to expose his exquisite forearms. A couple of soft brown curls graced his forehead, while the sides and back of his hair were freshly trimmed. My god, he was sexy – a perfect birthday gift, and I was desperate to unwrap him. I bit the inside of my cheek as his eyes met mine, then drifted slowly down my body.

"Happy birthday, Red Riding Hood," he said as he hugged me. His hands pressed into my bare back, and I considered dragging him out of the club right then and there. He leaned in, pushing my curls aside, his nose grazing my ear as he growled, wolf-like, "That dress is going to be the end of me."

He withdrew, a smouldering gaze lingering on me as he slid his hands down my back, squeezing my hip before letting me go. A vivid image of me riding Jake with my red dress hitched hastily up over my hips pulled into sharp focus in my mind. I needed another drink.

"This is for you." Jake handed me a small gift bag.

"Aww, you didn't need to get me anything," I said, pulling out the tissue paper and unfolding the T-shirt wrapped inside.

"Well, I couldn't *not* get this when I saw it – I hope you don't have it."

I held up the vintage black T-shirt, "Spice Girls" written across the top, with a large picture of the five women in colour on the front. On the back, "Spice Up Your Life" was printed in red block letters. A wide smile broke out on my face.

"Thank you. It's perfect." I reached up to give him another quick hug.

"Happy Birthday, V!" Ryan said, as he stepped away from saying hello to Mel and Jerry and leaned over to hug me.

"Thank you! I'm so glad you could all make it," I said, turning to give Lauren a hug. She sat down beside Mel and accepted a drink from Jerry, who had been busy making another round of doubles while guarding his makeshift bar on the table.

"Alright, everyone," Mel called. "A toast to the birthday girl…who's about to have her work featured at the Worth Gallery!"

There was a chorus of congratulations as Jake turned to me with a huge smile, his eyes crinkling at the corners. "You got it? Em, that's fantastic!" He clinked his glass with mine.

"It hasn't even sunk in yet," I said. "I just got the email in the car on the way here."

"Even more reason to celebrate tonight," he said. "I'm so proud of you."

A warm rush spread through me at his words. He'd always been able to make me feel like the only person in the room. I quickly pushed that thought aside – he would be gone soon enough, and I wasn't about to make this more complicated than it needed to be.

The next hour passed in a flurry of clinking glasses, boisterous laughter, spontaneous sing-alongs, and impromptu mini-dance breaks, fueled by the beats of our favourite throwbacks and the drinks Jerry kept flowing. I was warm and fuzzy around the edges, my inhibitions softening with every sip.

Drunk Jake was fucking adorable…and seriously fuckable. He wore a loose, goofy grin, and his eyes traced my every move. As the night unfolded, I found myself pressed closer to him, his hand tracing an intimate path along my bare back before travelling up my spine to squeeze the nape of my neck, the pressure sending goosebumps down my body as my nipples tightened.

Finally, he turned my head to his and pulled me into a lingering kiss, his tongue stroking mine as I ran my hand over his jaw. I pulled back when Lauren's playful whistle cut through the music.

"Alright, you horny teenagers, we came here to dance," Mel said, a gleam in her eye. "Off the couch." She clapped her hands at us as the opening beats of "Party Rock Anthem" pumped through the speakers.

I laughed in delight as Jake rose to his feet and tossed back the rest of his drink.

"Let's go, Anderson," he said. "This time, I'll make sure to catch you if you fall." One hand on my lower back, he guided me to the crowded dance floor behind our friends.

As we danced, Jake and I found it impossible to keep our hands off each other. When Ed Sheeran's "The Shape of You" seamlessly transitioned into the next song, we found ourselves tucked into a private corner at the back of the club, Jake's hands tracing the curves of my body as his mouth moved eagerly against mine.

He pulled back, his chest rising and falling. "Come home with me?" His voice was low, thick and raw.

I'd been fantasizing about this since Mel had interrupted us on Wednesday. If I was honest, long before that. But I needed to be clear – both with him and myself – about what this was. Given our history, I couldn't let it get messy again.

I nodded.

Jake's eyes flared with heat, his grip tightening on my hips as he dipped his head down to mine again. I stalled him with a hand on his chest.

"But, so we're clear – I'm not looking for anything serious." The words tumbled out quickly, like they'd been waiting all night for the right opening. I gestured between us. "This is just fun." And based on recent experience, it was going to be a *lot* of fun. "I've got the exhibition coming up and I need to focus. You're going back to Waterloo soon anyway, right?"

*There. Self-preservation mode activated. No way was I falling for him again, not after everything that happened last time.*

Jake blinked a few times as a momentary shadow passed over his face, and his hands stilled on my hips. "Um, yeah. Sure. Okay. If that's what you want."

That wasn't what I'd expected. He couldn't possibly think that we were going to start any sort of real relationship. "That's what I want."

I ran my hand over his abs, slow and deliberate, then down over the front of his jeans. He was already hard, straining beneath the denim. We were definitely on the same page.

Jake groaned, caught my wrist and yanked me back against him, crashing his mouth onto mine in a kiss that was all hunger and heat. Any lingering doubts about where we stood evaporated the second his body pressed into mine.

*Game on.*

*Fuck me soon.*

*Please.*

This entire evening had been torturous, glorious foreplay, and I was impatient for the main course.

Jake pulled back, running his hand through his hair as he took out his phone and ordered an Uber before steering me back to the couches to grab our things. I waved goodbye to our friends and mouthed "thank you, love you" at Mel and Jerry on the dance floor. Mel's smirk screamed "I love this journey for you!" in her best Alexis Rose as she watched us go.

I winked back at her. No doubts, no second-guessing. Tonight, I was in control.

Jake and I squeezed through the heaving club, his hand firm on my bare lower back, guiding me toward the exit. The Uber was already waiting at the curb. I was wound as tightly as a drum, tension resonating through every fiber, desperate for him. As soon as he closed the car door behind us, I turned to face him and slid one knee between his. My tight red dress rode up as he pulled me higher onto him, his hands gripping my hips, skillfully rocking me up and down his thick thigh. My body humming, I grabbed the back of his neck, breathing hard against his lips before feverishly pressing my mouth to his.

## Seventeen

# Surprisingly Athletic for an Optometrist

We burst into Jake's apartment, lips and hands frantic on each other. He shoved the door shut with one hand as our mouths clashed, clumsy and desperate, like we'd been waiting years for this.

Jake slid his hands down my spine, leaving a trail of fire in their wake. As they settled on my ass, he groaned into my mouth, "Emma, you have the most perfect ass I've ever seen."

He lifted me effortlessly, my legs wrapping around him, my mouth sealed to his as he walked me the few steps into his kitchen and set me down on the edge of the breakfast bar, the marble countertop cold against my rear.

Jake stepped closer between my legs, and his large frame blotted out my view of anything other than his eyes intent on mine. This was it. The only way to move on – to finally let go of the ache I'd never dealt with. I deserved this. I wanted it. Not just for the version of me that used to daydream about Jake Griffin, but for the one standing here now, bold enough to take what she wanted.

It was my birthday. I wasn't going to overthink it. I was going to enjoy every fucking second.

"This little red dress has been driving me crazy all night," he growled, as his hands glided down my sides, over my hips, and to the hem of my dress. "All I've been able to think about is what's underneath."

"Is that right?" I leaned back on my hands, a slow smile spreading across my face.

"You're so fucking sexy," he breathed, as his fingers started tracing the hem of my dress.

I shivered as each swipe of his fingers raised the hem a little, the soft sporadic touches on my bare skin making me tremble in anticipation. Ever so slowly, he nudged my dress upwards, until after what felt like endless minutes of this exquisite torture, he slid his warm hands under my dress and hooked his fingers under the sides of my thong, tugging it down. I lifted up, letting him draw it down my legs and off.

Grabbing my bare hips, he pulled my center securely against him. I pulled his head down to mine, biting his lower lip before sliding my tongue across it. I could taste the rum and Cokes he'd been drinking, but mostly I could taste him, the most intoxicating flavour I'd ever experienced.

His warm hand lifted my knee over his hip, tracing upward until his fingers curled around my thigh. He slowly started rocking against me, the impressive ridge of him making my need spike. A lock of hair fell over his forehead as he worked himself against me, the rough texture of his jeans on my bare skin teasing me closer to the edge. I slid my hands down to his chest and fumbled with his buttons, desperate to feel more of him. Unable to remember how buttons worked while Jake kissed me within an inch of my life, I got stuck.

"Having fun down there?" he panted, pulling away to look down at my hands, where they were halfway down his shirt and struggling.

"Why are you so hard to unwrap?" I frowned down at the offending button. "You're an extremely frustrating birthday present."

He chuckled against my ear, the gust of air sending shivers down my overheated body.

"I got it." Jake unbuttoned the last few buttons on his shirt, before drawing it open and sliding it off his shoulders, in the sexiest impromptu strip tease I'd ever witnessed.

*Had I witnessed an impromptu strip tease, previously? Unclear. Focus, Emma.*

Reaching for him, my eyes roamed over the sculpted planes of his chest that I'd dreamt of climbing every night since I'd seen him again at speed dating.

"You're an optometrist, for god's sake, how do you look like this?" I asked.

"Thursday night Zumba at the community centre," he quipped with a smile.

I slipped my hand into the waistband of his pants, my fingertips grazing his chiseled abs, and pulled him back where I needed him.

"I hope your pants don't have a button-fly." I smirked.

Jake laughed, then groaned as my fingers brushed across his chest, goosebumps rising on his skin. He drew my hands around his neck again, before pulling me close and capturing my lips, our kiss turning nuclear in a heartbeat. Everything felt infinitely better with his warm, bare chest pressed against me.

"Jesus, I need to get you to my bedroom before I decide that the kitchen counter is an acceptable location for our first time." Jake lifted me, his shoulder muscles flexing under my hands, my legs still wrapped around his waist.

A man on a mission now, he carried me down a hallway and through a doorway, my elbow bumping against the doorframe before he dropped me on a neatly made bed, his navy-blue duvet scratchy against my bare legs.

Pausing to study him, standing shirtless over me, his erection pressing against the denim of his jeans, I got to my knees before putting my hands on his hips and drawing him closer to me, my head level with his waist. I palmed him through his jeans, my hand rubbing up and down his erection, squeezing gently.

"Emma," he hissed, his stomach twitching at my touch.

I gave him a wicked grin, my fingers moving to the button of his jeans and flicking it open. Dexterous now, they brushed the narrow line of hair that arrowed down and disappeared under his waistband. Holding his eyes, I licked my lips as I drew his zipper down, before sliding my hands inside his black boxer briefs, one hand cupping the heavy weight of him while the other drew him out of his boxers, stroking gently but deliberately up and down his length before lowering my head to take him in my mouth.

He groaned and shut his eyes, threading his hands through my hair as I swirled and flicked my tongue around the smooth head, then took him deeper and sucked, his cock hot and impossibly hard in my mouth.

His eyes fluttered open, and fixed on mine, his jaw slack as he watched me work for a little while, before jerking his hips away.

"That feels too good." His gruff voice rasped across my nerves like sandpaper.

He shucked his pants and boxers down his legs, stepping out of them. Then he pulled his socks off, tossing them aside. Thank god. He lowered himself on top of me, the heavy weight of him anchoring me to this moment.

I gloried in the feel of his bare skin as I ran my hands around his broad back, clutching at him as his lips came down on me. His breath brushed across my damp skin as he nuzzled my neck, alternating licks with gentle nips. I gasped as he reached up and grabbed the shoulders of my dress, jerking it down. His lips trailed towards my breast until he took my nipple in his mouth, his tongue lashing across it as he sucked, the sharp tug making me whimper and arch into him.

"More," I breathed.

"Fuck," he groaned, his hand coming up to massage my other breast, pinching my nipple between his thumb and forefinger. This twin assault had me twisting against him.

"Jake, now," I panted, arching up to his mouth and hands, at a fever pitch now, desperate to feel all of him. I guided his head back up to mine, nipping his lower lip. "I need you inside me."

His eyes were dazed, the blue muted in the dim bedroom, lit only by the light of a Toronto night outside his windows.

"You're sure?" His voice was low and strained, his need pressing against the confines of his self-control.

"Please," I whispered, stroking my hand down his body to demonstrate exactly what I needed from him.

At my touch, he sprang into action, reaching across and yanking open the drawer on his nightstand, his muscles bunching under my seeking hands. I sat up and pulled my dress over my head from where it had been crumpled around my waist. Jake turned back, the condom successfully located and drew in a sharp breath.

"You are so beautiful." His voice slid like velvet over my skin, raising goosebumps.

He lay back on the bed, cupped my jaw with his hand, and guided me down over him. He kissed me slowly now, deliberately, his tongue dragging against mine, and I was helpless to do anything but follow his lead as he gently drew my leg over his hips. Together, we rolled the condom on, my hands trembling, Jake letting out a soft moan at my touch.

His stomach muscles flexed between my knees. His eyes held mine, soft but intent, as I lifted to position him and exhaled as I slid downwards, my eyes fluttering closed as I steadied myself with my hands on his chest. I paused to gather myself when he was fully seated, getting used to the unfamiliar size of him, before slowly drawing up and back down, a moan escaping my lips.

*Holy shit. This was happening.*

"Fuck, Emma," he groaned, laying back and gripping my hips to guide me up and down a little faster.

I leaned forward, my breasts grazing his chest, sucking his tongue into my mouth as I began to work myself up and down his cock, my need rising sharply. The next minutes were a blur, a kaleidoscope of feeling. The only sound Jake's whispers in my ear telling me how hot I was, how much he'd wanted this. His feelings were a perfect echo of the drumbeat that had been reverberating in me since I'd seen him again, shunting me closer to the edge as my hips rocked up and down more quickly.

"I'm so close," I gasped into Jake's mouth, desperate for release.

He trailed his hand down to the juncture of my thighs, his thumb rubbing firmly against my clit as he pumped his hips upward once, twice, and I shattered, crying out, my muscles going rigid, my mind the night sky scattered with a blanket of stars.

Slowly, I came back to myself, becoming aware of Jake's hands stroking gently down my back to my ass. I pressed myself up, my hands tracing his abs, feeling him still hard inside me. His jaw was tense, his eyes burning on mine, his hips twitching slightly like he couldn't keep himself from moving, his hands kneading my ass.

"You like making me come?" I wiggled my hips, trying to set him off. A cheeky laugh escaped my lips.

At this, Jake growled and flipped me onto my back, his large body on top as he slid his cock back inside me, my laughter cutting off as he jerked my legs up around his hips, one large hand on the underside of my knee, holding me wide open for him, the new angle abruptly rekindling my desire. His eyes boring into mine, he began moving, every stroke hitting a place deeper inside me that had me rapidly climbing to another peak.

"More than anything," he panted, his hips moving faster. His mouth trailed hungrily down to my breast as he grabbed my hands and stretched them above my head, one hand wrapping around my wrists to hold them there. I pushed my hands back against his, the pressure of him holding me captive spiking my need as he licked his way to my other breast. I moaned loudly and let my arms go slack as he brought his wild mouth to mine again. His chest pressed down against me as his hips sped up.

“Faster,” I panted. “Harder. Please, Jake.” I whimpered, writhing against his body as my desire intensified until I was gasping against his lips, frantic for release.

“Fuck,” he said as he dragged one hand down my body and curved it under my ass. He lifted me up to meet his powerful thrusts and I exploded, crying out into his mouth as he thrust once more before holding still deep inside me and groaning my name. He pressed his forehead against mine, and kissed my lips slowly.

As I floated gently down from the orgasmic cloud nine I’d been frolicking on, I disentangled my wrists, bringing my hands up to his hair to stroke through it, eliciting a murmur of pleasure from him.

“You have excellent manners,” he said, breath ragged. “Always saying please.” His sexy half smile lit up his face. As our breathing slowed and synchronized, I let my hands go on a walking tour of his damp skin. At the gentle scratch of my fingernails, Jake propped himself up and gazed down at me for several seconds, then pressed another slow kiss to my lips before he disappeared into the bathroom.

Emotion welled in my throat, sharp and sudden. For a split second, I was back in that sun-drenched field, our first kiss lingering between us – tender and certain. I swallowed hard and blinked the memory away with a deep breath. That was a lifetime ago. This was something else entirely.

Chilly without Jake’s large, warm body pressed against me, I scooted under the duvet. He returned a moment later and slid beneath the covers so that we were lying on our sides, facing each other.

“Not too shabby, Griffin,” I said. “Surprisingly athletic for an optometrist.”

Jake laughed. “Oh, it’s like that, huh? I guess I’ll have to work harder next time to get those approval ratings up.”

My mind boggled at the thought of Jake “working harder,” sending a shiver down my spine. He reached out and pulled me closer, so I was nestled against him. My eyes drifted closed, and we stayed like that for a while, his hand slowly stroking from my hip to my shoulder blades and back again, mapping the contours of my body.

I sighed, letting myself bask in the glow of finally having mind-blowing sex with Jake – even better than I’d imagined it could be – and without the messy emotional baggage. Just a few more pages and I’d be ready to finish this spicy Choose Your Own Adventure, closing his book for good. I wasn’t delusional enough to start something real with the man who’d shattered my self-confidence in high school, and his departure in a few weeks made sure of it.

At the bottom of this page, I had an important decision to make: turn to page 32 to heat things up in the kitchen, or flip ahead to 47 to soap up in the shower. I wasn't very hungry, but nothing worked up an appetite quite like getting taste-tested on the kitchen counter.

Yes, chef.

# Eighteen
# June 29, 11 Years Ago

## *Peak High School*

Jess' house reeked of weed, cheap beer, and greasy pizza – the holy trinity of high school suburban house parties. The sticky floor trembled beneath my feet, thanks to her older brother's shitty garage band thrashing around in the basement like they were headlining Coachella, not butchering the same three chords next to the laundry room. Jess' parents were at their cottage for the weekend, so this wasn't just any party – it was *the* unofficial start to summer. And I was, without question, the least cool person in the room. For the record, I didn't even want to be here. Sarah had dragged me along, since I was heading to camp on Sunday and we wouldn't get to see each other much this summer.

We were in the kitchen now, where she and Jess were doing tequila shots with two other girls from the dance team. I leaned against the island, sipping my Mike's Hard Lemonade. I hadn't planned on drinking, but Sarah had shoved one into my hand, saying, "Come on, you're allowed to have fun, you know." It was summer in a can, and I was on my second, which meant I was having twice the fun.

The band abruptly cut off. The sudden silence made it seem like someone had unmuted the party; everyone was shouting over each other as if the music were still playing. It only took a moment before "Get Lucky" blasted from the speakers in the room next to us and the basement door swung open. A couple of sweaty older guys stumbled out and beelined for the fridge, grabbing a couple of beers. Sarah slammed her shot glass down, just as one of them – the one with drumsticks jutting out of his back pocket, a damp, sleeveless *Blood Duct* T-shirt, and a smattering of facial hair – drifted over with a cocky grin.

"Sarah, this is Jeff," Jess said, angling Sarah towards him. "He's *Blood Duct*'s drummer."

"You guys are awesome," Sarah gushed as she leaned into him. "What was that last song you played?"

I tried not to roll my eyes, but the Mike's was making it harder to control my inside face.

Jeff grinned wider. "'Meat Window' – guaranteed mosh pit every time. We have our new demo, *Clogged with Suffering* downstairs. You want a copy?"

"Only if you sign it." Sarah took Jeff's beer out of his hand and sipped it while holding his gaze. He reached back into the fridge, grabbed another beer, then Sarah's hand, and led her toward the basement door. She gave me a little shrug before disappearing downstairs.

Jess tapped her can against mine, as if her work here were done, then headed into the living room to cozy up on the couch beside Kyle, Murray's "yes" man.

Okay. Well. This had been fun.

It was time for me to head home, now that I had been ditched by Sarah and was surrounded by people I didn't even like. I sent her a quick text letting her know I was heading out. I sighed, took a long sip of my magical lemony goodness and started toward the front door.

Then it opened.

My breath caught. Heat prickled at the back of my neck. There was a glitch in the matrix as the ground shifted beneath me. Or maybe that was just the vodka swirling in my stomach.

I hadn't expected him to be here.

He looked good. Too good. His grey zip-hoodie was pushed up his forearms, and his hair was a bit messy in that intentionally-unintentional way. He scanned the room like he wasn't sure why he'd come, and for one horrifying second, our eyes locked.

I turned away so fast I tripped, stumbling back into the kitchen. One wobbly step told me I was tipsier than I'd realized. I was in no shape to talk to Jake. We hadn't spoken much since Winterfest, just the bare minimum at awkward SAC meetings and careful avoidance in the hallways. I'd even switched to Mondays at the food bank. Our friendship was over, but I had a sinking feeling that if I spoke to him now, a little tipsy and a little lonely, I'd dive headlong back into my unrequited crush.

I edged past everyone in the kitchen and slipped out the sliding doors. The backyard was just as loud – Jess' brother was now jamming on an acoustic guitar, someone tumbled off a patio chair to thunderous applause, and a group was celebrating a come-from-behind Cornhole win. I took a few steps down the stairs to find a quiet corner to catch a few breaths, but Murray found me first.

He was unsteady, a red Solo cup in one hand and a joint in the other, eyes glazed over with a cocktail of drugs, alcohol, and sheer lack of brain activity. Fantastic. This night just kept getting better.

"Emmmmmaaaaaa!" he slurred, coming face to face with me. He leaned in, his breath warm and smelling like beer. "You're kinda hot, you know."

My stomach turned. Perfect – a wasted Murray with fermented pickup lines and no concept of personal space.

"You're kinda gross, you know," I said.

I took a step back, but it was no match for his incessant close-talking. He stumbled toward me and laughed, seemingly convinced this was going well.

"We should hang out. Just you and me. It's loud out here. Let's go find a room and talk." He put his joint between his lips, and reached for my hand.

"Yeah, that's never happening," I said, stepping out of his reach.

He was too drunk to stop his momentum, stumbled, and face-planted into the hydrangeas behind me, then promptly puked all over them.

"Charming," I muttered to myself as I took a couple of steps towards the back gate and texted my mom that I was heading home. She replied instantly, saying she'd walk over to meet me.

"Hey."

I turned at the sound of his voice – dizziness, then sharp focus as my eyes locked on him. Jake stood a few feet away, his expression somewhere between concerned and amused.

He nodded toward Murray, now groaning in the bushes, trying to sit up. "You good?"

I shrugged. "Better than the hydrangeas."

Jake laughed, and something fluttered in my chest.

"Peak high school."

Maybe it was the Mike's. Or the way he took a step closer, and I had to tilt my head to keep looking at him, but there was something different about him.

He rubbed the back of his neck.

We stood there, marinating in silence.

"Did you get taller? You look taller." I eyed him as I tipped my can up and slurped the last of my drink.

"Maybe?" He ran his hand through his hair. "It's been a while."

"Yeah." I let my gaze linger. "And your hair is shorter. And you have a tan."

Jake chuckled. "Baseball."

I nodded slowly. "And your eyes are doing that thing they do when they're happy. All soft and warm. You have beautiful eyes."

He lifted his eyebrows, as if he hadn't expected that.

I winced. "Did I say that out loud?" I would definitely be mortified about this tomorrow, but the Mike's was having a pleasant insulating effect on my emotions.

"You did." He broke into a wide, easy grin. "Are you leaving?"

"Well, I think it's almost time for *Blood Duct*'s next set, so…" I teetered my hand back and forth. "Definitely going home. My mom's on her way to meet me."

"Good call. Can I wait with you?"

I was a little buzzed, and very aware of how much I wanted to spend more time with him.

"Would Annika mind?"

Jake paused. "We aren't together anymore. She's off to Queen's in the fall and travelling with her family all summer, so it made sense."

"Oh," I said, the word catching in my throat. My brain scrambled to keep up – surprise, confusion and the tiniest thrill, all wrapped up in the fog of two Mike's and months of pretending I didn't care. "Sorry to hear that. Me and Kevin didn't work out either. Turns out he doesn't peel his cheese strings. Just bites them. Like a monster."

Jake laughed. "That's horrifying."

"Right?" I said, throwing my hands up in agreement. Kevin and I had broken up a month ago. I'd really tried to make it work with him after the Winterfest disaster, but it had become clear that I didn't feel the way I was supposed to.

I reached through the railing on the back porch, and dropped my can into the recycling bin, as Jake opened the gate.

"After you, Anderson," he said.

I cast one last glance back at Murray, now snoring on the grass, one hand still clutching his cup, then stepped through the gate into the narrow path between the houses.

We emerged onto the sidewalk in front of the house, just as the band started warming up in the basement. The night was cooling off, and Jake tugged down the sleeves on his hoodie. We sat on the curb, the streetlights buzzing faintly above.

"Do you have any summer plans?" Jake asked.

"Yeah, I'm heading to art camp in Muskoka for most of July. They have everything – photography, printmaking, painting, graphic design, and life drawing. I can't wait."

"That sounds amazing." He glanced over at me. "You're so talented."

"Thanks," I said, feeling my cheeks warm. My buzz had mellowed into something soft, and sitting beside Jake felt almost…normal. "I've never been to an overnight camp before, so I'm kind of nervous. There's this one workshop where you work with some of the music campers and design an album cover for them. Concept, visuals, everything. I think that'll be cool."

"You should do one for *Blood Duct*." He grinned. "They could use all the help they can get."

I snorted. "What about you? Big summer plans or endless baseball?"

He exhaled, looking ahead. "Besides work, pretty much just baseball. Lots of practice and traveling for tournaments."

"Work?" I asked. "Where are you working?"

He hesitated long enough to make me suspicious.

"Promise you won't laugh?"

"No, absolutely not." I broke into a wide grin.

He smirked. "Dairy Queen – yours truly is the proud dispenser of cones, Blizzards, and Dilly Bars. I've even started writing on the cakes."

"That's incredible. Do you have to flip the blizzards upside down when you serve them?"

"Only if I want to keep my job." He grinned. "Company policy."

"Have you ever lost one?"

He nodded solemnly. "A Reese's Pieces. Medium. Tragic day."

I burst out laughing. "Floor or counter?"

"Floor. Full splatter. A kid cried."

"No!" I covered my mouth, still laughing. "Did you give them a new one?"

"Of course. Double stuff." He quirked a smile at me as I shook my head at him.

"Heroic."

God, I'd missed him.

I looked up to see my mom rounding the corner across the street, before turning around to admire the garden at the neighbour's house. Jake sighed, like he wasn't quite ready for this to end either.

"So, you're gone for July?"

"Yeah," I nodded, as we stood up. "Then we're doing some family things, but I'll be around mid-August when we need to plan the SAC back-to-school stuff."

He rubbed the back of his neck, hesitating for a second. "It was really good to talk to you again."

"You too."

He took a small step backward, his eyes still on me. "Night, Anderson. Have fun at camp. Text me when you're back."

"Sure. Night, Blizzard boy."

He laughed under his breath and turned to head into the backyard. I smiled as I crossed the road to meet my mom, the sound of his laugh echoing in my chest as if it had never left.

# Nineteen

# Grandma-Has-Some-Fun-Before-the-End-of-Summer

I dropped into the bleachers beside Mel with a dramatic sigh, clutching my iced coffee like it was holy water. I'd arrived just in time to see the end of the warm-up and peered toward the court. Jerry tripped over his own feet trying to serve and nearly hit Ryan in the back of the head with the volleyball. They were a player short tonight and had begged Jerry to fill in as a last resort – something none of us should have allowed.

Mel sipped her drink and pointed toward Jerry. "If that man doesn't snap an ankle tonight, it'll be a miracle."

I laughed. "I almost wish my shoot had run longer today so I wouldn't have to witness the carnage."

I glanced over at Jake, who was stretching out his quads in a loose pair of athletic shorts. Watching Jerry play a sport was painful enough, but that wasn't the only reason I'd been hoping to avoid coming tonight. This was the first time I'd seen Jake since I'd left his apartment yesterday morning, and the post-sex nerves were making me antsy. The weekend had been amazing. We'd spent the entire time together, surfacing only long enough for me to grab fresh clothes and takeout, but we hadn't made any plans to see each other again. As far as I was concerned, the sequel was already in pre-production, coming soon to a bedroom near me. I just needed the green light from Jake.

Across the gym, Jerry attempted another practice serve and sent the ball careening into the net. Ryan offered a few words of encouragement as he picked it up and tossed it back to him. Jake headed toward Jerry with a grin, and my gaze lingered on his perfect ass.

"So." Mel drew the word out as she eyed me with a smirk. "How was it, finally getting your hands on your long-lost Jake-shaped fantasy?"

I groaned quietly, making Mel laugh. I'd texted her to let her know I'd be staying with him for the weekend, but this was the first time we'd had a chance to chat.

At that moment, Jake looked up and spotted me. His face broke out in a broad grin and he lifted his hand in a wave. He'd texted earlier to ask if I'd be coming, but I'd been on set shooting web content for a children's clothing line and hadn't had a chance to respond.

"From that grin, I'm guessing it's all systems go in the 'grandma-has-some-fun-before-the-end-of-summer' plan?"

"Oh yeah," I said, sighing. "That man should come with a warning. It was like a portal to another dimension."

Mel nearly choked on her drink, laughing.

On the court, the whistle blew, and the game began. I leaned against the bleachers, leisurely perusing Jake's perfect body. His shirt was already sticking to his back, his forearms flexing as he received the serve and passed the ball to the setter. I took a long sip of my drink.

"Any potential for something more there?" Mel asked, her tone fake-casual.

I shot her a look. "Mel, he's leaving in a few weeks. I'm not interested in a long-distance relationship."

As the ball was hit back over the net, Jerry dove and missed it by a solid two feet, landing with a dramatic "oof" that echoed throughout the gym. The whistle blew. Mel and I cringed, then clapped and shouted some encouragement at Jerry as Jake helped him up.

"Poor Jerry," I said, deflecting. "He texted me five times, begging me to come for emotional support. You'd think he was playing in the Olympics."

Mel sipped her Coke, watching as Ryan returned a serve. "Waterloo's a two-hour train ride away, not on another continent. You guys seem to be vibing. Why not see what it could be?"

I didn't answer. I really didn't want my best friend trying to convince me that this could be something real. Because when Jake touched me, when he looked at me like I was the only thing he could see, it didn't feel temporary. And that terrified me. Already my unruly brain had started to fantasize about what a relationship with him might look like – the power of truly incredible sex – but if I started letting him in again, I'd have only myself to blame if he pulled another disappearing act.

On the court, Jake jumped up for a block and landed lightly on his feet, winking as he looked over and caught me staring. My heart did a weird flutter-flip and I couldn't help grinning back.

"It doesn't have to have an end date, you know?" Mel said.

The thing was, I did know. I knew exactly how it had ended the last time. On my front porch, with a kiss, a promise and a silence that had lasted years.

But Mel didn't know that.

"We'll see," I said. *Not a chance in hell.* Past experience had taught me that Jake was a classic "I'm here for a good time, not a long time" guy.

Mel and I winced in unison as Jerry lunged for a ball and slammed into the net post with a theatrical grunt. Thank goodness it was padded.

The sun was setting by the time the game wrapped up, casting a warm glow over the cracked asphalt in the parking lot behind Central Tech. Ryan grabbed a Bluetooth speaker from his car, and music drifted through the air as the team spilled out of the school, sweaty and flushed.

Jake did some quick introductions of the other three players, who then went on their way, and Ryan pulled a couple of camping chairs out of his trunk. Jerry immediately collapsed into one like he'd just survived war.

"My body," he groaned. "My soul."

"You looked like a crash-test dummy out there," I chuckled, offering him my water bottle. "A very determined crash-test dummy. Good game, Jer-bear."

"You dove three times," Mel said, grinning at him. "And you missed every ball."

"I sacrificed myself for morale," Jerry wheezed. "And for beer. Ry said there'd be beer."

Ryan laughed. "We appreciate you coming out, man. We would've had to forfeit without you, and now we're sailing into the playoffs."

"I don't have to 'play-off' do I?" Jerry asked. "Volleyball is a lawless sport. No one tells you where to go, the ball comes out of nowhere, and everyone's yelling 'mine' like we're in divorce court."

"You did try to catch it like a football," I said, grinning.

"I panicked," Jerry said. "You know I hate ball sports."

Ryan pulled a bag full of snacks and a small cooler out of his trunk. He reached into the cooler, handed Jerry a beer, and patted him on the shoulder.

"Honestly, I was impressed you stayed upright most of the time," Mel said. "And you almost made contact on that last dive."

"That one wasn't intentional. That was gravity claiming me." Jerry twisted open his bottle and took a gulp before leaning his head back and closing his eyes. "Can someone please feed me a chip? My arms are noodles."

Ryan popped open a bag and tossed one directly into Jerry's open mouth. He caught it like a seal and raised a lazy fist in triumph.

Mel flopped into a chair next to Ryan and passed the rest of us drinks. Jake eased into the chair on my left, his hair still damp with sweat. I shivered as I imagined soaping him up in his glass-enclosed shower. I was ready to wring everything I could out of this summer fling, but Jake hadn't mentioned anything when I'd left on Sunday. It was maddening not knowing exactly where we stood, even though I kept telling myself I shouldn't care.

"I'm glad you could make it." Jake tapped his knee against mine, sending sparks through me like the snap of static. "It's nice having you here."

I flicked a glance at him. "What are you up to tonight?"

"No plans after this," he said, a grin on his lips as he looked intently at me.

I nodded. "Me neither. I've got a busy week, though. Now that I have the exhibit to prep for, I need to choose my final prints and finish editing. Plus, I've got a full day of mini sessions at High Park on Friday, so I should definitely make use of the time off tonight while I have it."

"I'd love to see the shots from the other night. So I can take credit for being an amazing assistant, obviously."

I laughed. "Sorry, I never let anyone see my work before a show."

"No problem." His smile was warm, eyes lingering just long enough to make my pulse tick faster. "I'm sure it'll be worth the wait."

His words hung in the air for a moment, settling between us. It seemed like he meant more than the photos. Something stirred inside me, alongside a warning that maybe this wasn't turning out to be as casual as I needed it to be. But I wasn't ready to give up on the idea that a fling with Jake might finally help me get past the fear that had always kept my relationships superficial. And spending the night having sex intense enough for my Apple Watch to politely interrupt with, "It looks like you're working out. Want to start a High Intensity Interval Training session?" felt like a solid way to avoid mulling over Mel's inconvenient questions.

Time to stop acting like a teenager with a crush and just ask for what I wanted. "I'd still love to come over, though."

Jake's smile widened, and he abruptly stood up, reaching down to grab my hand and tug me upwards.

"Sorry to cut out early, but Emma and I have plans," he said, taking the half-empty bottle from my hand and passing it to Ryan.

"Where are you guys going? Maybe we could all join." Ryan grinned.

Mel whacked him on the chest. "Do not listen to him. Go, have fun, we'll make sure Noodle Arms makes it home safe." She winked at me.

Jake grabbed his bag, and slung it over his shoulder before turning and threading his fingers through mine.

My heart stuttered, then sped up at his touch. "Night everyone," I called, as Jake and I started walking toward Borden Street.

Jake dumped his duffle bag inside the door. "I'm just going to jump in the shower. I need to get out of these sweaty clothes."

I reached up and tugged his head down for a kiss. "Yeah, you do," I grinned. "I'll race you." I couldn't wait to soap him up with whatever made him smell like a cold glass of lemonade on a sun-drenched dock.

Jake's eyes widened, and he groaned low in his throat.

"Ready, set!" I dashed for his bedroom, aware that in a fair race I would have no hope of winning against Jake's athleticism.

"You didn't say 'go,' Anderson!" Jake bellowed from behind me. I could hear him chasing me.

With a frantic peal of laughter, I rounded the corner into his bedroom, Jake right behind me. I screeched as he grabbed for my dress, his fingers clutching the fabric and slowing me down so that his long legs let him overtake me. He reached the bathroom door just before me, turning and catching me as I slammed into his chest.

"Cheater!" I was out of breath, from the brief sprint and the feeling of him pressed against me.

Jake threw back his head and laughed. "We can go again if you want, Anderson."

I ran my hands down his back to his ass, pulling him against me. "I'm pretty sure we can think of better ways to get our heart rate up."

"Oh yeah? What did you have in mind?" Jake's grin turned wicked, a dare in his sparkling blue eyes.

I stepped back from him and in one swift motion, pulled my maxi dress over my head, revealing a black lace bra and thong. As Jake's grin fell away, I reached up and removed the elastic and bobby pins securing my bun, dropping them on the floor as I shook my hair down my back. His gaze bounced around my body, moving from my lips to my breasts to the junction between my thighs. He licked his lips like he couldn't decide what needed his attention first.

I sauntered past him into the bathroom, reveling in the fact that he seemed speechless as I brushed up against him and sent him a challenging look. "You're wearing too many clothes, Griffin."

With that, I stepped into the large glass shower and turned it on, gasping as the cold water hit my overheated body, turning my nipples into points, pressing against the lace of my bra. I turned to look at Jake through the glass, raising my hands to run them through my hair as the water turned warm. Jake sprung into action and rid himself of his clothing, pushing down his boxers and stepping out of them and into the shower.

"Come here," he growled, grabbing my hips and pulling me close, his cock long and thick against my stomach. "You make me fucking crazy."

He manoeuvred us beneath the shower head, licking into my mouth as the water pounded down on us. His hands were everywhere, kneading my ass before one hand traveled up and yanked the cup of my bra down, palming my breast as his thumb rubbed across my nipple. Jake lowered his head, keeping me tight against him with his other hand on my ass, as he licked across my nipple before sucking it, swirling his tongue around. He reached behind me and flicked open my bra, drawing the wet fabric from my body and tossing it on the shower floor before turning his attention to the other breast.

Jake's body inched closer to me until I was pressed up against the glass shower wall, out from under the direct spray from the shower head. He kissed slowly down my body until he was kneeling in front of me. He leaned forward, his tongue tracing the edge of my thong with a slow, teasing lick before he breathed against me, a soft gust of warm air. His eyes locked onto mine with an intense, hungry gaze as he reached up and peeled it off.

He leaned forward and licked into my folds, then circled his tongue around my clit, the soft, wet contact driving my desire sharply upwards, before he gently began to suck.

"Oh my god," I moaned as my head fell back, one hand pressing back against the shower glass to steady me while the other hand threaded through his hair to press his head closer to me.

He groaned and slid his hands around the back of my legs, one hand gripping the back of my knee to lift it and rest it over his muscular shoulder. He had access to all of me and I flashed hot, my nipples tightening further as he dove down and thrust his tongue into me, before dragging it upwards again to flick my clit. His teasing rhythm pushed me to the brink, burning hotter with each stroke.

"Jake, please," I whimpered, my hands tugging at his hair.

He pulled back. "Emma." His low voice made me shiver. "Look at me."

Trembling with desire, frantic to come, my eyes locked on his, a hot blue flame in their depths. Slowly, he brought one hand up and slid a finger inside me, curling it as he withdrew it before sliding it back in again. I moaned and my eyes fluttered closed as I clenched around his finger.

"Eyes, Em." The slight hint of command in his tone ratcheted up my desire. My gaze dropped again, in time to see him slide a second finger in, bringing me right to the edge.

"Fuck, Jake, please," I whined, willing to do anything he asked.

Intense and unyielding, he watched me as he sucked strongly on my clit, and pumped his fingers in and out of me. I clutched his hair and lost my mind, crying out as my orgasm washed over me in a wave so intense it left me breathless and weak.

As I emerged from the undertow, Jake's mouth and hands gentled on me. I reached down and drew him upwards, unsteady on my feet. He stood, nuzzling into my neck as his hard cock rubbed my stomach.

"I want to go down on you every fucking day." His low murmur in my ear raised goosebumps across my sensitized body.

Turning my face to his, our lips met in a heated kiss that quickly turned wild. The ticking clock on our time together made me want this even more. I grabbed his cock, pumping it roughly, making Jake groan into my mouth. He slid his hands down and palmed my ass, before lifting me up and pressing me against the glass, positioning his cock at my entrance.

He captured my lips again, his tongue thrusting into my mouth as his cock slid inside, not stopping until his hips were flush with mine. His chest pressed against me as he set up a steady rhythm. The pounding of the shower and the slapping of our wet skin mixed with our gasps and moans. I ran my hands over his wet shoulders and back, the feel of his muscles flexing under my hands turning me on even more.

Abruptly, Jake pulled out of me, making me whimper in protest. He set me down on the ground before spinning me around and coming up behind me, his wet cock sliding against my ass. One hand came up to cradle my breast while the other dived down between my legs, parting my folds and thrusting two fingers inside. I moaned and bent forward, bracing my hands on the bench in front of me.

"Jesus, I can't get enough of you," Jake groaned as he pulled his fingers out and slid his cock back inside. He bent over me, one hand on the bench beside mine while the other one drifted across my hip until his fingers found my clit. He circled slowly, his fingers slippery, as his thrusts increased in tempo. The stimulation was too much and I came apart in his arms, crying out right as he thrust one last time and groaned into my hair.

We breathed together for long moments. Jake kissed the nape of my neck before slowly withdrawing. He collapsed onto the bench beside me and pulled me onto his lap. "Pretty sure you're going to kill me one of these days, Anderson."

*Not if you kill me first.*

It was like our sex was choreographed, designed to give me maximum pleasure. This was the best sex I'd ever had and it wasn't even close. I tried to tell myself it was just our physical chemistry, not an emotional connection. There was no possibility of something real between us, so it was time to stuff any inconvenient feelings way down deep where they wouldn't see the light of day.

# Twenty
## September 2, 11 years ago

# If You Died, I'd Kill You

The bus jerked to a stop as Sarah and I waited on the back step. We pushed the door open wide, hopped out onto Lawrence Avenue just as the light changed, and hurried across the street toward the baseball diamond at Heron Park.

The late afternoon sun beat down on the infield, glinting off helmets and the chain-link fence surrounding the diamond. The air buzzed with excitement as the crowd's hum rose and fell, friends and family filling the bleachers. The Scarborough Stingers 18U Elite baseball team was warming up for their East Conference Final. A win today would send them to the Toronto Finals in two weeks.

I could spot Jake a mile away, taller and broader than most of his teammates, working in the bullpen in his tight white baseball pants, his stance easy but focused. He fired a pitch into the catcher's mitt with a solid pop, his eyes locked on the target, jaw set with fierce focus.

"Jesus, put your tongue back in your mouth," Sarah muttered, shooting me a sidelong look, one eyebrow raised in amusement.

"What?" I clasped my hand to my chest. "I'm just here to support the team. They need a win to make the finals."

"And?" She looked at me expectantly.

"And to see if Jake throws a few of the sliders he's been working on with his coach."

"And…"

"Fine…*and* to check out his ass in those tiny white pants. Take it up with the complaints department."

Sarah snorted as we clanged our way up the section of metal bleachers behind home plate, choosing a spot at the top. I dropped my bag full of water and snacks with a thud at my feet.

About halfway through camp this past summer, I'd started texting with Jake again – just silly stuff at first. I'd send him photos of what I was working on, and he would reply with something funny or thoughtful that made me smile at my phone like an idiot. After I'd gotten home, the texts had become more regular. Longer. Later at night. There was no one else in the picture this time – no Kevin, no Annika – and without them, it was easier to just be ourselves. We'd never really talked about what had happened at Winterfest, but it was like we'd picked up where we left off, only without the tension and guilt layered on top.

I pulled the massive poster I'd spent way too long making out of my bag.

"You can't be serious," Sarah said, not hiding her embarrassment. "Why are you so extra? You definitely don't need that sign."

"Oh, but I do." I unrolled the poster to reveal my hyper-realistic drawing of the Scarborough Stingers logo – a fierce, stylized yellow and black hornet in mid-flight, wings spread wide, poised to strike. The bold script curved beneath it in dynamic lettering, edged in red to match the team's intensity, read: "It's a sting operation!"

"Okay, that actually looks cool," Sarah said. "Maybe I don't have to go sit with Jess after all."

She said it like a joke, but the pause while her gaze drifted down to the lower bleachers stretched a little too long. Jess had just arrived, tossing her hair over her shoulder as she laughed at something Kyle said. The only thing I hated about going to Jake's games was seeing Murray and his collection of mouth-breathers outside of school. Murray's dad was an assistant coach, so he'd lucked into the Stingers' right field spot, and Kyle was never far behind.

"I think she was expecting me to sit with them." Sarah fiddled with the edge of her sleeve.

Something prickled at the base of my neck. Part jealousy, part annoyance that she was friends with them, and part hurt that I always seemed to come in second place now.

"Nope, you're stuck with me, you promised."

I flipped the poster over to show her the other side. It was a stunningly detailed mythical griffin – Jake was the starting pitcher today. It had the body of a powerful lion, a crest of full plumage around its neck, wide feathered wings outstretched, and Jake's face morphed halfway into an eagle, a proud beak exaggerating the determined look on his face. The griffin wore a black Stingers cap and clutched a ball in one claw and wore a baseball glove on the other.

"Majestic as an eagle, powerful as a lion." I grinned.

"You're insane," Sara shook her head. "He's going to be so embarrassed."

"He's used to me," I said, shrugging. This wasn't the first Jake-inspired baseball sign I'd made, but it was the most intricate.

Sarah raised an eyebrow. "So, you're both single, right? Why aren't you two hooking up yet?"

Her question caught me by surprise. "We're friends." I shook my head, the words coming out fast, but not fully capturing what we were. Jake could never be a casual hook-up.

Sarah's skeptical look was a challenge, her lips curling into a teasing smirk. "Uh-huh, just friends. Keep telling yourself that."

"It's the truth," I said automatically, my eyes returning to Jake. I did want to be more than friends. But I just didn't know what the next step was, or whether I was brave enough to put myself out there. I didn't want to risk losing what we had for a second time.

Jake rolled his shoulders, the tension easing out of his frame. A decisive nod to his coach and a sharp exhale – like he was forcing out anything weighing on him. As he jogged to the mound, he looked fluid, practiced. Ready. But I knew about the cracks beneath the surface.

I knew how much it bothered him that his dad never made it to a game, that his mom was always overworked and overstressed. That he missed his brother, who had been away at school for years and rarely made it home anymore.

I told him about the pressure and loneliness I sometimes felt as an only child – my parents often joked that they hadn't had a second one because they'd "nailed it on the first try" – and how Sarah had been off with me lately, sharp around the edges, and I didn't know if we were okay.

Somehow, with Jake, I didn't have to explain much. He just got it. We were building something quiet and invisible between us, a little world where we didn't have to pretend.

Jake threw a couple of warm-up pitches right in the strike zone. He adjusted his cap in between, his usual habit when he was focused.

"He's dialed in," I said, unable to take my eyes off him.

Just before the umpire called the first batter, Jake glanced up into the stands and blew out a deep breath. His gaze swept the rows until it landed on me, and the corner of his mouth lifted in a smile that made my heart flutter.

I jumped to my feet and let out a big "Wooooooo!" holding the poster a little higher.

When his gaze shifted to my drawing, he laughed out loud – the warm, unguarded sound carrying across the diamond. A couple of his teammates glanced over, but I couldn't look away from the way his eyes crinkled as he shook his head at me, grinning.

Sarah jabbed me in the ribs with her elbow. "Just friends, gotcha."

Jake pitched the first few innings with precision, his fastball snapping into the catcher's mitt like a whip, the occasional slider slicing through the air with a sharp break. The Lions' swings were desperate, always a fraction too late. With each strikeout, we stomped on the metal bleachers, and I held up my sign, screaming for Jake as the crowd's roar grew louder.

The Stingers' offense was grinding in a tough battle. Rohan worked a full count before drilling one into right field, barely beating the throw to second. Weston followed with a hard hit to centre, but the Lions' outfielder quickly closed in, keeping us from breaking the game open. The score stayed close, neither side able to pull away.

The game stretched on under the late-afternoon heat, and Jake's pitches began to lose their edge. His jaw tightened with frustration as he stepped back onto the rubber with two out in the bottom of the sixth, pushing to finish the inning. I could see the strain on his face, the faint glimmer of sweat beading on his forehead, and my heart lurched with every pitch. Sarah gave my arm a quick squeeze, concerned, but I knew he had this. The count was two and two, runner on second, Stingers up by one.

Jake had pitched a fantastic game; one more out, and the closer would take over.

I leaned forward, muttering under my breath, "Come on, Jake, one more."

He wound up and threw a fastball. The batter swung and hit it with a deafening crack. The ball rocketed straight back toward the mound, and before Jake could raise his glove, it slammed into the side of his face with a sickening thud. He crumpled instantly.

"Oh my god." My heart leapt into my throat, and I shot to my feet. My body moved on instinct, legs carrying me toward the steps, desperate to reach him.

A collective gasp rippled through the bleachers, followed by a heavy, suffocating silence. The first baseman scooped up the ball to make the third out. Players rushed towards the mound, and coaches sprinted onto the field.

I crashed into the metal chain link, my body wired with panic as I scanned the backstop, searching for a way to reach him. Jake was on the ground with Coach Chambers kneeling beside him. He was moving – barely – his hands clutched to his face, blood seeping between his fingers. My pulse hammered in my ears. Every part of me was screaming to run to him, but the fence was a prison; I was trapped.

"Em." Sarah's voice cut through, but I couldn't tear my eyes away from Jake.

He had to be okay. He had to be. I willed him to stand up, to laugh it off, but he didn't move. Please, please, please be okay.

The siren wailed in the distance, but it was taking too long.

"I need to–" I sputtered, frantic.

"You can't. They've got him, he's gonna be okay."

Her words were meant to comfort, but they barely pierced the wall tightening around my lungs. I was drowning, unable to catch my breath.

I stood frozen against the fence, stomach twisting as the paramedics arrived and lifted him onto a stretcher. Jake held a bloody thumb up as they took him off the field and into the ambulance with Coach Chambers.

Even as he gave that small gesture, my mind raced with images of what that impact could have done to him.

Holy shit, it was bad.

After the ambulance left, Sarah pulled me toward the bottom bleacher – right into the middle of Jess and her friends, who were all laughing and joking like nothing had happened. I sat stiffly, surrounded by perfect ponytails and glossed lips. Sarah nudged me at one point and told me to focus on the last inning so I could give Jake a play-by-play later, but the words slid right past. I wasn't able to concentrate on anything but the growing pit in my stomach.

"I just can't shake the image of him." I swallowed hard. "That sound, when the ball hit." I couldn't finish the thought.

"Well, if he can't get his glove up, maybe baseball's not his thing," Kyle said, smirking.

Jess laughed and Sarah snickered, then looked at me, uncomfortable.

"You're such an asshole, Kyle," she said.

He held up his hands. "What? I'm just saying."

Sarah rolled her eyes, but didn't press it. Jess was still grinning when she turned to chat with the other girls. I had no idea what Sarah saw in these people. I said nothing, having learned a long time ago that engaging with dickheads like Kyle only made things worse.

I sat in silence, my phone gripped in my hand, as if holding it tight enough would somehow make him text me to say he was fine. But there was nothing. All I could do was wait.

The Stingers ended up winning, but it didn't really feel like a victory. A few players cheered, trying to lift the mood, but no one could forget what had just happened. For me, it was all a blur. I was trapped in a storm of anxiety, my entire being consumed with waiting to hear that Jake was okay.

It wasn't until later that night that my phone finally buzzed. I'd been checking it obsessively all evening, willing Jake to text me. My mom's "no phones at the dinner table" policy was out the window once I'd filled her in on what had happened at the game. After dinner, which I hadn't eaten, my dad suggested we watch a movie, but I couldn't focus. I sat there, the laughter of the characters on the screen muffled by the overwhelming worry pressing on me.

When my phone finally vibrated, my hands shook as I unlocked the screen, already knowing who it was.

**Jake:**
You can relax now, Anderson. I'm not dead.

My eyes stung. I exhaled sharply, marching upstairs and flopping onto my bed as I tapped my reply.

**Emma:**
You scared the shit out of me. Are you okay? How's your face?

**Jake:**
Stitched up, massive goose-egg, headache from hell, and monitoring for concussion. Doc says I'll survive, though.

**Emma:**
Good, because if you died, I'd kill you.

**Jake:**
Ha. That's dramatic, even for you.

**Jake:**
Great poster by the way.

I huffed out a laugh, my body sinking deeper into the bed as I rolled onto my side and pulled my duvet over my back. Fluffy stared back at me, hovering at the front of the bowl like she knew something was off. I was relieved, but I couldn't shake the lingering worry, the tension still tight in my shoulders. My fingers hovered over my phone before I finally typed what had been sitting on my chest all night.

**Emma:**
I wanted to be there. I couldn't get to you.

A few seconds passed. My heart thundered as I waited for his reply.

**Jake:**
I know.

**Emma:**
I was really worried. It was awful.

More silence. I swallowed hard.

**Jake:**
I know.

I paused, my thumb nervously hovering above the screen. I wanted to say more – so much more – but this wasn't the time.

**Emma:**
Are you even supposed to be texting right now?

**Jake:**
Nope. Just needed to talk to you.

I groaned, rolling onto my back. My cheeks tingled as I stared up at the ceiling. The cool night air brushed against my skin, but it did nothing to calm the whirlwind inside me.

**Emma:**
Rest your brain, Jake. You probably have a concussion.

**Jake:**
Fine. But only if you promise to check on me tomorrow. Come over, don't text. Doctor's orders.

**Emma:**
Of course. Rest up. I'm so glad you're okay. ♥

**Jake:**
Thanks Em. Me too. ♥

## Twenty-One

# Like Sunlight Through the Blinds

The late August sun blazed down on my shoulders as we sprawled across two beach blankets, waves lapping at the shore and hungry seagulls squawking overhead. Lauren dug through the cooler for a cold bottle of water while the rest of us tossed around ideas for what to do this afternoon before we met up for happy hour at the Toronto Island BBQ and Beer Co.

"Kayaking?" Jake asked, eyebrows raised in my direction.

*Time alone with Jake that didn't involve hooking up? Too risky.*

"Sorry, small watercraft and I have a hate-hate relationship," I said.

Jake grinned. "I'm getting a mental image of you leaning out too far to get the perfect shot of a majestic Canada Goose and tipping right over."

"Hmmm, it's like you were at our cottage weekend last year, where I did exactly that. Except it was a moose. Thank god for waterproof cameras!"

"Biking?" Mel suggested.

"Done," I said quickly. Biking with the group was safely in fling territory.

"You guys have fun, I'm off to meet my future wife," Lauren said. "I'll see you later."

Her one date with Zoe hadn't gone anywhere, so Lauren laced up her sneakers and joined a new 2SLGBTQIA+ run club. Before meeting them for the first time, she'd suggested we all get together for a picnic at Centre Island. I'd enthusiastically jumped on board. Jake, shirtless at the beach? A little sweaty, a little sun-kissed? *Yes, please*. And having our friends here would hopefully help me keep him at an emotional distance, something that was becoming harder and harder to do.

We'd spent every night together this past week, exploring multiple surfaces in both his apartment and mine. From the outside, everything seemed to be going according to plan. But Jake had started to make off-hand comments that hinted at a future beyond this summer, like asking when to start planning a route for Nuit Blanche – the all-night, city-wide art festival in October. He'd even suggested he'd help me set up an installation. I had no idea if he was serious – probably not – but his comments had me entertaining dangerous thoughts. Like maybe Mel had been right when she'd suggested this didn't need to have an end date, that I could just see where things went.

But I couldn't. I knew that, because Jake wasn't the type to stick around. So, I was redoubling my efforts on "Operation Hit It and Quit It." It shouldn't be difficult – keeping my emotional distance from men was my signature move.

As Jake grabbed his backpack and tossed waters and granola bars in, his phone buzzed in his pocket. He pulled it out, and his brow furrowed as he read an incoming text.

"Oh, shit," he said, scrolling down as a buzz announced a second message.

"Everything okay?" I asked.

"It's my mom – she's getting married next Sunday, and their friend who was supposed to take photos had to cancel," he said, typing. "His sister was in a bad car accident, so he's going to Ottawa to stay with her kids until she's out of the hospital."

"Oh, that's terrible," I said, with a pang of sympathy.

"Yeah, really," Jake said, looking down at his phone. "Right now, she's just worried about her friend, but I know how much she wanted proper photographs."

"What about Emma?" Mel asked, looking up from where she had been putting away the picnic leftovers in the cooler. "You left next weekend free to prep for your show."

I turned and gave her an "are you fucking kidding me?" look.

As much as I felt for Jake's mom – it would suck not to have someone to capture your wedding – spending the entire day with his family, photographing the intimacy of a second-chance marriage, did not sound like a great way to avoid getting more emotionally entangled with him.

Jake glanced at me before turning to Mel. "I don't want to interfere with Emma's work. I know how important the show is."

His respect for my work made my heart melt just a little bit.

"It's probably good if she keeps busy," Mel said, with a mischievous look in my direction. "You've never seen her right before a show. She's basically Leslie Knope, obsessing over every detail like she's planning Lil Sebastian's state funeral."

I huffed out a laugh. *Okay, fair.*

As much as I didn't want to overstep the bounds of my situation-ship with Jake, I couldn't figure out a way to get out of this gracefully. If I made an excuse, I'd seem selfish. And Julia deserved a stress-free day.

I took a deep breath and smiled at Jake. "Honestly, Mel's right. Focusing on something else will help. But no pressure if it would be weird to have me there."

I caught Mel's self-satisfied smirk before she turned away.

"Are you kidding? My mom will be thrilled she doesn't have to scramble for a photographer," Jake said, a relieved breath pouring out of him. "And I'd love to have you there."

"I'm happy to help." *Sort of.* "Just ask her what time she needs me and send her my number."

His smile grew as if it had been nurtured, watered, and placed in a sunny window. "You are the absolute best. What would I do without you?"

Jake started tapping out another reply to his mom as his last words banged around inside my chest. *What would he do without me?* We had a shelf life, and we were two weeks from the expiration date.

I cleared my throat. "Alright, who's up for convincing the teenager renting the quad bikes that we can all fit on one?"

"So, your mom's getting remarried?" I asked, as the five of us walked towards the bike rental place. Mel, Jerry and Ryan were in a spirited three-way game of rock, paper, scissors to determine who would get to steer, and Jake and I had fallen behind. As much as I shouldn't want to learn more about Jake's life now – that way lay emotional entanglement – I needed some background on the couple before the wedding.

"Yeah. She and Brian have been together for a couple of years. Not sure if you remember, but my parents' marriage was a mess. My dad was barely around until he just…wasn't." Jake sighed before his mouth lifted at the corners. "But Brian brought out this side of her I'd never seen before."

"Now that they're both retired, they've been travelling, they have a whole group of friends in the neighbourhood, and they play pickleball at the PanAm Centre. Of all the classic retired-people hobbies," he said with a grin.

"That's adorable," I said.

"She's laughing more than I've ever seen. They're best friends." He paused. "That's what I want in a relationship now."

My heart stumbled. "You want a relationship now?" My voice cracked despite my best effort to sound steady.

He glanced at me, his smile soft. "I mean, yeah. I want it all, Em. Eventually."

He turned back toward the lake, where a couple of kayakers paddled along the shore. I hid behind my camera, aimlessly pointing and clicking without absorbing any of the scenery in front of me.

I really needed him to stop talking about relationships. That kind of talk – mixed with the emotional hangover from high school, the wild pheromones he was radiating, and the fact that the sex was easily a million times better than anything I'd experienced – was messing with me.

We reached the bike rental shack, a small wooden building with a faded "Island Wheels" sign nailed crookedly over the window. A teenager in a sun-bleached Jays cap looked up from his phone just long enough to mumble, "ID and a credit card," before his attention dropped back to Clash of Clans.

Mel plunked her cards on the counter. "Driving, called it."

"I'm driving, I won fair and square," Ryan shot back. "You can't use dynamite in rock, paper, scissors, Melanie."

"Can, too," Mel said. "Besides, you'll drive us into the lake."

"Then we'll beat the heat." Ryan grinned.

Mel laughed and rolled her eyes as she signed the paperwork and led us outside. We scored a red, four-seater quadricycle with a worn yellow sunshade, convinced we could all cram onto the two narrow bench-style seats.

The sign read, "Max: four adult riders and two small children (under fifty pounds each)." Jerry's math was that Mel and I together equaled one adult and two malnourished fifth graders, which, according to him, made us perfectly legal under island traffic law.

Mel and Ryan hopped in the front, and I was sandwiched between Jerry and Jake in the back. I crossed my legs to take up less space, which resulted in my calf hooked around Jake's shin. His arm stretched casually along the back of the seat, his fingers curling lightly over my shoulder to steady me over each bump as we made our way towards O'Bumbles Ice Cream Parlour.

We were pressed tight together, his body heat radiating into me, and with every jolt and turn, I leaned closer. The four of them pedaled, the constant up and down of Jake's bare leg brushing against mine sending shocks through me, making it impossible to focus on anything but the way our bodies fit together.

Vivid memories of the past week spun through my mind – straddling him on the couch, my nails clawing at the back of his neck as he gripped my hips; my legs wrapped around him as we christened his kitchen counter; my hands slammed against the top of his dresser as he fucked me from behind, his reflection in the mirror whispering all the filthy things he wanted to do next. It had been a wonderfully busy week.

My fingers twitched against his thigh, and I dragged my nails lightly over his skin. He turned to look at me with his irresistible half-smile and ran his hand over my shoulder and squeezed the nape of my neck in a teasing, silent one-up.

I slid my hand–

"Dog!" Ryan yelled, pulling the hand break as a blur of shaggy brown fur shot in front of the bike. Mel yanked the wheel hard to the left and the bike lurched violently. Pedals slammed into shins as we skidded off the path and onto the grass, the frame rattling beneath us. If Jerry's weight calculations were off, this thing was about to fold like a cheap lawn chair. Jake's arm tightened around me, pulling me flush against him as we bounced to a stop.

He released me, and it was like someone had unplugged my power source.

"You good?" he breathed.

"Fine," I said, though my pulse was still racing, and not just from the near-miss.

"Loki!" The yell came from behind us, where a young boy and small woman hurried down the path. The boy clutched a green leash with a collar still attached in his hand, tears streaming down his face.

"That dog has a death wish," Ryan said, watching Loki run in wide circles, weaving between other bikes.

"So do you!" Mel said, twisting to glare at him, and whacking him on the shoulder with the back of her hand. "You could have at least yelled 'stop' before pulling the brake like that. You think you're Vin Diesel or something? Fast and the Furious: Centre Island Drift? Jesus, my shins!"

"Well, if you had been paying attention, or let me drive like I was supposed to – you can't use dynamite! – none of this would have happened!" Ryan leaned closer to her as he finished his sentence through gritted teeth.

Mel leaned in too, eyes flashing, chest heaving, and for a second it looked like she might slap him…or kiss him? I glanced between Jerry and Jake and none of us could tell which. Jake raised his eyebrows, trying to hide a grin.

"Okay kids, let's save the murder for after ice cream," Jerry said.

My laugh broke the spell between Mel and Ryan. They swivelled toward the back seat, as if they'd suddenly remembered we were there. Loki's playful barks drew our attention back to the field, where the little boy chased after him.

"Okay, well, I'm gonna go help catch the dog," Jake said, looking between Mel and Ryan with interest. "Jer, come help." He dug a package of beef jerky out of Ryan's backpack, then hopped off the bike and jogged away.

Loki zigzagged between groups of people relaxing on the lawn, barking gleefully as he darted in front of a couple of teenagers on scooters, cutting them off and driving one off the path and into the grass.

Jake clapped his hands and whistled. "Here, buddy! You want a treat?"

Loki stopped at the word, ears perking up as he tilted his head at Jake. Jake held up the beef jerky, but the dog darted the other way, easily avoiding Jerry's open arms as he dove towards him.

Jerry hit the ground and grunted. "He's like the Roadrunner, and I'm Wile E. Coyote."

Jake laughed and waved the jerky like a matador's cape. For one glorious second, it seemed to work. Loki slowed and sniffed the air, then peeled past Jake, nipping at the jerky while he jumped.

"Jesus, I almost lost a finger!" Jake checked his hand as he recoiled.

"That's why you have ten," Jerry said, half-laughing as he got to his feet.

"Loki, come!" The little boy called through his tears. He spun around as Loki ran circles around him, having the time of his life.

"Okay, buddy. Game's over, you win." Jake waved the jerky like a white flag. "Come claim your prize."

Loki froze a few meters away and wagged his tail suspiciously. He barked twice, then charged full speed, straight at Jake.

"Wait!" Jake crouched low, bracing for impact. Loki collided nose-first into his chest with a thud, knocking Jake off his feet, then flipped onto his back.

Jake laughed, rubbing the dog's belly with one hand while keeping the other wrapped around him in case he bolted again. He tossed the jerky into Loki's mouth as he sat up, and patted him on the back.

The little boy finally caught up, breathless and red-faced. He clipped Loki's collar on, and hugged the dog tight around the neck.

Jake stood, brushing off his knees, just in time for the world's tiniest Grandma to shuffle up and fling her arms around his hips in a tight embrace.

"Thank you, young man!" she cried, holding on a moment too long.

I laughed out loud as she finally released him and began rifling through her enormous purse.

Jake waved his hands in protest, but a moment later, she put something in his hand. He nodded his thanks, scratched the dog behind the ears, then jogged back towards us.

"She pinched my ass and gave me a handful of butterscotch candies," he said, pink-cheeked, through an incredulous laugh, as he squeezed himself back onto the bike. "The audacity!"

I howled in delight as he handed us each a Werther's Original.

"I feel so cheap!" he said, eyes twinkling.

"I can't blame her," I said. "You have a fantastic ass."

"I'm not a piece of meat, Anderson," he said, smiling, as he knocked his knee against mine.

"You know you're the whole package," I said. "But your ass definitely makes the highlight reel."

"Dang, I hope I have that much game when I'm eighty," Mel said. "Her phone number's on this wrapper." She held it up as she popped the candy into her mouth with a grin.

Jake groaned, shaking his head.

The rest of the afternoon passed in a blur of sunshine and laughter. When we reached the patio for happy hour, Mel recounted our quad bike misadventure to Lauren. She texted everyone the group selfie we'd taken after Jerry had insisted he was the most responsible driver on the way to return the bike: Mel was in hysterics, Jerry firmly at ten and two, and Ryan was pretending to nap with his hands under his chin, tucked against Jerry's chest. Jake and I smiled from the back seat.

I stole a glance at Jake as he finished telling the Tiny Grandma story, his eyes sparkling as he tossed a candy to Lauren. It hit me like sunlight through the blinds, sudden, and inconvenient: I hadn't been this happy in a long time.

Stepping back, I lifted my camera and framed the group against the Toronto skyline, trying to freeze this one perfect moment in time, before it slipped away.

# Twenty-Two
## October 30, 11 Years Ago

## What Fresh Hell Was This!?

I touched up my makeup for the hundredth time, annoyed that Sarah was already half an hour late. I had wanted to arrive early to check that all the decorations were still in place and the DJ had a couple of water bottles and no issues setting up. I'd been to all of the school dances over the last two years, but now that I was in grade eleven and part of the planning committee, there was more pressure to make sure tonight ran smoothly.

Finally, her telltale knock sounded, and the front door clicked open. I dropped my makeup brush in the pile on my cluttered bathroom counter and dashed down the stairs to find Sarah letting herself in as she always did.

"Woah, what are you wearing?" I gave her a once-over as she stopped beside the mirrored sliding closet doors in the front hall, wobbling just enough to make me wonder if she'd already been drinking.

She tucked her phone into a thigh holster with one hand and held a half-empty bottle of murky blue liquid in the other – all signs pointed to yes.

Her eyes widened. "What am *I* wearing?! What is that?!" She flapped her hands around my homemade one-piece Ninja-Turtle costume, complete with built-in muscles and a thick, soft shell.

I glanced at myself in the mirrored door, admiring my green face with Raphael's red mask painted around my eyes and his trademark bared teeth over my left cheek. Sharp black and white lines gave it that comic-book flair, bringing his personality to life. My dark hair was pulled into a tight bun and sprayed green.

"Uh, I look incredible!" I withdrew my cardboard twin sai from my belt and held them up. "I thought we were being Ninja Turtles," I said as I tucked my sai back into my belt. "I figured you'd be a cute turtle with a tutu or something, but you ditched me to be a…sexy cop?"

She was dressed head to toe in black: heeled boots, thigh-high socks, fishnet stockings and booty shorts. The top two buttons of her tight, collared shirt were open to reveal a bit of cleavage, and there was a silver badge pinned to her chest and a pair of handcuffs swinging from her belt. Her long, sleek blonde hair swayed from under a police officer's hat as she slid off her mirrored aviators.

Sarah giggled and stumbled slightly as she headed up to my room, waving off my comment with a lazy hand. "You were serious about that?" she asked, dragging out her words. "Whatever. Jess had these, and the whole team was getting ready at her place, so what was I supposed to do? Say no to a group costume?"

I sighed, following her. Lately, it had seemed pretty easy for her to say no to me, without actually saying the word. Sarah gripped the banister as she wobbled up the stairs, nearly missing a step at the top, before bumping the door frame on the way into my bedroom. She sat down on my bed and twisted the cap off her drink.

"We should get going – we're already late," I said, looking dubiously at her as she guzzled and grimaced, before offering it to me, wiping her mouth with the back of her other hand. I sniffed.

"Ugh, what is that?" The scent stung my nostrils and triggered my overactive gag reflex.

"Jess called it 'killer Kool-Aid,' but I have no idea. Kool-Aid and whiskey, maybe? Whatever she could take from her parents without them noticing. I need a minute to finish this, then we can go. You'll survive not seeing Jake for five extra minutes." She rolled her eyes like I was the one being ridiculous.

So "drunk sexy police officer Sarah" was kind of a bitch.

"Wow. Okay." I was annoyed and hurt. Sarah and I had spent every

Halloween together since we were six, and I'd been looking forward to going to the dance with her, but not like this.

Fluffy stared at me from her bowl on top of my dresser, her bulging eyes fixed in a disapproving stare. She turned her back on me, flicking her tail as she swam in a contemptuous circle, like this drama was somehow beneath her. "Just please don't puke."

Sarah knew that seeing or hearing someone vomit always made me sick. Just ask our grade two class what had happened after Brandon Jones threw up on the carpet during a read-aloud.

Sarah downed the rest of her concoction and put the empty bottle on my desk. She adjusted her hat and smoothed her hair in the mirror above my dresser while pursing her lips before following me down to the front door.

"Mom! We're ready to go!" I called, slipping my feet into my green Converse, tightening the laces and praying she wouldn't comment on Sarah's attire, balance, or breath.

"Photo first!" My mom glanced up from her digital camera as she powered it on, walking towards us with a wide smile, my dad a few steps behind her.

"Hi Sarah! You both look great!" she said, not missing a beat but holding my eye for a moment afterward. She knew I'd expected Sarah to be the Michaelangelo to my Raphael. My mom was going to ask me about this later, but I appreciated her tact in keeping her concern close to the vest for now. I posed with my sai as Sarah twirled her handcuffs suggestively around her finger. We headed out to the car as my mom kissed my dad goodbye, and promised to bring him back a Reese's Blizzard from Dairy Queen – his favourite.

"Oh, there's Jess and them." Sarah pointed to the scantily clad SWAT team, turning heads as they entered a couple of minutes after we did. "I'm going to go say hi."

Sarah blew me a kiss and skipped off towards Jess and her crew. I spotted Dev and a couple of my other friends by the snack table, dressed as Avengers, and stealthily approached.

Steps away from surprising them, Jake's delighted chuckle came from somewhere on my left. Shell pressed against the wall, I swiveled my head around and withdrew my sai, preparing for attack. His laugh grew louder and closer as I scanned the hallway, my ninja skills proving ineffective in pinpointing his location.

"My god, Anderson, you are my favourite." He grinned as he stepped toward me out of the crowd. "You look incredible! Did you make this?!" he asked, squeezing my foam biceps. "I love it." He lifted his purple-framed sunglasses off his face, his vibrant blue eyes captivating mine.

A laugh burst from my lips. "Are you performing tonight?" I lifted the white string from his purple hoodie with the tip of one sai. "Taking requests?"

He looked like he'd just stepped off the stage of his "My World" tour. Fitted, skinny white jeans were bunched above purple velcro high-tops, a white denim jacket buttoned over the hoodie, with bedazzled silver hearts on the sleeves. He wore a perfect brownish blonde "Bieber" swoop wig and a performance headset with a small microphone in front of his lips.

*God, he was hot.*

"We'll see how the night unfolds," he said, replacing his sunglasses before showcasing some mediocre pop-lock moves. "How about you? Ninja skills on the dance floor? At least if you fall, you'll have a nice soft landing." He reached one hand over each of my shoulders to squeeze the top edge of my shell. "It's so soft. If I get sleepy, can I borrow this?"

"What?! The Biebs doesn't sleep. He's the hardest working kid in show business. And I plan to end the night without injury, so no flips unless Bebop and Rocksteady show up."

He lowered his hands from my shell as I pressed my lips together and squinted to accentuate the detail in my makeup. I did a quick spin, a high front kick, and then brought my fists up in front of my chest, ready for battle.

A low laugh escaped him, and his face softened into the kind of smile that made my heart stutter. "Where did you come from?"

I bit my lip, smiling up at him as hope bloomed in my chest. Maybe – finally – tonight could be the night things shifted between us. September had been brutal. Jake's concussion had been mild, thank god, but it had sidelined him for the first few weeks of school. He'd been cleared in time to pitch in the Toronto finals, but the team had lost a nail-biter. Between concussion recovery, baseball, and trying to stay on top of his classes, he'd been swamped. Aside from prepping for tonight's dance, we'd barely seen each other. We still texted every night, but even those conversations had been cut short while he'd recovered.

Both of our phones buzzed at once, slicing through the moment.

"It's time!" I squealed, excitement overflowing, as Jake released a small groan. "Suck it up, buttercup!" I silenced my phone and tucked it back into the pouch on my belt before grabbing his hand and pulling him towards the centre of the gym.

As we moved to our spots, Sarah and her dance crew had already scattered around the gym. A bunch of others were in their positions as the eerie groan of Rihanna's "Disturbia" intensified.

The pulsating rhythm reverberated through the gym, resonating with each throb of the bass. Sarah, despite the "killer Kool-Aid," led a small group of dancers towards the center of the gym with a captivating strut. With each eight-count, a fresh wave of dancers joined the group, and soon, unsuspecting students and staff in the gym began to catch on to the flash mob unfolding around them, some recording it with their cameras and cell phones.

When it was my turn to join the group, the clash between my dancing prowess and the comical reality of my bulky, overstuffed costume became abundantly clear. I'd never rehearsed in my turtle suit – I'd only finished stuffing it last night – so I went all out, clumsily popping my shell like there was no tomorrow, trying not to crack up. Jake did a double-take at my over-the-top moves. His guffaw cut through the music before he pulled himself together, adjusting his microphone and lip syncing as he performed the routine, surprisingly believable as a pop star.

I remembered his adamant "never in a million years" from a few weeks ago after I'd approached him about my flash mob idea and begged him to participate along with the rest of the council. He was confident and popular, but far more reserved and introspective than he let on. Yet, here he was – immersed in the delightful chaos that had previously only lived inside my head. Sarah had supported my idea from the start, convinced the dance team to participate, and choreographed the entire routine with me.

Whistles and cheers cut through the sweaty gym air as the refrain began again, all of us spreading into the crowd to encourage others to join us before repeating the routine twice more. As Rihanna's vocal runs signalled the end of the song, we all sauntered back to our starting positions as if nothing had happened, though our collective heavy breathing said otherwise. A wave of cheers swept through the crowd, and after a moment, we all joined in, clapping, high-fiving, and hugging each other.

"That was all you, Anderson." Jake breathed hard as he slung his arm over my shell and pulled me close for a side-hug.

"I am shook! You nailed it!" I slapped Jake on the chest with my hand, beaming. I revelled in the contact with his warm body, as he chuckled and shook his head. I grinned up at him, high on adrenaline as I looped my other arm around his waist and squeezed him back. As the DJ called for one final round of applause for all of us, a jubilant crowd began to gather around Sarah and the other dancers.

"I think I blacked out," he said as Weston and Rohan approached him, astonished.

I laughed as I pressed my hand against his chest and reluctantly pushed away, sliding out from under his arm like a wave receding from the shore. I needed to find Sarah to thank her, and I also needed a moment to collect myself before the depth of my feelings for Jake threatened to pull me under his relentless tide. *Breathe.*

"Sair!" I called, as I approached her group. "You were amazing! Thank you, that was perfect!"

Sarah smiled back at me and opened her mouth to reply, just as Murray *Fucking* Fraser stepped up behind her and slithered his hands around her hips, tightening possessively around her waist. She gasped as she looked behind her, then broke out into a grin and stepped back to settle against him.

*What fresh hell was this!?*

My eyes widened as he leaned into her neck and whispered something into her ear, his hands creeping up toward her breasts. She giggled and placed her hands on top of his before they reached their destination, and then she pulled his arms tighter around her body.

I stood there, an actor who'd forgotten her lines while the studio audience waited in suspense, the imminent laugh track ringing in my ears.

"Let's go," he murmured into the crook of her neck, releasing one of his hands from her chest, and tugging her away with the other. She went with him, without a glance back at me.

*Plot twist.*

Yes, Sarah had been spending more and more time with Jess and the dance crew, and Jess was famously on-again-off-again dating Murray's number one meathead, Kyle. But I'd thought Sarah and I had been on the same page about Murray – slimeball with a hefty dash of misogyny and a sprinkling of entitlement – the exact kind of guy we'd always sworn we'd protect each other from.

As I slogged toward the gym door in disbelief, my friend Carla, dressed as Black Widow, came barrelling toward me, shrieking about how much she'd loved the flash mob, and dragged me over to where Dev and the rest of the Avengers were dancing.

The weight of whatever was going on with Sarah pressed on my shoulders, but when "Shake It Off" came on, I took Taylor's advice and let it go – for now – dancing and singing along with my friends for what felt like hours. Jake was working behind the snack table, but I kept checking the clock, counting down until 9:30 when he would be free.

As "We Are Young" wrapped up, and we all belted out the "na-na's," I felt a tap on my shell. I turned to find Jake grinning at me, holding out an iced tea.

"My hero! Thank you!" I grabbed the can and pulled Jake into a quick hug before chugging it down, the cold drink soothing my dry throat. I was so thirsty, but I hadn't been able to bring myself to leave our corner of the dance floor, afraid of running into Sarah and Murray.

"I need something in return, though." He looked around, panicked. "Protection."

"Shredder?!" I pulled out a floppy, overworked sai with my empty hand, and pushed Jake behind the safety of my shell with my other arm, careful not to spill what was left of my drink on him.

"Worse," he said. He spun me around to face him as I sipped my drink. "Beliebers." He tilted his head towards a small group of grade nine girls, huddled nearby, staring at him the way I tried hard not to, whispering and smiling.

I pressed my lips together, but it was too late. A cackle escaped, the last swallow of iced tea spraying out the sides of my mouth as I brought my elbow up too late to cover it. Jake looked helpless as he took the can from me, finished it off, then tossed it into the recycling bin as I coughed and choked through my laughter. He patted the back of my thick shell in a feeble attempt to help me clear my windpipe, but this was useless and made us laugh harder.

"That's the price of fame, Justin," I said around a laugh, once I'd caught my breath.

The delicate, ethereal cascading piano at the beginning of Beyoncé's "Halo" filled the gym as the bravest Belieber stepped forward.

"One of them's coming," I told him out of the corner of my mouth. I turned towards him as he looked at me, wide-eyed but smiling.

"Dance with me?" He extended his hand.

My heart free-fell from my chest and landed with a splat at my feet. I grasped his hand, stepping close to him as my smile faded.

*Finally.*

Jake's warm hands settled above my hips, my shell an overbearing chaperone, preventing them from wrapping around my back the way they did in my dreams.

Of course, I was dressed like a ridiculous Ninja Turtle the first time I danced with Jake – fate wouldn't have it any other way. I met his gaze as

I set my hands at the base of his neck. He brought one of his hands up to guide my head to rest against his shoulder before returning it to my waist.

"I don't wanna get green stuff on you." I lifted my head to look up at him.

"Right, 'cause I was planning to wear this outfit to Grad." He smiled. "It's fine, Em."

The mere mention of his graduation, eight months from now, hit me hard. I nestled my head against his chest, enveloped by the warm, seductive scent of his Axe Dark Temptation.

We swayed in slow circles to the gentle rhythm and Beyoncé's soulful voice. His heartbeat thudded against my ear, steady and low – almost in time with the music. He rested his cheek against the top of my head and took a couple of slow, deep breaths. When I looked up and met his eyes, there was a sadness there that I hadn't seen before.

"You okay?"

"Not really," he said after a pause.

"Worried about Grad?"

"Not yet."

A quiet moment stretched between us as I tucked my head against his chest. We held on to each other, turning slowly on the dance floor, my cheek resting on his shoulder, right where I was meant to be. His hands shifted and he pulled me closer, as if seeking solace in a stormy sea.

"My mom's sick."

# Twenty-Three

# *Too Good to Pass Up*

I grabbed my camera bag and hopped out of my assistant Kristina's car as it stopped in front of Julia and Brian's house on Flagstone Terrace. After a quick wave to Kristina, who was on her way to Owen's house to photograph Brian and the groomsmen, I adjusted the bag on my shoulder and turned towards the quaint bungalow. I would take the standard photographs of the bridal party here, then document the limo ride to the Guild Inn for the wedding.

Walking up the stone pathway, a mix of nerves and excitement churned in my stomach. I told myself it was my usual pre-wedding adrenaline, but today was different. I was about to spend time with Jake's family again – at his mom's wedding – which meant stepping right into the centre of their lives. I wasn't sure what Jake had told them about us. Did they remember me as the girl who used to watch reruns of *The Office* in their basement? Was I just the photographer? Or had he somehow explained this in-between space we were in now?

I glanced up at the sky – puffy white clouds against a bright summer blue – and forced myself to feel the warm breeze and smell the freshly cut grass drifting from a neighbour's lawn. Little grounding tricks to keep my nerves in check.

As I stepped up to the front door, my phone buzzed with an incoming text, Jake's name popping up on my home screen. I rang the doorbell, then swiped up to see a photo of him wearing his glasses, a crisp white dress shirt open over his bare chest, abs on display, black tie hanging around his neck, directing a mischievous smile at the camera. Jesus.

A fantasy reel played in fast forward through my mind: him helping me check out books at the library before leading me behind the stacks and lecturing me about the Dewey Decimal system while he fucked me. I brought the phone closer, needing a better look.

The door swung open. I jumped, fumbling to kill the screen, but I lost my grip. The phone slipped from my hand and hit the dense welcome mat with a soft thud, landing face up. Jake's perfect torso and sexy grin stared up at me – and the tall, slender young woman who'd opened the door.

"Is that Jake?" she asked, bending down to pick up the phone.

*Kill me now.*

Her perfect brows arched over large, dark brown eyes. "Owen said he'd been working out more…" she mused, before looking back at me with a wide smile on her berry-coloured lips. "You must be Emma, Jake's friend from high school." She smirked.

Cringing with mortification – but relieved she couldn't read my mind – I stuck my hand out and she dropped the phone back into it. "That's me. I promise, I'm less clumsy with my camera equipment," I said, trying to regain a semblance of professionalism.

"Oh, I'm not worried," the young woman said with a peal of laughter. "We're so thankful you stepped in today." She opened the door wider, gesturing for me to step inside. She closed the door behind me as a little girl around three came through the front hall, tap dancing in a neon dinosaur-patterned dress and sparkly ballet flats.

"I'm Meera, Owen's wife, and this is our daughter Amaya. Julia's in the kitchen finishing up her makeup. I'll take you back."

"It's great to meet you both," I said, relieved that it hadn't been Jake's mom to open the door. "Amaya, I love your dress! Dinosaurs are the coolest."

"I have a fancy dress for the wedding but this one spins too. Watch," Amaya said, twirling in circles as her skirt fluttered around her. "That's how you know if your dress works."

"Definitely," I said, breaking into a smile and wishing I had my Nikon out to capture this moment. I could already tell the camera was going to eat her up. Amaya spun into the kitchen and right into Julia's arms.

Julia was glowing in a white silk robe, her long brown bob in loose waves, the brilliant blue eyes she'd passed on to her son shining as she held her wobbly, giggling granddaughter upright and tickled her.

Julia lifted Amaya onto the kitchen island stool in front of the hairdresser. "Time for your flower crown, peanut!" she said as Amaya squealed in excitement.

"Emma!" Julia beamed, turning and closing the space between us with her arms open wide before wrapping me into them, my camera equipment bumping awkwardly between us. "Thank you, thank you, thank you! I was worried I'd have to get the boys to take photos with their phones. I can't thank you enough for coming at such short notice."

Her gratitude eased some of the knot in my chest. I smiled, hoping *I'M HAVING THE BEST SEX OF MY LIFE WITH YOUR SON* wasn't scrolling across my forehead like an electronic billboard. I caught a glimpse of Meera in my peripheral vision, smirking.

"I'm so happy to be able to help!"

"Grandma, look!"

Julia turned to Amaya to exclaim over her gorgeous headband of creamy white and dusty pink baby roses interspersed with burgundy ranunculus. I set my equipment down in a corner and pulled my Nikon out of its bag to take a few close-ups of the two of them.

"Okay, people, let's get this party started! I'm here and looking faaa-bu-lous!" A vivacious woman sashayed into the kitchen. With a bottle of champagne clutched in each hand and a grin on her face, she strutted towards me in her floor-length, wine-coloured gown, smizing for the camera with the finesse of a top model. A laugh bubbled out of me as I captured several shots of Jake's aunt Cheryle, the matron of honour.

Cheryle executed one last "Blue Steel" face before plunking the bottles down on the counter beside a tray of champagne glasses. Meera came over and started peeling the foil off one bottle.

"Hi, Aunt Cheryle," I said, grinning. I'd only met her once before, but she'd made an impression.

"Emma!" Cheryle cried, throwing her arms around me. "I heard you were back in Jake's life and ready to paparazzi this shindig!"

I jumped as Meera popped the champagne cork, then started filling several glasses. Julia handed them out to the hairstylist and makeup artist before handing one to me.

"Yes, we're so happy you and Jake have reconnected. And not only because we now have a proper photographer for our wedding!" Julia said with a laugh.

She turned to Cheryle and Meera. "Jake had *such* a huge crush on her in high school." She grinned at me. "He was always up in his room texting or talking to you. I was really surprised you lost touch when he went away to school."

*Not as surprised as I was.*

I blinked, that familiar ache twisting inside me, but I shook it off and smiled at Julia.

"It's been nice to see him again," I said. "Jake's great."

My brain skipped over the word "great" like a needle on a vinyl record. That counter sex was *really* great. Jake was great with his hands, his lips, his tongue, his co–

I snapped back to the present as Meera nudged my arm with her elbow.

"That great, huh?" she quipped under her breath, eyebrows raised. "Lost you there for a moment."

My breath was shaky, and I raised my champagne to hide my warm cheeks. Meera grinned at me as she handed glasses to Cheryle and Julia, before picking up the last one herself. I put my glass down and raised my camera as I framed up Julia, Cheryle, Meera and Amaya for Cheryle's toast.

"To Julia – a new chapter, filled with love, joy, and your happily ever after," she said. "Cheers!"

Their glasses clinked and I captured their radiant smiles, resolving to keep my focus on work for the rest of the day.

Julia caught my eye and lifted her glass towards me with a bright smile. "And to Emma – who somehow always shows up when we need her."

I lifted my glass toward her, a flicker of belonging brushing against me – then I tossed back my champagne before the idea could take root.

Jake beamed as he and Owen gave their speech, candlelight flickering across the tables draped in ivory linens with bursts of pendulum dahlias, ranunculus, roses, and soft greenery spilling from low vases. I swivelled between them, capturing Julia's candid laughter and Owen's straight face as he finished up a story about her legendary performance as "concerned mom" in his straight-to-home-DVD teenaged directorial debut, a no-budget slasher flick titled "Cottage Freak."

"It was terrible," he laughed. "But she threw herself into the role, like everything else she did. Even after grueling shifts in the ER, she'd drive

Jake to early baseball practice, and stay up late to argue with me through debate prep. She did it practically on her own, no complaints, just pure love."

"And stubbornness," Jake coughed out, to an eyeroll from Julia and a room full of laughter. "Seeing her today – happy and glowing – makes me realize how much she's sacrificed for us over the years, how determined she's always been, and how perfect Brian is for her. Not just because he makes her laugh or lets her take the last piece of garlic bread, but because he sees the strong, endlessly giving woman that we are so lucky to call our mom. Their kind of love makes you believe in second chances."

Jake swallowed as he scanned the crowd, and for a moment, his eyes landed on mine – brief, electric. I froze behind my camera, breath caught somewhere between my ribs. "In lasting love. In finding your person."

The world stilled. The clink of cutlery, the buzz of low conversation and murmurs of agreement muffled under the weight of his words. A piece of the wall I'd built around my heart chipped at the top.

It wasn't just what he'd said, but the way he'd said it. Steady, open, and with conviction.

Like he meant it for me.

This wasn't how it was supposed to be. But the way he looked at me, like he wanted that love too, made it easy to imagine what it would be like to let him in.

And for the first time, I didn't want to run from that.

"To the bride and groom," Owen added, lifting his glass. "For showing us it's never too late to begin again."

Jake tilted his glass toward me in a quiet, deliberate toast, his half smile jump-starting my heartbeat again.

I was quick to refocus on the shutter, capturing Julia and Brian as they stood to hug Jake and Owen, before taking the mic to thank their family and friends for their love and support. I snapped a photo just as Julia looked at Brian with that soft, open smile – like she was letting him see every part of her.

When they finished their speech, the room buzzed to life as the DJ dropped the punchy opening guitar riff of "The Best." Tina Turner's gravelly voice crackled through the air, adding to my emotional turmoil.

I weaved between the tables, photographing guests as they danced. I caught candid moments – Cheryle wiping her eyes, Amaya licking her lips as she piled her plate high with cookies and cupcakes. Through the lens, there was clarity, even as my thoughts tangled around Jake's words and what they could mean.

Waterloo wasn't that far.

We could make it work.

I zoomed in on Owen, tipping his head back in laughter with Jake, who was a freaking four-course meal in his fitted navy suit, relaxed under the soft chandeliers and candlelight. I caught myself smiling behind my camera, imagining him in that suit, nervously adjusting his tie before walking down the aisle. Our friends filling the seats, my dad winking at me from the front row and my mom blinking back tears. Someone else holding the camera, capturing us.

I looked back at Julia, laughing with Brian and a friend, her eyes crinkled in joy.

If she could find this kind of love and happiness after everything she'd been through, maybe it was out there for me too. I wasn't the same girl I'd been in high school, and Jake wasn't the same boy.

I exhaled, steadying my hands on my camera as I sat on one of the gold chairs to get a close-up of the centrepiece, the guests having drifted towards the dessert buffet. It gave me a quiet moment to breathe, just long enough to settle into the possibility that maybe I didn't have to keep pushing Jake away. Maybe there was something more for us.

"So…did you decide about the job in B.C.? Doesn't it start soon?" Owen's voice came from behind me. I looked over my shoulder to see him pulling out the chair next to Jake at the table, their backs to me. Owen handed Jake a beer.

*B.C.? As in British Columbia?*

I froze, my camera suspended, pulse hammering in my throat. Jake's response was swallowed by the sudden clinking of silverware, guests calling for Julia and Brian to kiss. I pulled my camera up to cover my face, moving on instinct, adjusting the focus to catch the image in time. My hands trembled as the room seemed to narrow around me.

A burst of cheers followed, and through the noise I only caught a fragment of Jake's voice, "–too good to pass up."

The words clanged through me, louder than the silverware. I popped up from my chair and started walking away from them, heading for the terrace, my mind dropping into a free-fall.

Jake was taking a job in B.C. I slowed my breathing and flexed my fingers, letting my camera dangle around my neck. I needed to get outside.

He hadn't told me. I wasn't important enough. I was over here picking out fucking baby names and he'd been planning to vanish without warning – again.

It was like a trap door opening under me. Same dizzying drop. Same sick thud at the bottom. I was back in high school again, at the centre of a shit-storm, and the boy I'd loved had just disappeared.

It wasn't rational. I knew that. But that didn't stop me from unravelling in real time, the coldness inside me expanding, and my vision tunneling in the familiar but hated sensation of an oncoming panic attack.

I pushed out through the doors to the terrace and began the box breathing exercise that was the only reliable way I'd found to potentially avert it. *Inhale…two, three, four; hold…two, three, four; exhale…two, three, four; hold…two, three, four.* I focused on counting and naming things I could see, feel, hear, smell, and taste, grounding myself in the present moment. Slowly, my awareness expanded out. The warm night air brushed along my skin. The fairy lights strung around the terrace twinkled. The murmur of voices and occasional bursts of laughter reached me from the reception.

As my breathing returned to normal, I steeled myself to finish the job I'd been hired to do. But as I pasted a smile on my face and walked back into the reception, one question kept echoing through my mind.

*How had I let this happen again?*

## Twenty-Four
## February 4, 10 Years Ago

# Feet on the Floor

I stood on the front porch of Jake's house, a foil-covered tray of my dad's lasagna in my mittened hands. Jake had texted me that his mom was finally home and resting after her surgery, and I was anxious to see him. He'd taken a couple of days off school so that he could stay with her during the day while his dad worked. I assumed they had zero food in the fridge and no energy to cook, so I'd grabbed the lasagna from our freezer and headed over to drop it off.

The door opened and Jake stood there, with dark circles under his eyes and his usually intentionally messy hair just plain messy. His face relaxed into a smile when he saw me.

"Hey, Em. You didn't have to come by."

I held out the lasagna. "I'm just here to drop off food. I know you all must be exhausted, but I figured you and your Dad might not want to cook tonight."

"You're the literal best. Thank you." He opened the door and gestured for me to step inside, taking the tray from my hands. "My Aunt Cheryle's here for a few days to help my mom while she recovers, so she took care of dinner. But more food is never a bad thing."

A tall woman with purple streaks in her hair who resembled Jake's mom sailed into the front hallway. "Did I hear you say more food? Brilliant. I'm not used to feeding teenagers."

"Hello!" She stretched out her hand to me. "I'm Cheryle, Jake's favourite aunt."

"Nice to meet you. I'm Emma, Jake's friend from school," I said, shaking her hand.

"Emma! We've heard so much about you! Jake's told us how helpful you and your family have been while Julia's been sick." She took the tray from Jake. "I can pop this in the fridge and you two can head downstairs."

I looked over at Jake. "Oh, no, I'm not staying. I'm sure you all need a quiet night."

"Don't be silly," Cheryle said. "Jakey needs a night off from worrying about his mom."

"Yeah, stay," Jake said, opening the basement door. "I need an update about Valentine's Day. Has Monica convinced Mrs. Driscoll to do Matchomatics yet?"

I followed Jake downstairs to the rec room as Cheryle disappeared into the kitchen. "Yes! She finally got her on board by highlighting how gender-inclusive it is. The surveys are going out next week, and on Valentine's Day, everyone's going to find out who their ideal matches are."

"I can only imagine the chaos. Monica only proposed this because she's had a thing for Avery since they were lab partners in grade ten biology."

I laughed. "Let's just hope the money we raise will be worth the broken hearts."

As Jake and I settled down on opposite ends of the squishy leather couch, I caught him up on the rest of the inconsequential Bondar gossip from the few days he'd been away, my sole goal erasing the furrow between his brows and the worry in his eyes.

After wince-laughing through my imitation of Mr. Whitehead getting stuck halfway through a backwards somersault that he'd attempted to prove that "physicality was an important tool in every actor's toolkit," Jake leaned his head back against the couch and sighed, the tension melting from his shoulders. "I'm so glad you came over tonight."

*Goal achieved.*

"It's great that your Aunt Cheryle is here for a few days."

"Yeah. My dad apparently couldn't take any time off work because it's nearing the end of a quarter or some shit." He rolled his eyes. "He's leaving for a work trip this weekend."

"Wow – that's shitty." I was outraged on Julia's behalf. What kind of asshole doesn't take time off work after his wife has a mastectomy?

"My dad's always been pretty checked out. But fuck, he can't even step up when my mom has cancer?" His voice cracked and he put his hand over his eyes.

My heart twisted. I couldn't imagine not being able to count on my dad. I scooched over and wrapped my arms around him. "I'm sorry your dad is, like, the worst partner in a group project ever."

Jake gave a half-hearted laugh before wiping his hand across his cheek and sliding his arm around me. "I don't know what I'd do without you," he said, his voice quiet in the cool, dim basement.

Above us, the floorboards creaked, followed by the faint shuffle of Cheryle's feet as she puttered around. He pressed his lips to my hair.

"You make everything better," he murmured. "Lighter."

I settled into Jake's side slowly. When I looked up, he was watching me. His eyes were still damp, their blue soft and familiar like worn denim. But the look in them was new – unguarded and raw. Like he was asking me for something. Permission, maybe.

Everything I felt for him – every inch of longing that I'd tucked away out of respect for what he was going through – came rushing to the surface.

His head dipped slightly toward mine, slowly, like he was making sure I had time to pull away. My lashes fluttered shut, my heart thudding–

And then came the screech of hinges and the unmistakable groan of the basement door being yanked open.

"Feet on the floor, kids, I'm coming down!" Cheryle's voice rang out, bright and breezy, like she wasn't interrupting the moment I'd been waiting literal years for.

I launched myself to the far end of the couch, my pulse racing, as Jake blinked like someone had pressed pause on his brain. I yanked a blanket over my knees and tried to look extremely normal and not like I'd been about to kiss my best friend.

Cheryle thumped down the stairs in a hot pink fleece robe and fluffy socks with wine glasses on them. "Don't mind me," she said, eyeing the two feet of space between us with visible amusement. "Just grabbing a beer. Your mom's asleep, and your dad has retreated to his cave of spreadsheets. That man's priorities need work."

She bustled behind the bar tucked in a corner of the basement and grabbed a can from the mini fridge.

"You two are awfully cozy down here. I'll go ahead and assume your respective parents have had 'the talk' with you and I will not be called upon to provide either romantic advice or birth control for the rest of the evening, correct?" Cheryle said.

My brain spontaneously combusted from the heat of my embarrassment. I had not been prepared for Aunt Cheryle's chaotic "fun aunt" energy tonight.

Jake cleared his throat. "We were just about to watch a movie, Aunt Cheryle."

"Excellent. It's time for my murder show, and I'd prefer not to be disturbed while Detective Benson puts another scumbag behind bars." With that, Cheryle winked at me before heading back upstairs.

Jake shifted, scratching at the back of his neck while I tried not to melt into the couch.

"So…How did Aunt Cheryle take it when Detective Stabler left *SVU*? 'Cause my mom was fully devastated," I said.

Jake laughed. "She mourned like she'd lost her long-time partner in a fatal shootout."

I chanced a look at him, my cheeks still flushed. His grin reassured me that we were okay.

"Did you wanna watch something?" Jake asked. "*21 Jump Street* just came out on Netflix."

"Channing Tatum exercising his comedy chops? Yes, please."

We settled into our usual positions on the couch – each at one end, legs stretched out and overlapping in the middle. I tossed one corner of the blanket to Jake, and he draped it across our legs before hitting play.

The opening credits rolled. Within minutes, Jake was asleep. His head lolled to the side, his chest rising and falling in slow breaths. But even asleep, he looked tired, and the faint crease between his brows wasn't fully erased. The sounds of Channing Tatum and Jonah Hill bluffing their way through high school receded into the background.

The past few months, as Jake had tried to keep it together and I'd done my best to be a good friend, something between us had changed. Grown deeper. Stronger. He was my best friend – and I was so in love with him it ached.

Sometimes – like earlier – I was sure he felt it too.

But I wouldn't make the first move, not when everything in his life was so stressful. What we might be to each other could wait.

If I had to, I'd wait forever.

# Twenty-Five

# Not Now, You Brilliant Ginger

Bickford House was lit up against the midnight blue of the sky, the chandeliers inside casting a warm glow over the small crowd visible through the large windows. I'd just waved Kristina off with the equipment and turned back towards the terrace, the music and laughter growing louder as I climbed the stairs. I'd been barely keeping it together since I'd overheard Jake's comment about B.C., going through the motions as I photographed the reception.

Jake was lounging on one of the wicker couches, a relaxed smile on his face and two glasses of white wine sitting on the low table in front of him. He stood as I approached, the only one left on the deserted terrace, then reached down to pick up the drinks.

I scanned the dark sky, determined not to break down again. It was my own stupidity that had let him do this to me again, but I was resolved to call him out on his selfish bullshit. This time, I had the chance to confront him, and I wasn't going to pass it up.

"You saved our asses today, Anderson." He handed me one, his eyes tracing the lines of my face as he clinked his glass against mine.

I added a mental tally to the number of times I had come through for his family, and made a note in the margin that I still couldn't count on him.

From inside, Ed Sheeran's "Perfect" drifted out into the night, the familiar melody amplifying my heartbreak.

*Not now, you brilliant Ginger.*

"I'm glad you're here," Jake said, his lopsided smile threatening to pull me in.

I set my wine glass on the table, not sure what to do with my hands, let alone my heart. I was in deeper than I'd planned. I'd worked so hard to keep things light, to pretend that this fling didn't mean anything. But it did. Of course it did. I already felt more for him than I'd felt for anyone since…well, him.

And somewhere along the way, I'd started to imagine a world where Jake would just stay. He felt like home, but now the lease was up.

"So, were you going to tell me about B.C.?"

His eyebrows shot up. "B.C.?" He put his glass on the table.

"Yeah." I met his eyes, my voice sharp. "Were you ever planning to tell me, or were you just going to disappear again?"

Jake blinked, his easy smile gone. "Woah, slow down. That's not what's happening."

"No?" The word was bitter. I folded my arms so he couldn't see my trembling hands. "Because it kind of feels like déjà vu. You said you were going back to Waterloo." My voice cracked. "God, Jake, is anything you say true?"

He flinched. "What are you talking about? Why don't we sit down so I can explain?"

"There's nothing to explain. It's clear." My voice was shaking, but I kept it low, not wanting to make a scene. "I always show up for you, and you always let me down."

"Are you serious?"

"You're allowed to leave. It's fine. It's what you do."

Jake stared at me like something had just clicked into place. The confusion in his eyes gave way to hurt, then hardened into something distant. Like he was pulling away before I could push him further.

"That's what this is really about, isn't it?" His jaw tightened. "Because you didn't let me explain then, either. One stupid misstep and you cut me off like I didn't matter. I've already apologized, and you said we were past it."

"I cut *you* off?" I said, my pulse spiking. "You fucking abandoned me, Jake, at the worst time in my life!"

"It's not like I didn't try!" He threw up his hands. "I don't know what you want from me. You said this was just a fling, Em. You told me to keep it casual. You scripted the whole thing. Why are you acting like I broke some kind of promise I never made?"

The truth struck like a dagger.

I'd been lying to everyone, most of all myself.

But my breaking heart didn't care. I'd let him in, and now I was bleeding for it, even though nothing had changed for him.

I laughed, sharp and humourless. "I can't believe I let a few good fucks make me forget who you really are."

His lips parted like I'd slapped him, a strangled sound caught in his throat. I turned on my heel, leaving Jake behind on the terrace, the lyrics to "Perfect" dissolving into the night like a cruel joke.

He called my name, raw and desperate, as I stalked away. My breath was uneven, every inhale scraping against the lump in my throat. I dashed away the tears, taking the steps two at a time. There was only one place I could go that would keep me from a total collapse.

# Twenty-Six

## June 22, 10 years ago

## Bold, Anderson

The warm air crackled with an electric buzz as the throbbing bass from the DJ's speakers reverberated around us. Students were scattered across the sun-bathed school grounds for our carnival, the final SAC event of the school year. The anticipation of summer hung thick in the air, and I was on a high after Jake had shared the best news this morning: his mom's recent scans were clear of cancer. It was the ideal kickoff to summer after navigating a taxing eight months of treatment and her surgery in February. When I'd thrown my arms around him to celebrate, I'd felt his relief and joy as easily as I'd felt his broad shoulders beneath my hands.

Now, as I headed over to the inflatable obstacle course to meet Jake for our shared shift – the last one of the day – I was still giddy from what had so far been a perfect day.

The crowd around the games and activities had thinned, with the majority of students taking advantage of the half-priced, end-of-day samosas, and sitting around in the field signing each other's yearbooks. With the obstacle course deserted, Jake and I sat together and exchanged ours. He scribbled intently, a cheeky grin on his lips. I didn't know where to start or what to write, so I watched him for a moment. There was a vibrant energy about him today, a glow that made him more beautiful than usual.

I pulled my eyes away and wrote with abandon, honesty about what he meant to me flowing from my pen. I was afraid it was going to demolish me when he left for the University of Waterloo in two months, but I had faith that what we had could survive a little distance. We weren't dating. But we spent every spare minute together. And now that Jake's mom had the all-clear, the last barrier to us being together was finally gone. I was determined that by the end of the day, Jake would finally know how I felt about him.

Obnoxious shouts and spirited trash-talk drew near, jolting me out of my writing haze. Sarah, Jess, Murray, and Kyle were approaching the obstacle course.

"Gross," I said, glancing up at them as I snapped Jake's yearbook shut. A sinking feeling dragged me down, as if I were caught in an undertow, a familiar sensation whenever I saw Sarah these days. It had been months since I'd talked to her, but it still hurt to see how much she'd changed to fit in with the popular crowd. And what she saw in Murray Fucking Fraser was a complete mystery to me since he was objectively the worst. Cue the Jean-Ralphio GIF. *Ugh.*

Jake saw them and groaned. "We should have unplugged this thing when we got here." He nodded toward the inflatable. "I'll do the start; you take the end. They'll be gone soon."

He closed my yearbook and returned it to my backpack before reaching out a hand to help me up.

I reluctantly went to the end of the course, as Jake went to welcome our unwelcome guests. He gave Kyle and Murray the go signal, then turned a thumbs-up my way. The inflatable wobbled back and forth as various curse words were shouted from inside. I waited for them to appear at the end, hoping they were only here for one race. Sarah and Jess lined up next, laughing at their inability to stay upright once they stepped onto the inflatable. I missed Sarah for a moment until Murray's stupid face peered over the top of the slide at the end of the course, and I remembered she'd chosen him over me. Once Kyle made it over the top, they slid down.

I flashed Jake a thumbs-up to send Sarah and Jess along, as Murray and Kyle reached the bottom of the slide. I turned my back to the slide exit, just as Murray bounced through it, launching himself behind me and grabbing a handful of my ass.

I threw a sharp elbow behind me, smashing into his nose with a resounding crack. He stumbled one step back, then flashed a nasty smirk and lunged toward me. I spun around wildly, catching Sarah at the top of the slide, gaping down at us. The rhythm of Jake's footsteps grew louder as he sprinted toward us.

"Your ass feels better than it looks," Murray said with a sneer, stepping close as blood dripped from his nose. "And it looks incredible in those shorts." He wiped at his nose with the back of his hand, as Jake flew between us, pushing Murray backwards with two hands before tucking me behind him.

"Never touch her." He stepped towards Murray, the intensity of his words leaving no room for negotiation. "Ever."

"What the fuck, Emma?" Sarah's voice cut through the chaos as she scrambled off the inflatable. "Everything's always about you, isn't it?!" She glared at me as she moved to tend to Murray.

My jaw dropped. Did she honestly believe this was *my* fault? If I'd needed any more evidence that the person I'd known and loved since the first day of kindergarten had changed irrevocably, this was fucking it.

"She was all over me, then she hit me when I told her to stop," Murray spat. "Psycho bitch." He looked venomous as he blotted his nose gingerly with the Kleenex that Sarah handed him.

Jake strode towards him, making him stumble backwards, before he turned and scrambled away.

Sarah shook her head and muttered "skank" as she turned to follow him, throwing one last disgusted look my way. Jess and Kyle slithered behind them, leaving Jake and me alone, his chest still heaving with adrenaline and me trembling with shock and burning at the injustice of Sarah's accusation. Jake ran both hands through his hair, then held the back of his head as he turned towards me, his face pale.

"Are you okay? Do you want to report that?" He breathed heavily. "Can I?"

Jake looked tortured, his eyes searching my face before he reached for me and pulled me into a tight hug.

"No, I'm okay," I said, wrapping my arms around his waist and leaning into him. "He's graduating, so I won't have to deal with him again."

For me, the worst part was that Sarah had taken his side. At some point, I'd have to contend with the reality of my former best friend being a total jerkoff, but for now, I wanted to forget about them.

Jake nodded before pulling back. He leaned against the side of the inflatable, then slid down to sit on the grass, knees bent, feet on the ground. We were tucked away in the field, far from the school, on the opposite side where no one could see. The quiet privacy settled me, like the whole world had shrunk down to the two of us. I mirrored him, pressing the right side of my body close to his, revelling in the comfort and connection between us.

"I'm not a violent person, but I wanted to fucking kill him, Em."

"Well, I'm glad you didn't," I said, bumping my shoulder against his. "Minimum wage at the Dairy Queen probably isn't enough to make bail."

Jake chuckled before tipping his head back to rest against the inflatable and closing his eyes. I rested my head on his shoulder, inhaling the scent of his soap and sunscreen. We sat like that for a while, adrenaline from the run-in with Murray and Sarah dissipating as the warm breeze caressed my skin and my love for the boy beside me coursed through me, stronger than ever.

I wanted, more than anything, to climb onto Jake's lap and kiss him. He was graduating too.

We were running out of time.

I turned and swung my leg over him, so I was straddling his hips. His eyes were warm, and his face relaxed into a slight smile as I lowered myself onto his lap. He slid his hands up my thighs, to where the edges of my cut-offs surrendered to the warmth of my bare skin. His thumbs moved in slow, deliberate strokes, just beneath the hem, then glided over my shorts, his fingers pressing behind my hips to draw me closer to him. My stomach fluttered with anticipation, my breath catching with every touch. I wasn't nervous. This had been building between us for months.

"Is that okay?"

I nodded and ran my fingers over the back of his neck, my other hand sliding down his collarbone to his chest. His heart pounded under my palm. I stared at him as one side of his mouth turned upwards.

"Can you just kiss me already?" His low, husky voice sent shivers through me as his eyes fluttered closed, his lashes casting a gentle shadow on his cheeks.

I leaned forward, every inch of me drawn to him as his warm hands slid higher up my back, urging me closer with a gentle yet undeniable pressure. I closed my eyes, my trembling lips parting as I pressed them against his. The touch sent sparks flying through me, forcing me back, his taste of carnival cotton candy left on my lips.

"Bold, Anderson," he murmured as he broke into an approving grin. His gaze dipped to my lips, lingering there for a moment before he brought his hand up, fingers brushing the back of my neck.

"Come here," he whispered. He brought his other hand up to my chin and tipped it up with a possessive slowness that made my breath catch. Our lips connected again, his warm and sweet. His tongue brushed my bottom lip. Slowly, softly, I followed his lead until we found a rhythm. His hand settled behind my ear, drawing me closer and kissing me again – deeper this time, more certain. Every glide of his tongue sent my heart skittering down my spine. The charge between us flared, sharp and electric.

*Holy shit, this was finally happening.*

*And it was everything.*

# Twenty-Seven

# We Listen and We Don't Judge

I fumbled with my keys at the front door, the Uber's headlights flickering past as it backed out of my parents' driveway and disappeared down the street. I'd tried to make myself look presentable so my parents wouldn't ask too many questions, but it had been difficult in the dim light of the car. I always wore waterproof mascara to weddings, but the amount of rage-sobbing I'd done after I'd stormed off the terrace had left my eyes puffy and red. I couldn't believe I was back here again – literally and metaphorically – but there was no way I could go home after telling Mel I'd be at Jake's tonight. She'd want to know the whole story, and I wasn't ready to share it.

I just needed to get inside, past my parents who would launch into a dozen questions about why I was surprising them at eleven at night, and find my old art therapy folder tucked away in my bedroom.

I hadn't needed it since I'd moved out, but I hadn't faced a full-blown panic attack since then, either. I couldn't even remember the last time I'd had one, but I had to stop it before it crushed me. The heavy heat of someone sitting on my chest pressed tighter with every second, their hot, unrelenting breath right in my face, making it impossible to fill my lungs. I needed something concrete to hold onto, to remind me of what I'd learned. There was a reason art therapy worked for me when talking alone never did.

I pushed the door open, stepped inside, and kicked off my shoes. I named a few things as I sensed them – the smooth metal doorknob, the cool tile under my feet, my dad's nachos from the oven, and forced a couple of long, even breaths.

*Only Murders in the Building* played from the living room TV – my parents had been binging it all week. Oliver Putnam shrieked, mid-meltdown. My mom let out a delighted laugh from the couch, as I peeked my head into the room.

"Hi," I said, aiming for casual.

She clutched her wine as it sloshed over the rim in a jump scare.

"Emma!" She scanned me head to toe like I might be bleeding. "What are you doing here? Is everything okay?"

My dad coughed, choking on a nacho he'd inhaled, then took a swallow of his beer to clear his throat. "Hey, kiddo. You didn't say you were coming by." He picked up the remote and paused the show.

"I had a wedding at the Guild," I said, my breathing a little more controlled. "I didn't feel like making the trek across the city, so I figured I'd crash here." I was desperate for the quiet of my room, and my hands itched for my folder. It held visual reminders of how far I'd come, and grounding exercises that worked when panic took hold.

My mom tilted her head. "Julia's wedding?"

Of course, she knew where and when Julia was getting married – Wine Club. She studied me like she could see right through me, her eyes landing on the bags under mine. I'd deliberately kept everything about Jake quiet with my parents. The thought of disappointing them if they found out I'd been spending time with him again made my throat tighten.

I hesitated. "Yeah."

She nodded, her expression curious. "How'd you get that gig?"

"Mom…" All the exhaustion and emotion I'd been trying to hide pushed to the surface, my right eye twitching. "Can we talk tomorrow? I'm really tired. I'm going to head up."

She reached out and gave my arm a light squeeze. "Okay, honey, love you." She glanced at my dad as he said he loved me too.

"Love you," I murmured, already halfway up the stairs.

I shut the bedroom door with a quiet click and crossed my room, eyeing the top shelf of my closet. The folder was right where I'd left it years ago, wedged between an old shoebox and my stack of yearbooks. I stretched up on my toes and slid it out, then settled back on my bed.

I opened the folder with a slow, deep breath. It was a lifeline – packed with messy self-portraits from darker days, and calmer watercolours, proof that those times didn't last. I flipped through my old journal, filled with scribbled prompts from Dr. Kuri and shaky sketches I'd made when I didn't have the words. I paused and practised some of my breathing and grounding techniques, slowly and deliberately. I pulled out the identity collage and timeline I'd made back in high school. For several minutes, I focused on the rhythm of my breath, the papers on my lap, the colors in the collage.

"This feeling is temporary – it will pass," I murmured. Running my fingers over the timeline, I traced the texture of the intricate work I'd done with Dr. Kuri, as a way to process my emotions, years ago. The linear progression of my words and doodles, layered with different colours and media, followed the winding path of my high school years. Arrows stretched past heartbreak and healing to what I wanted to feel one day: *safe, loved, chosen.*

I was proud of the progress I'd made, and I was not going to let what happened with Jake make me regress – to slip back into the darkness and chaos that I'd fought so hard to escape. The timeline wasn't just a record; it was proof I could change, a reminder that I could keep moving forward when everything tried to pull me back.

I wasn't helpless. I had tools, and for the first time since I walked through that door, my breath found a steady rhythm.

And tonight, that was enough.

I pushed my eyebrows high on my forehead to force my scratchy eyes open, and reached for my phone on my nightstand. Squinting at the bright screen, I saw the time: 9:48 am – and one unread text from Jake.

**Jake:**
Can we talk about what happened?

I rolled back onto my bed with a sigh. There was no point in talking. I'd already said everything I needed to say. I cleared the notification, stretched, slid my feet into my middle-school SpongeBob slippers, and headed down to breakfast. I wasn't looking forward to an interrogation from my parents, but I needed food and the alternative was curling up in my bed and avoiding this forever – appealing, but impossible.

My dad was pulling a sheet of bacon out of the oven as I shuffled towards the coffee pot. I poured myself a full mug and took a few gulps.

"Morning," he said, raising his eyebrows, flipping a couple of pancakes onto a plate, and adding bacon on the side. "Hungry?"

I sat down, and he slid the plate in front of me. "Thanks, Dad," I said, reaching for the syrup.

"Em, help me with the Wordle." My mom flipped her phone towards me to show me her latest guess: *FARTS*.

"Strong choice," I laughed.

"I was fishing, give me a break." She rolled her eyes.

I scanned her previous guesses and leftover letters. "Try 'FAINT,'" I mumbled, through a mouthful of pancake.

"Ooh, good one." She typed the word in. "Yes! Thank you!"

My mom dropped her phone on the table and grabbed her coffee. "So, how was the wedding?" She smiled, subtle as a sledgehammer to the head.

"The wedding was beautiful." *And horrible, and heart-breaking, and I wish I'd never gone*. I stuffed another forkful of pancake in my mouth.

"That's nice." She paused. "So, are you and Jake seeing each other, or–" my mom took a sip of her coffee, pretending to be neutral.

"No. Definitely not." I swallowed the pancake and chased it with another long sip of coffee. "We started hanging out a bit, but it was a bad idea, so I called it. It's no big deal." That's how it should have been, and I hated that I'd let it mean more than that.

She studied me. "So, why do you look like Sad Keanu?"

I huffed out a laugh, dropped my gaze to my pancakes, and gave one a half-hearted poke. I didn't want to talk about Jake or admit how much our fight had hurt.

"I don't know. I guess I'm just stressed about the show." That wasn't the reason I was here, but it also wasn't a lie.

My mom gave me a skeptical look. "Are you sure that's all it is?"

"Mom, I'm fine."

"You've done lots of shows and usually you're running around like the Energizer Bunny, not looking like you're about to drown yourself in a puddle of maple syrup."

"There's just a lot on the line with this one. Working with Teo Castillo would be a dream, and I'm a little in my head about it."

My mom glanced at my dad. It was clear she wasn't buying it.

"Well, sitting here moping isn't going to help," my dad said, ruffling my hair as he sat down beside me. "Start checking things off your list. Clear some space on that mental shelf of yours." He poured syrup over his pancakes.

I directed a grateful smile at him. My sweet dad could always help me focus when he knew I was struggling.

"The adjudication is Thursday, right? Need a hand with anything?"

"No, I'm picking up the prints today and Mel is going to help me frame them tonight," I said. My dad was right. I needed to get over this emotional breakdown, stat, so that I could re-focus on the show. If I didn't do my best work and missed out on the chance to work with Teo Castillo because of the fucking melodrama that was my love life, I'd never forgive myself.

My phone buzzed beside my plate. I wiped my fingers on a napkin and picked it up. Mel. I knew I couldn't hide from her for long.

**Mel:**
WTF, Em. Jake came by to talk to you – I thought you were with him??

Another buzz.

**Mel:**
Are you laying in a gutter somewhere or sitting at your parents' kitchen table? Not cool, going MIA.

I sighed and replied:

**Emma:**
Eating Scotty's pancakes. Sorry, I'm fine.

**Mel:**
You're definitely not fine. Jake told me about your fight.

Oh, god. Concerned best friend was Mel's final form, and it was intense.

**Emma:**
I'm fine, Mel. It's over, as scheduled.

**Mel:**
Calling your bluff. See you soon. Love you.

Mel and Jerry arrived about an hour later, armed with three iced coffees and a cake for my parents, who were outside weeding the garden.

"I didn't know you were coming too," I said, taking the cake box from Jerry. "Thanks for the cake. My parents love Jac and Jill's." I set it on the kitchen counter and led the way to the living room.

"I was already on the way to your place to help Mel test her markers for back-to-school when I got her SOS text. So, I just picked her up and we swung by the bakery on the way. You know I can't show up empty-handed. I'm Scotty's favourite."

Mel snorted as she dropped onto the couch and turned to face me.

"So, what happened? Jake showed up looking like he'd been mauled by a raccoon. Talk." She pushed an iced coffee into my hand.

I hesitated, swallowing hard. Where did I even begin? How much could I say without falling apart completely?

Mel blinked. "You're in love with him, start there."

"Mel–" I started, feeling a sting at the back of my eyes. "Whatever we were…it's over."

"Why? You're being stupid." Mel's voice was sharp. She always called me out on my shit, no matter how much I didn't want to hear it. "You're running your same old playbook, Em. Pull away, pretend you're fine, burn the whole thing down before anyone gets a chance to hurt you." She stared intently at me until I met her eyes. "Or love you."

She was right. Of course, she was right. But she was pushing me because she didn't understand. She didn't know that, of all people, Jake Griffin couldn't be the person that I finally let down my guard for.

"Ouch. Well, to start, he got a job in B.C. that he didn't tell me about."

"For sure?" Jerry asked.

I shrugged. Technically, I didn't know all the details, but it had sounded pretty cut-and-dried to me.

"You don't know?" Mel looked at me like I had two heads. "Why are you jumping to conclusions? Ask him to make sure, before you start spiraling."

"I can't trust him. He says one thing and does another. It's the same thing he did before."

"I promise you, it's not. He might have looked like death this morning, but he isn't trying to ghost you this time. It's pretty clear he loves you, too."

I shook my head, not trusting my voice, two seconds away from breaking down again. Someone who loved me wouldn't make me feel like this.

Mel's voice softened. "I'm not letting you shut down and deflect this time. If I'm wrong about him, tell me why."

I stared at the ceiling, blinking back tears. The words were there, heavy on my tongue, and for the first time, I wanted to let them out.

*I can do hard things.*

Mel leaned back on the couch and swung her feet up on the ottoman like she was settling in for the long haul. "Start from the beginning. Give us the whole story."

"We listen, and we don't judge," Jerry said, with a sympathetic smile.

I took a deep breath, then told them everything that had happened the day of the carnival…and about the fallout that had nearly destroyed me.

# Twenty-Eight
## June 22, 10 years ago

## #MessyAF

Sarah's sardonic laugh jolted us back to reality and forced our lips apart. My breathing was heavy as Jake wrapped his arms protectively around me.

"Must have dropped this," she said, tilting her phone up. She looked between us before her eyes landed on me. "You finally got a taste, huh? Does it bug you that he's slumming it before he leaves for school?" She smirked.

I had fucking had it with her bullshit. I had never done anything but show her love, patience, and kindness, and I couldn't understand why she had become so toxic. I climbed awkwardly off Jake's lap and stood to face her.

"You're nasty when you're jealous." My voice shook, but I didn't care. "Go hang off Murray, your sketchy creep who can't keep his hands to himself, and leave us the fuck alone."

Sarah blinked, a flicker of surprise crossing her face before her usual smirk slid back on. "Jealous?" She glanced at Jake, who stood beside me. "Of your one friend who only decided to make out with you because he knows he has an out in a couple of months? Hilarious." She snickered.

"Whatever," I said, wishing she would disappear. She didn't know what she was talking about. Her opinion didn't matter anymore. "Nobody cares what you have to say."

She stepped forward so she was right in my face. "You're not tough, Em. Don't test me." She held my gaze a moment longer before flicking her hair over her shoulder and strutting away.

I wrapped my arms around Jake as tears stung my eyes. Our first kiss would be forever tainted by her bullshit.

"You know she's full of it." Jake pressed a kiss to the top of my head. "I don't know everything that happened between you two, but I do know that you're the best person I've ever met, and if she's choosing Murray and those obnoxious assholes over you, it's her loss." His voice was soft as he looked steadily back at me, his care and respect shining out.

I nodded, Jake's words echoing what my mom and I had been discussing for months: my friendship with Sarah was over. She'd fallen in with that crowd and changed – skipping class, smoking weed at lunch, taking every chance to tear me down. I didn't understand it, but the girl I'd loved like a sister since we were four was gone. A wave of sadness hit me, and I closed my eyes, devastated that it had gotten this bad.

Jake nudged me gently. "Alright, Anderson, back to work," Jake said, his grin like quicksilver before he pressed another quick kiss to my lips. "We gotta get this thing deflated before all the samosas are gone."

I let out a small laugh, the tension easing just a bit. Despite my sadness over my lost friendship, my mind was still spinning with that perfect kiss and all the possibilities waiting for us. Just a few more days of exams, then Jake and I could finally have the whole summer to ourselves, away from all this drama.

I bounced to school after lunch the next day, unable to keep a silly grin off my face, ready to get my English exam out of the way so I could find Jake after his music exam. I felt like the lead at the end of a romantic comedy, all of the shenanigans out of the way so that the main characters could finally be together.

After Jake had walked me home last night, my mom had been a captive audience as I'd recounted my eventful day to her. She gasped in all the right places, narrowed her eyes when I told her about Murray (I toned that part down – I didn't need my mom storming into the school to call out a seventeen-year-old), and shook her head sadly at Sarah's betrayal. I'd texted Jake before bed, like we did each night, but I hadn't heard back from him yet, so I couldn't wait to see him today. Our summer together before he left for university was going to be amazing, and I was sure my parents would let me visit him in Waterloo.

I hurried straight up the stairs once I got to school. I was a bit later than I'd planned, and there were only a few minutes before my exam. I nodded at a couple of people on the stairs, who raised their eyebrows at each other as they passed me. I opened the door to level C with my hip and started down the hall, reaching into my bag to fish out my phone as it buzzed. That had to be Jake – we hadn't gone this long without texting in months. I pulled out my phone and squinted at the message.

**Unknown Number:**
Lol, thot alert. Nobody's gonna want you after this.

My stomach dropped, my feet dragged through wet cement. I read it again.

What the hell? Who was this? The number wasn't in my contacts. My hand trembled as I swiped left and blocked it.

A couple of grade twelve girls sitting across the hall whispered to each other, before sizing me up with sharp, curious eyes. They glanced at their phones, then back at me, laughing. My spidey senses tingled – something in the air was off. I scanned the hallway and quickened my pace on the way to C 62. Heads turned to follow me, whispers trailing behind.

As I approached the classroom, Dev stood in the hallway, checking his phone.

"Dev, hey!" I called as I sped up, trying to escape the hallway. I met him at the door and peered around him to see that students were still milling around the classroom and Mrs. Schindler hadn't handed out our English exams yet.

"Em," Dev said, grabbing me by the arm and steering me a few steps down the hall. His jaw was tense, his eyes flicked past me, restless.

"What's going on?"

"Uhh…" He paused and blew out a breath. "There's a picture. Of you.

Someone sent it to me and, like, a bunch of other people. Have you seen it?"

"No," I said, uncomprehending, but with a tremor of foreboding at Dev's serious expression. Why would someone send a picture of me to other people?

At that, he turned his phone around to reveal a picture. The word "SLUT," written across the top in bright red capital letters, seared itself into my retinas like a branding iron.

Underneath was a picture of me on Jake's lap, kissing him, in perfect focus. I gasped as I grabbed the phone from Dev. There was only one person who could have taken this picture, one person who saw us yesterday…one person who must have written that disgusting word and sent it around to everyone. The depth of Sarah's betrayal was impossible to understand.

"None of your friends think that about you. It's a total dick move that someone would do this." Dev's face was twisted in sympathy as he lifted his phone from my limp hand. "Trust me, this'll blow over soon. High school douchebags have the attention span of that dog from *Up*." He gave a reassuring grin.

I couldn't understand it. If Sarah was hateful enough to go after me like this, I was doubtful this was going to blow over anytime soon.

Oh god – Jake. Had he seen the photo yet? I fumbled for my phone, desperate to have him tell me it would all be okay.

"Umm, the exam's gonna start in a couple of minutes. We should probably go in…" Dev trailed off.

"Can you tell Mrs. Schindler I'll be there in a minute?" I frantically typed out a text to Jake.

**Emma:**
Have you seen the photo?

He still hadn't texted me, so he couldn't have seen the picture yet. Dev nodded and headed into the classroom.

My text showed as "delivered" and I willed Jake to read it before his exam. I kept my eyes trained on my phone, heart thumping, right eyelid twitching, and my breakfast considering making a surprise reappearance, until Mrs. Schindler popped her head out of the classroom and let me know that the exam was starting in one minute.

Conversations thinned as I entered the classroom, every pair of eyes on me. Amaya, a friend of Sarah's on the dance team, leaned over to Brad and whispered something. He snickered and gave me an appraising glance. There was a white-hot spotlight shining directly on me, and my classmates were speculating, regardless of the truth. My cheeks flamed as I dropped into a seat near the front of the classroom beside the windows as Mrs. Schindler finished handing out the exams, face down.

"Okay, everyone, you will have two hours to complete the exam. There are three sections: Short Answer, Short Essay, and Creative Response. Please read the questions carefully. You can turn your paper over now."

I flipped over the page, and the words swam. My mind was utterly blank. I blinked and tried to breathe the text into focus, reading and re-reading the Short Answer questions over and over, none of it making sense. I skipped to the Essay section, the prompt staring back at me like a gun to my head.

*Analyze the central themes in Monkey Beach by Eden Robinson. Discuss how Robinson develops these themes through character development, setting, and plot structure.*

The lines I'd reviewed last night, the literary devices I thought I knew – gone. I tried to focus, tried to summon some scrap of insight or memory of Lisa's life, but it receded every time it got close, like a wave crashing against the shore. The shore. Yes! There was an ocean.

A beach.

Jimmy.

A hot sting behind my eyes warned me that tears were coming. I dabbed at them with the neckline of my T-shirt, then forced my hand back to the page. I scribbled a sentence, then another. They were vague, flat, but they were there.

The scratch of pens around me grew louder, a swarm of bees closing in. I was going to fail this exam. Maybe Mrs. Schindler would understand. She was my favourite teacher, and I wanted to do well on this one. I'd loved *Monkey Beach*. It was beautiful and devastating, and we'd spent hours after class discussing it.

She was going to be so disappointed in me.

So would my parents. I was supposed to be their perfect daughter, and now I would have to explain all of this to them.

A cough from the back corner carried a sharp, disguised, "slut," followed by a ripple of quiet laughter.

My stomach twisted, my hand shook. I kept writing, not sure if any of it made sense, but I didn't stop until I answered every question. I needed to finish so I could find Jake. He'd know what to do.

I handed in my exam, one of the first to finish. As I grabbed my backpack and headed towards the door, Brad looked directly at me and made a fist beside his open mouth, moving it back and forth with his tongue poking out the opposite cheek, his eyebrows raised. I ducked my head and rushed out of the classroom, cheeks burning. I sped towards the stairwell, needing to get to Jake's locker on level B.

All I wanted was his arms wrapped around me. I was trying not to get so upset about a stupid picture and trust what Dev said, that those assholes would find someone else to torment soon…but this was personal, and the thought that this picture had been sent around the school devastated me.

As I hurried down the stairs, I pulled my phone out of my backpack to check whether he'd texted.

Nothing.

It wasn't like him not to reply. Maybe he'd seen the photo and decided I wasn't worth the trouble. I lowered my phone as I went through the doorway, then it buzzed in my hand. I blew out a shaky breath and looked again, hoping it was finally him.

**Unknown Number:**
My dick is inflated and ready for you to jump on. 😜🍆💦

My fingers froze on my phone, my chest tightening with every shallow breath. What the actual fuck was going on? Who were these people, and how had they gotten my number? Sarah had to be behind this, but could she be that cruel?

I rounded the corner into the hallway, only to stop short. Printouts of the photo were everywhere: pinned on the SAC bulletin board, taped to lockers, even plastered across the glass case in front of the art room, my number scrawled on each one next to a string of suggestive emojis. I stared, my heart thumping in my ears. My throat closed. I wanted to scream, to run, but my legs were lead. Every eye in the hallway was on me, as if half the school had shown up to watch me unravel.

*New plan: Leave as quickly as possible and call Jake when I get home.*

I ripped the picture off his locker, crumpled it, and dropped it into the nearest recycling bin before spinning through the doors to the stairwell.

I stumbled backward to avoid crashing into Kyle's chest, as he and Murray stepped off the bottom stair and into the doorway. As if this day could get worse.

"Hey Em," Kyle said, smirking. His beady little eyes looked me up and down, his snake-like tongue flicking out to wet his thin lips.

"Fuck off, Kyle."

I started to push past him, but he put his arm out, wrapped it around my shoulder, and steered me into the nook under the staircase. He stepped forward so my back was against the wall, then ran his hand down my arm. Murray stood beside him with a filthy grin.

"What's the hurry? I just wanted to check on you – thought you might be having a rough day." Kyle's eyes lingered on me, then travelled down my body, making my skin crawl. "Jake said you like it rough, though, right?" He snickered, and Murray laughed in agreement.

The air thinned to nothing as my lungs collapsed, and for a second, I just stood there, stunned and hollowed out. Then I shoved past Kyle, out the doors of the school, and into the sunlight – the beautiful June day mocking my inner turmoil. I gulped air like I'd been underwater too long, but it did nothing to steady me.

*What the fuck was happening?*

*Where was Jake?*

I stumbled into my house and slammed the door shut behind me. My bag slid off my shoulder as I clicked the lock, then leaned against it, trying to steady myself. My head was spinning.

I toed off my shoes, grabbed my phone, and headed upstairs. The house was silent – my dad was supervising exams at his school, and my mom was still at work. They would be home soon, so I didn't have much time to get a hold of Jake and get myself together before I had to talk to them.

I dropped onto my bed and stared at my unread messages to him, then tapped his name and hit call. It rang once. Twice. Three times. I pictured him looking at my name and deciding not to answer it. His voicemail picked up.

"It's me. I–" I tried to take a deep breath, but the tears started falling, my breath ragged. "I need you. I don't know if you've seen it yet, but please call me. Please." I hung up and sent him another text. He would read that before he heard the voicemail and would get back to me faster.

**Emma:**
Have you finished your exam? Where are you? I came home because of the bullshit at school, call me when you can. Preferably now please.

I grabbed my laptop off my desk and opened Facebook. I could send him a message there, just in case there was something wrong with his phone. A notification pinged as soon as the page loaded.

**Jess MacIntosh** invited you to join the group *Emma Anderson is a SLUT!*

The profile picture was the one I'd seen at school today, the cover photo was a candid someone had taken this morning as I stood in the hallway surrounded by the sea of photocopies. Another ping made me jump, drawing my attention to a new notification. I clicked to find my name tagged dozens of times in the comments. I went back to the page and scrolled. There were over a hundred members already. There was a new post from Sarah.

Emma really thought she could pull Murray from me.
#MessyAF #Nastybitch

My pulse roared in my ears as I started checking names, scrolling members, and the comments – people I'd sat next to in class, girls I'd eaten lunch with, guys I'd never even spoken to. Wave after wave of nausea hit me when I'd see a name I thought was a friend. I fired off another text to Jake. Where the hell was he?

**Emma:**
I'm freaking out. People are saying all kinds of shit about me.
Are you alive? Where are you?

I scrolled down some more, past a photo of me taken before my exam today, when I was looking in my bag for my pen. The caption: Searching for her dignity 🙄 #Trainwreck

Then, a post from Kyle.

Emma sucked my dick in the stairwell 🤤🍆💦 pics coming lol

There were dozens of comments underneath.

**Whore.**

**Skank.**

**Been there, done that, not worth the Kleenex 😂😋😋**

Laughing emojis, eggplant emojis, my name tagged over and over. What the fuck.

I dropped to my knees, crawled to my trash can, and gripped the rim, retching until my stomach was empty.

"Emmie?" My mom's voice was close.

I lifted my head to see her coming through the doorway, a crease between her eyebrows. She kneeled beside me and rubbed my back. I leaned into her, immediately bursting into tears as she wrapped her arms around me.

My dad came in behind her. "What's going on, kiddo? Something you ate?"

I shook my head, not able to form words. I glanced at my laptop, still open on my bed, then squeezed my eyes shut, fresh tears streaming down my cheeks.

"Oh my god," my mom said when she saw the screen.

My dad sucked in a sharp breath. He reached for my laptop without a word, snapped it shut, and tucked it under his arm. He disappeared into the hallway as my mom helped me back onto my bed.

"Honey, you're shaking." She wrapped me in her arms again. "What happened?"

## Twenty-Nine

# Emma's Emotional Breakdown

Mel and Jerry stared at me, appalled.

"I will rearrange their bones in alphabetical order. Starting with that absolute piece of garbage, Sarah."

Always my fiercest defender, Mel's jaw was set, and she was using her teacher voice.

I accepted a Kleenex from Jerry and leaned my head onto his shoulder, his flannel shirt soft and comforting against my cheek.

"My parents had the group taken down pretty quickly, then deleted my Facebook account. They took my phone a few days later because as soon as I blocked one number, a new message would come from another. The disgusting things that were written on that page and texted to me are still imprinted on my brain."

My phone buzzed and I flipped it over to see that Jake had texted again. I couldn't deal with him right now.

"That summer, I started having panic attacks, mostly when I had to go somewhere I might run into someone from school. Friends from SAC and the art club reached out to me before my parents took my phone, but I was too embarrassed and overwhelmed to reply. I had so much anxiety about walking into school again in September that I could barely leave my room. Thank god my parents found an alternative high school with an arts focus I could transfer to for grade twelve."

"That's why you had to switch schools," Mel said. "Why didn't the teachers or admin at your school do something?! We have zero tolerance for that kind of bullying now."

"I don't know. My parents reported it, but I shut down and have no idea what the consequences were. I was off social media, and they were handling it."

A few more tears escaped as I remembered that desolate summer when I'd been abandoned by everyone except my parents. Jerry hugged me closer to his side, and I wrapped my arm around his middle, drawing comfort from his steady presence.

"And where was Jake through all of this?" he asked softly but with an undercurrent of "I will fuck him up if he wasn't there for you."

I scoffed. "I have no idea."

"What?" Mel said, flat disbelief in her tone, as she sat up straighter, her eyebrows drawing down.

"He was gone. Poof!" I snapped my fingers. "I called and texted him multiple times, increasingly frantic, and he never responded. I blocked him when he hadn't replied after a couple of days, so we've never talked about it. What Sarah and Kyle had said was bouncing around in my brain, getting louder and more convincing every day." I shrugged. The pain of Jake's disappearance back then was like a fist squeezing my heart.

"But he must have seen the picture. Even if he didn't want to be with me, he was my best friend, and it was pretty fucked up that he would ghost me at the worst possible time."

"Are you fucking kidding me?" Jerry said, his voice rising in disbelief.

"The next time I had any contact with him was when he sat down in front of me at speed dating."

Movement in the doorway caught our attention. We turned to see my mom, tugging loose the drawstring from her gardening hat and pulling it off as she entered the room. She looked between us with a furrowed brow as my dad followed behind her, the cake box in his hands.

"Mel! Jerry! Are you kidding me? Strawberry Shortcake from Jac and Jill's? What's the occasion?" My dad beamed as he set the cake down on the dining room table across the room.

"Emma's emotional breakdown," Jerry quipped, shooting my dad a half grin as he put his arm around me for a side hug.

"Oh–" my dad's eyes widened as he looked between us, finally reading the room. "Uh…I'll go get plates?" He disappeared into the kitchen.

"Is this about Jake?" my mom asked, carefully sitting on the couch beside me, her gaze shifting between the three of us.

"Yeah, Emma's finally filling us in on their history," Mel said. "I can't believe he was such an asshole." She turned to me. "I'm sorry for encouraging you to give him a chance. I wouldn't have, if I'd known."

There was a huge sense of relief at sharing this part of myself with my best friends. It was ridiculous that I hadn't told them this before. But when we'd first met, I was still recovering from the whole experience, and the last thing I'd wanted was for them to view me differently because of it. I hadn't trusted that someone as confident as Mel wouldn't judge me, at least a little bit, for not standing up for myself. Eventually, it had felt unnecessary to tell them.

"I know," I said, looking down. "I was ashamed, even though I knew it wasn't my fault. And it was so much worse since Jake basically threw me to the wolves."

"Well," my mom said. "About that." She paused. "I didn't tell you at the time, but he did come by the house shortly after the shit hit the fan with that disgusting Facebook group."

Mel and Jerry snapped their heads towards me.

"What?" I stared at her. "When?"

"Several days after the bullying started. I know that we'd already taken your phone and deleted your Facebook."

"But…where was I?" I asked. I'd been holed up in my bedroom for a solid month after everything that had happened. It was impossible that he'd come by then. I would have known.

"I think it was when your dad took you to Algonquin to do nature photography to get away from the situation."

*Ohhhh*. I'd forgotten about that. We'd been gone for a couple of days before I'd had to come back to finish my exams.

"What the hell, Mom?" I couldn't believe that she had kept this from me. "What did you say to him?"

"I can't remember exactly – but I let him know that you didn't want to see him."

This revelation hit like a hailstorm, whipping my emotions into a frenzy. "You knew how much he meant to me. Why didn't you tell me?"

I caught a glance between Mel and Jerry as they tried to disappear into the furniture.

"Sweetheart. You specifically told us that you didn't want to see or hear from anyone from school, especially Jake. I wasn't sure what his role was – for all I knew, he was involved in it. I was doing what I could to protect my daughter." My mom's voice was firm. "Once we made the decision to switch schools, and you were meeting with Dr. Kuri and slowly getting better, I thought it would be counter-productive to tell you at that point."

"Mom, you should have told me!" My voice rose, my heart hammering in my throat. Knowing this could have changed everything. I got up and paced. "Why would you listen to me? I was a mess!"

My mom paused. "It was the decision that I had to make then, and I would do it again. But I'm sorry that it's coloured your impression of Jake now, especially after hearing from Julia what they went through around the same time." Her distress was clear.

My brain switched gears like a racecar on a drag strip. This was too much, too fast.

"What do you mean?"

"It's not my story to tell, but it does sound like you and Jake have some things to discuss."

I sat down as my mom excused herself to go shower, my brain trying to reconcile this new information with the narrative that I'd held onto for ten years, that the boy I'd loved had abandoned me when it mattered most. The story was starting to crack, and I didn't know if I was ready for what might be underneath.

I looked at Mel and Jerry. "All along, I thought he just disappeared. And now…" My voice trailed off.

"I think you need to talk to him. It sounds like there's more to the story," Jerry said.

"And once he's gone, you might not have another chance." Mel's voice was soft. "It's clear he cares about you. Lauren said that she's never seen him like this before."

I believed that Jake cared about me. I just didn't know if it was enough.

I heaved a big sigh. "I'm such an idiot. Falling for the guy who broke my heart? Right before he moves across the country? Genius."

"You're not an idiot," Mel said. "Maybe a little masochistic, but not an idiot."

I laughed and dropped my head onto Jerry's damp shoulder.

"I'm sorry I got you all snotty, Jer-bear."

"No worries. This isn't the first time you've cried all over me. Remember the sad chicken ball?"

I snort-laughed at the memory as Mel mimicked the loud "Booooo!" I'd yelled before bursting into tears as the last chicken ball from my leftover Chinese food, perfectly coated in sweet and sour sauce, had rolled off my plate and across our dirty kitchen floor to nestle into the dust bunnies against the baseboard.

"This is nothing compared to how devastated you were about that," Jerry said.

As our laughter subsided, my friends let the subject drop. Mel started making a "To Do" list to help me get my shit together for the show, while my dad served us each a hefty slice of cake. Jerry put on *The Great Canadian Baking Show*, getting in a spirited argument with Mel about the best comfort TV shows. Mel preferred her relaxation to come in the form of watching hot people do stupid things, so her vote was for *Too Hot to Handle*. The familiar sound of them bickering was helping me regain my equilibrium, as I turned the Jake problem over and over in my mind.

Maybe I would get actual closure by talking to him about what had happened and asking him point blank why he'd abandoned me when I was going through the shittiest time of my life. I wasn't sure what he could say that would make what happened back then better. If he confirmed what I'd always believed – that I hadn't been important enough for him to stay – it would only make me feel worse.

But I was sick of feeling like this. Sick of not being able to let my guard down in relationships. Tired to death of the niggling voice in the back of my mind reminding me that I wasn't worthy of sticking around when things got tough. Enraged that the thought of Jake leaving could send me spiraling into a panic attack when I hadn't had one for years.

And all of those messy, unwanted feelings could be traced back to him and the fact that he hadn't been there when I'd needed him. Except… maybe he'd tried?

I took a deep breath and picked up my phone to text him.

**Emma:**
Can I come by later? We need to talk.

I caught Mel's gaze as I put my phone down.

"You ready to see him?" she said after a beat.

"Nope," I said, taking a bite of cake.

"You're stronger than you think, Em. Whatever happens, I'll be home when you get back and we'll attack that list. We got this."

## Thirty

# The Sand Was Shifting

Jake opened the door, handsome as ever, but the dark circles under his eyes told me he hadn't slept last night. His hair was still damp from a shower, and he wore a threadbare baby blue Toronto Blue Jays tee – Halladay, 32, on the back. He'd worn one just like it in high school, back when we'd spent entire afternoons in his basement, talking about everything and nothing. Back when he'd been my everything and I hadn't been able to imagine a time when he wouldn't be. My heart cracked a little more for the sweet, naive girl I'd been.

"Hi," I said, barely above a whisper, as he closed the door behind me.

"Hi." The usual warmth in his eyes when he looked at me was gone, the blue opaque. "Can I get you a drink?"

"I'm sorry–" I blurted, at the same time.

His brows lifted slightly, but he didn't say anything right away.

"I shouldn't have blown up at you at the wedding. I was hurt, but I overreacted. I–" I sighed. "Can I just explain?"

"Please." He gestured toward the living room, and we both sat down on the couch.

"When I overheard you telling Owen you were going to B.C., it brought me right back to when you left before, which is why I panicked and said things I regret. I'm sorry."

He was quiet for a moment. "There's no B.C.," he said.

My eyes flicked up to meet his. "What?"

Jake sighed. "A friend from my program started a practice in Victoria last year. It took off, so he reached out to offer me a position back when I graduated in May. There was no rush to decide, so I'd just been sitting on it. But after this summer back in Toronto, I realized that I didn't want to move that far away from my family. I turned it down a couple of weeks ago, but forgot to tell Owen." His gaze flicked over me with a faint smile. "I was busy."

"Oh." The word came out flat. All that fire I'd been carrying around, the certainty that he was about to disappear again, for nothing. A flush of embarrassment prickled at my neck, but under it was guilt. I'd jumped to conclusions and hadn't given him the chance to explain.

But the pain of being left behind before didn't just vanish because this time was different.

"I didn't tell you because it didn't matter." He paused. "And I was afraid you'd think I was staying for you, when you'd made it clear you wanted something casual. I didn't want to scare you away before I had a chance to convince you we could be something real."

He looked at me like he wanted to say more but wasn't sure if he should. The air between us was loaded, like all the things we'd never said were finally catching up to us.

"It was never casual to me, Emma," he said, quietly.

It hadn't been casual to me either. Of course it hadn't. But I wasn't here to explore what we might be to each other now – I was here to finally understand what had happened in the past.

I set my glass down and took a deep breath. "No matter what I feel for you now, I need to understand what happened in high school. When you left me back then, it gutted me." I looked up at him. The tears that had been threatening finally welled up, blurring the edges of his face. "I was sixteen, completely in love, and I couldn't understand how someone who made me feel so safe could just vanish, like I was nothing. There were days I didn't know if I was going to survive it." I wiped my cheek with the back of my hand.

He ran a hand through his damp hair, searching my face, trying to piece something together. "But – you pushed me away. What are you talking about?"

I began from the moment he'd left my porch, ten years ago. I told him everything I'd told Mel and Jerry, not sure what he knew about and what was news to him. His face fell, silent as my words washed over him. He blinked rapidly with glassy eyes, breaths sharp and uneven. He shifted uncomfortably – leaning back on the couch, staring blankly at the ceiling, running his hands through his hair. He sat upright, elbows on his knees, burying his face in his hands as he took slow, deep breaths. I wrapped up, revealing that my mom had told me only yesterday that he'd come to our house back then. His eyes snapped up to meet mine in shock as he thumbed away a couple of tears before they touched his cheeks.

"I get it – you were eighteen, I wasn't officially your girlfriend, you didn't owe me anything. But that didn't change the fact that I'd been abandoned by the boy I loved." My voice shook. I was freshly heartbroken in a way I hadn't seen coming.

With that, he exhaled fully, closed his eyes, and leaned back on the couch. He made no attempt to stop his tears as they trickled down his cheeks this time.

"Em." His voice cracked as he turned his head to look at me, still resting it on the back of the couch, as if the weight of lifting it was too difficult. "If I had known any of that, I'd have slept on your fucking porch until you came home. I didn't know about anything other than the picture. I'm so, so sorry."

His words were a shock. I'd convinced myself he knew – about the picture, the Facebook group, the harassment, having to switch schools – and just hadn't cared enough to stay. The sand was shifting beneath me, the ground on which I'd based my whole fucked up view of men and relationships was crumbling in the tremors before an earthquake.

I reeled, momentarily slipping into an alternate universe where he'd come to my house before my dad and I had left on our trip.

The question that had lived inside me for ten years finally clawed its way out.

"Where were you?" I choked, my words dissolving into a sob.

## Thirty-One
## June 22, 10 years ago
## Jake

# My Dad the Trash Panda

If there had ever been a perfect day in the history of the world, this had to be it. I was grinning like a fucking idiot. My mom was healthy, summer was starting, and Emma was holding my hand. As long as I'd known that I loved her, I'd had to hold back, and it had slowly been draining the life out of me.

Now, with our hands intertwined as I walked her home from the carnival, my thumb gently tracing hers, an overwhelming sense of peace settled over me.

*Finally.*

I'd been planning to ask her out at Halloween, but with my mom's diagnosis, I'd had to change my priorities. My dad was useless, and with Owen away at university, I was the one my mom had relied on. I'd taken her to most of her appointments and cooked for us. With school and work too, I couldn't be in a relationship. And I wanted to do it right, because

I thought she could be it for me – a wild idea at eighteen, but I couldn't picture myself without her.

For the last couple of weeks, as my mom's health had improved, I'd been trying to convince myself that it was unfair to start something more with Emma now, knowing I'd be away at school for the next few years. But today, her beautiful face – sunkissed and brimming with hope – had shattered any rational restraint I had left. I couldn't stop myself anymore, and honestly, I didn't want to. It was right.

"Here's you, Anderson," I said as we walked up her front steps.

She leaned against the wall beside her door and turned me, one hand tugging on each side of my T-shirt. "I don't want you to go," she said.

"Trust me, I don't want to leave, but I need to get home. Dinner out with my parents to celebrate my mom being cancer free." I smiled as Emma pulled me flush against her, my hands gliding over her hips as warmth spread through my body.

She grinned giddily up at me, her hands tucking under my T-shirt to grip the bare skin at my sides, holding me tight and guiding me closer. I dipped my head down as I curved one arm around her lower back, indulging in the warmth of her skin and the scent of her apple shampoo. I pressed my mouth to hers, savouring a few slow kisses before angling my head and parting my lips to take her in.

*How did I get so lucky?*

Em was my favourite person. The one I texted first and last. The one whose pink cheeks and boisterous laugh had knocked the breath out of me when I'd shared the story of getting locked in the walk-in freezer during my shift at Dairy Queen, surviving a cold, desolate twenty minutes on rations of chocolate chip cookie dough topping. The one whose ridiculous Ninja Turtle costume had split my heart wide open. The one who made me dance.

"I gotta go," I whispered, reluctantly drawing back as dopey grins lingered on both our faces. "I'll call you tonight."

My eyes sank to her full lips again, and she leaned in for another long kiss. I tugged her into a hug and kissed the top of her head, holding her, priceless and more precious than a mint 1952 Topps Mickey Mantle. "Bye, Em."

"Bye, Jake." She stepped backward inside her house, her smile overflowing, as she closed the door.

"Mom?" I called as I stepped through my front door, dropping my backpack and stepping on the heel of my sneaker to slide one foot out, then the other. The house was quiet, my dad's car missing from the driveway, so maybe they were still out. Mom had been elated this morning when he'd taken the day off. She had poured them both a second cup of coffee and was finishing off the last piece of bacon, dancing around the kitchen to Madonna as I got ready to leave. She'd beamed as she'd hugged me tight, planted a big kiss on each of my cheeks, and held my face in her hands as she'd told me how much she loved me and how proud she was of me.

I called her again as I headed up to my room, taking the stairs two at a time, looking forward to a quick shower before dinner after being outside in the sun all day. As I passed by my parents' room, a soft sob drifted out. I paused before knocking.

No answer. I slowly pushed the door open.

"Mom?" I asked, as she rolled over on her bed to face me, eyes red and puffy, tissues scattered all over. "What's wrong?" I stepped toward her and knelt beside the bed. "Are you okay? What's going on? Did the doctor call?"

A thousand thoughts raced through my mind, all of them worst-case scenarios – the results had been wrong, the cancer was back, she was dying.

"It's not that." Her voice cracked as she sobbed again. I sat on the bed beside her and wrapped her in a hug, rubbing her back.

"Mom, what is it?" I asked, desperate to know before my mind started fucking with me again.

"He's gone," she said.

I drew in a sharp breath. "Dad? What do you mean? Was there an accident?" The car was missing. I pictured it – obliterated by a semi on the 401 or flipped into the Don River from the DVP. Maybe the driver's side had been T-boned at an intersection by a drunk driver.

"He's not dead, Jake, he's just an asshole," she said, letting out a bitter laugh as she wiped the tears still slipping down her face. "He took the day off to pack so that he could move in with the woman he's been spending his weekends with. All that travel he's been doing for 'work.'"

She stood up and paced the room. "It's been *years*," she said, her voice cracking.

I sat, stunned, on their bed, and glanced around the room. His clock radio that he snoozed for forty minutes every morning – gone; the James Patterson book he'd been reading – gone. Left behind in its place, his platinum wedding band.

*Holy shit, this was for real.*

My dad had always been missing-in-action, even when he'd been around, but I still hadn't suspected this.

I was an idiot.

I flushed hot as rage swept over me. *That fucking coward.* I bet he was proud of himself for waiting until she was better, which only made me hate him more.

I willed my breathing to slow down. I had to keep it together. With Owen away, I was the steady hand in our shaky world, but now I was one tremor away from crumbling, a precarious Jenga tower waiting for the final blow to send me crashing down. I didn't think I could do it again.

But there was no choice. My mom was frantic, throwing open her drawers and tossing random clothes into a haphazard pile at the foot of their bed. I was suffocating, a strangling vine tightening around me with every piece of clothing she threw.

"I can't stay here, Jake. I can't sleep in that bed." Her eyes were wild as they darted around the room.

"Okay. Let's just slow down. I'm going to go make you some tea, and I'll text Aunt Cheryle."

She nodded as I gathered the tissues and threw them in the garbage can before heading down to the kitchen. Hands shaking, I texted my aunt. I put the kettle on, grabbed a mug from the cupboard, and threw a tea bag into it while I waited for her reply.

A series of events from the last year paraded across my brain. My dad missing the city finals in September. My dad missing Owen's graduation in October. My dad explaining that I'd have to take time off school to take my mom to her chemo appointments. My dad leaving for a "work trip" three days after my mom's mastectomy.

He'd abandoned us long ago, I just hadn't seen it.

My mom came into the kitchen and sat at the table, put her head in her hands, and took a couple of deep breaths. I poured the boiling water into her mug, then grabbed her a couple of cookies as my phone vibrated.

"Aunt Cheryle wants us to come stay with her." I poured a bit of milk into her tea and handed it to her, the vines loosening their grip on me slightly now that I wasn't in this alone. "I'll pack your things," I said, sliding the plate of cookies toward her.

I grabbed a bag from the basement and dumped her pile of clothes into it along with some toiletries. I stuffed my backpack with enough to last me a couple of days and carried our bags to the car.

I was running on autopilot, not fully grasping what was going on, only knowing that my rage at my father was all-consuming. My hands fumbled with the car keys, dropping them twice before finally sliding the right one into the ignition.

It would take about two and a half hours to get to my aunt's house in London if we left now.

When would Owen see the text I'd sent him? Could he meet us there?

I could blow off my music exam tomorrow morning, but I needed to be back Monday for Calc and Bio.

How did this go from the best day of my life to complete shit?

Once we arrived at Aunt Cheryle's, she gave me a hard hug and called me a "good egg, not like your asshole of a father," before whisking my mom to their den, where the sofa bed had already been made up for her. The double french doors rattled as she closed them, leaving me standing in the front hall in a daze.

I lumbered down to the basement family room and dropped myself onto the couch. The adrenaline that had kept me running for the past three hours left my body all at once, leaving me limp and tired. All I wanted to do was talk to Emma.

I dug around in my bag, searching for my phone. When I couldn't find it, I dumped it out and rifled through my stuff.

Oh shit, shit, *shit*. I'd tossed it onto my bed after I'd texted Owen, and I had a terrible feeling it was still sitting there. I could send her a Facebook message, but Aunt Cheryle's computer was in the den. Damn it, why hadn't I memorized her number?

It was official: I was marooned, in a fucking dead zone, my dad the trash panda that had gnawed through the electrical wires and caused a transformer, aka my life, to blow.

I blinked my sticky eyes open after a long night of tossing and turning on the slowly deflating air mattress in the basement, shocked that it was already noon. I headed to the kitchen for something to eat, passing my Uncle Dave sitting in the den peacefully playing solitaire, the old man's Candy Crush, on their only desktop computer as if my life wasn't imploding.

Jesus, I'd have to add my name to the waitlist.

"Morning, Uncle Dave. Do you think I could use the computer for a minute when you're done?"

"Sure thing, kid, I'll let you know," he said, not taking his eyes off the screen.

But before my uncle was finished, Aunt Cheryle took my mom and me to the Covent Garden Market to pick up fresh ingredients for dinner, then to the Old East Village. We spent the entire day out, trying to distract my mom and keep her spirits up. The whole time, I was crawling out of my skin, desperate to talk to Em. When *Nikita* finally started at nine, and my aunt, uncle, and mom huddled around the TV, I was able to hop on the computer to send her a Facebook message.

**Jake:**
Hey you. I miss you, and I have no doubt you kicked your exam's ass. I'm at my aunt's place in London until Sunday – my dad is a total POS, but I'll fill you in when I get back. I forgot my phone at home, so can't text you. I'll call you when I get back. I miss you and can't wait to see you.

That would have to do for now. I waited for a couple of minutes, but when she didn't open the message, I headed to the living room to see what kind of crazy shit Nikita was up to.

The weekend at my aunt's place was great for my mom, but I was dying to leave. I hadn't gone three days without talking to Emma since the party at Jess' house, and my life was fucking weird and sad without her.

On Sunday, Owen arrived, so I finally drove home with only my mental chaos to keep me company. The emotional toll of the last few days made it feel like weeks had passed, and all I wanted to do was wrap my arms around Emma and breathe in her apple shampoo. My parents' relationship was never what I'd call loving, and my mom would be better off without my dad in the long run. But he had bailed on Owen and me too, without a word. I shouldn't care – he'd never been there for me – but the anger and hurt were still making my gut churn.

I breathed a huge sigh of relief as I unlocked my front door and bounded up to my bedroom, finding my phone lying on my bed where I'd left it, dead. I plugged it into the charger as I booted up my laptop to check Facebook again. My message had gone unread all weekend, which was weird.

*What the hell?*

All of her messages were gone. My side of the chat history was still visible, but now the conversation was with "Facebook User," and the photo of the awesome self-portrait she'd painted for her art class had been replaced with a gender-neutral, white silhouette on a light blue background.

I shut my laptop and grabbed my phone, the black screen with the dead battery icon still filling the screen, giving me the finger for being such a dumbass and leaving it here. Finally, my phone lit up, missed calls and texts from Emma pouring onto the screen, followed by a couple from my group chat with Wes and Ro. I swiped my phone open and read hers first.

**Wednesday 10:47 PM**

**Emma:**
Hope dinner was great and your mom is living her best sushi and sake life. :) You didn't call but you can make it up to me tomorrow, I'll come by your locker after my exam. :D Sweet dreams. XO

**Thursday 12:58 PM**

**Emma:**
Have you seen the photo?

**Thursday 3:28 PM**

**Emma:**
Have you finished your exam? Where are you? I came home because of the bullshit at school, call me when you can. Preferably now please.

**Thursday 3:49 PM**

**Emma:**
Jake, I'm freaking out. People are saying all kinds of shit about me. Are you alive? Where are you?

**Friday 11:05 AM**

**Emma:**
I'm not sure what's going on with you but I need you and you haven't texted me back. My phone is blowing up. Are you ok?

**Saturday 4:33 PM**

**Emma:**
Why are you ignoring me?

**Saturday 11:50 PM**

**Emma:**
WTF, are you actually ghosting me? Wow.

I was out of body reading those messages, none of it making any sense. I switched to the group chat with my friends, hoping for a little insight.

**Thursday 3:42 PM**

**Ro:**
Dude what's up with you and Em?

**Wes:**
Glad you two got together but that pic was rough. Is she pissed?

And that was it. Leave it to my two best friends not to notice that I was MIA for four days. I sent a message to try to figure out what the fuck was going on.

**Jake:**
I was away for a few days with my mom. What pic?

**Wes:**
You didn't see it?

A couple seconds later, the photo popped up on my phone. My stomach dropped. My sweet Emma had been dealing with this on her own while I was gone? Of course, she was pissed.

**Jake:**
WTF. Who sent it?

**Ro:**
I got it from like 6 ppl. I don't know who started it.

**Wes:**
Same.

*Fuck.*

I knew. Emma must be devastated. And she thought I'd deserted her. I hung onto the hope that she knew me better than that. She knew me better than anyone.

I flipped back to my conversation with her so I could reply.

**Jake:**
I am absolutely not ghosting you. I just saw your messages and the picture. Are you okay? Of course you're not. I'm so sorry, some shit went down with my family, and I had to leave with my mom for a few days. I forgot my phone at home. I messaged you on Facebook, but you disappeared. I'm calling now.

I tapped send and then her number, my heart in my throat. My body wasn't built to move from one crisis to another. I breathed. She was going to answer, and I was going to see her, and everything would be all right. It had to be.

But the phone rang through to voicemail, time after time. I left a string of apologies, pleading for her to call me. A sinking feeling brewed in the pit of my stomach. At least for now, this was a dead end. I flipped back to my texts. The one I'd sent to her was undelivered, amplifying the roaring silence in my chest. Hollow and seething, I unplugged my phone, now charged to a healthy 7%, threw it in my pocket, and headed to her house.

I pressed her doorbell, its chime resonating through the wood. Glancing around the porch, memories flooded back – one of the best moments in my life had been here, a few days ago.

*How had it come to this?*

I needed to find Emma and make sure she was okay, but in the back of my nagging mind, a voice persisted, telling me I wasn't supposed to be happy. Each time I got close, it slipped away from me as I reached for it. I tried to be a good person and maybe I put too much faith in karma. It was starting to feel like some sort of higher power was punishing me for something I knew nothing about. Maybe some past life bullshit.

*Please, Em, open the door.*

The lock clicked, and my breath caught in my throat, ready to throw my arms around her and apologize for not being here. The door opened, but it wasn't Emma. Mrs. Anderson looked as wrung out as I felt.

"Jake," she said, her face impassive.

"Hi, Mrs. Anderson. Is Emma home? I need to talk to her, please." I said, my voice wavering. "I know she's upset with me, and I want to apologize and explain. Please."

Mrs. Anderson shook her head.

"She's not home, Jake. She's gone away with her dad for a couple of days." Her expression shifted, unreadable now. "But she made it clear she didn't want to speak to you. The last few days have been terrible, and there's still a lot we're dealing with."

"I'm so sorry. This was all totally out of my control." Hoping for some understanding, I silently pleaded for her to give me a chance.

"Honestly, seeing you right now would make it worse. I hope you can respect that and give her some space."

"I understand," I said, *not at all* understanding how things had gotten so fucked so fast. The fact that this single photo could jeopardize everything we were to each other was mind-blowing. Emma believing she was better off without me was even more devastating. If she knew me at all – she had to know that I wouldn't bail on her when things were shitty and that I would do everything I could to support her, the way she had for me.

"Can you please tell her I came by and ask her to call me if she changes her mind?" I wasn't about to give up on her. I knew her exam schedule, and I would find her at school on Tuesday.

"Sure, Jake." Mrs. Anderson said. "Take care of yourself." She closed the door, leaving me dumbfounded on the porch.

## Thirty-Two

# I'd Give You Everything

I focused on my breathing, my mind a cyclone of new information, each revelation from Jake whipping up debris from the wreckage of beliefs I'd clung to for years. I latched onto my first coherent thought.

"Your dad left you right when your mom finished her treatment? My god." I couldn't believe that had happened to him, to Julia, to Owen.

"He'd always been an asshole, so it was par for the course. But I still didn't see it coming."

My chest ached for the boy he'd been.

Jake sighed and ran his hand through his hair. "Then you weren't at your exam, and I didn't know what had happened to you. It was like you'd disappeared."

"I was trying to, with everything going on," I admitted. "I wrote them in the office after my parents met with the Principal."

Jake nodded. "I almost went back to your house so many times that summer, but I thought you didn't want to see me. I just kept telling myself you'd call when you were ready." He looked up, those beautiful blue eyes that I had fallen in love with all those years ago pleading with me. "If I'd known about even half of what you were dealing with, I would have come back every day."

I blinked back at him, a ventriloquist's dummy, no words of my own.

The only thing I had wanted, then, was him.

"Then I went away to school, and I was a fucking mess. I didn't think I was going to make it through the first month, but I met Lauren in one of my tutorials. She called me 'Saddy McSadface' and told me to stop moping over whatever girl broke my heart because she was my best friend now." Jake huffed out a laugh. "She reminded me so much of you."

Tears welled up again. How could I have given up on him so easily? I'd deserted him too. I could see it from his side now, guilt pulling me under like quicksand.

"I saw you that Christmas, you know."

"What?" I snapped my head up.

"At the movies. I was sitting at the back with Wes and Ro, and then there you were, bouncing down the aisle to the front of the theatre with a group of friends I'd never seen before." He rubbed his jaw. "You were laughing, popcorn in one hand, Sour Patch Kids and a pop in the other. You looked happy."

I shook my head. "I wasn't, not then. I probably wasn't happy again until I met Mel and Jerry."

Jake nodded. "I watched you dump your candy into your popcorn, shake it around, and offer it to the guy beside you. I wanted to be him so badly. It took everything I had not to come up and talk to you. I left before the movie ended so I wouldn't do something stupid. I thought you wanted nothing to do with me."

I shook my head. One more missed connection stacked on top of all the others that had altered the course of my life. If any small thing had gone differently back then, everything would have changed going forward. If he hadn't forgotten his phone, if I had been home when he came, if I hadn't blocked him so quickly, if my parents hadn't deleted my Facebook or taken my phone, if he had come back to the house a second time, or if he'd said hello at the movie theatre. If only my mom had told me he'd come by. If I'd bothered to find out what had happened to him.

If, if, if.

"Emma, I would go back and change it all if I could," he said, an echo of the thought running through my mind. "I don't know where to go from here."

"Me neither," I said.

"I want something real with you. But I understand if that's not possible for you right now or if I'm the last person you'd want to take a risk on." His voice cracked.

I wanted to burrow into him and let myself trust that he was the safest place for me. But the voice in my head – still sixteen – told me he couldn't possibly be. It reminded me how quickly it had all evaporated before, how deep it had hurt, whispering that letting him in again meant opening the door to the same heartache. I should keep my distance, because hope was so much harder to lose the second time.

I reached out and took his hand. The energy that had always crackled between us was still there. "I wish I had known what you were going through back then, and given you a chance to explain."

"Jesus, it wasn't your fault," Jake said. "Not with everything that you were dealing with. Those fucking assholes."

I surprised myself by laughing. "They were fucking assholes, weren't they?"

*Laughing about past trauma? Progress.*

Jake intertwined his fingers with mine and waited, his eyes steady on mine. I took a deep breath. Every instinct built on a foundation of trauma was screaming at me to cut him loose, to let him know that I didn't want anything more than friendship. But the braver part of me – the part that had been nurtured by my parents, Mel, Jerry, and Dr. Kuri – had piped up, and was gently insisting that Jake might be worth the discomfort and work of trusting someone.

I caught sight of the clock and swore under my breath. "Shit – I've got to grab my prints before the shop closes, then head home to frame them with Mel. The adjudication for the show is on Thursday, and I'm already behind." That, and I wasn't ready to untangle all of this with him yet.

"Can we talk after the show? I need some time," I said. "Can you give me that?"

He exhaled and nodded. "Of course."

I stood, and he walked me to the door, our hands still intertwined.

"I'd give you everything," he said softly. "I just need you to let me prove it."

## Thirty-Three

# A Photograph Emerging in the Darkroom

I had been looking forward to this for so long that it still didn't feel real. Opening night. The gallery lights, the polished floors, the quiet hum of anticipation. I'd spent the entire week forcing myself to compartmentalize. On Tuesday and Wednesday, Mel and I had finished all the prep work and set up my space, fueled by dill pickle Crispers and lime Bubly. Thursday, the adjudication for the competition had consumed every ounce of my focus, as I'd talked to the judges about my photos. The pressure I'd put on myself to win this competition made every detail – from the spacing of the frames to the lighting on each photograph – feel critical.

Now, standing in the gallery, I surveyed the culmination of all that work. My exhibit, "In the Heart of the City: Capturing Community in Toronto," highlighted moments of connection I'd photographed across the city. I was proud of the collection: messy, joyful, human.

The two winners of the internship would be announced tonight, and if I won, I'd be on a plane in a few weeks, heading to Panama with

Teo Castillo. Everything I'd ever wanted – professionally, at least – was within reach.

But personally, I was still lost, grappling with my feelings for Jake. My mind and heart waged a relentless tug-of-war, my heart begging me to fall into his arms while my brain bleated, "Danger! He'll break you again." Earlier today, Dr. Kuri and I had walked through my timeline, questioning whether my protective instincts were really necessary. Still, my thoughts tangled like overgrown weeds, choking out any clear path forward.

I needed a machete. Or maybe another glass of wine.

I shifted my weight to my other foot, a glass of Villa Sparina Gavi in my right hand, a fixed smile on my face. I nodded along to a dark-haired, plum coloured button-down and matching sweater vest-wearing art snob. Pastry crumbs shifted in his moustache as he mansplained the differences between film and digital photography, insisting my photos could be "elevated" if only I worked with film. I swiped a second glass of wine off a tray as a server passed by, so that my hands were too full to throat-punch him.

"Rowan uses film, over there." I nodded toward another artist as he "hmmmmed" and sauntered off. I took a gulp of my right-hand wine, smiled at a couple as they stepped closer to my shot of Sarko to read the title and caption, then checked my watch. My parents had already come and gone, leaving behind a comically large vase of flowers, now standing in the corner.

Right on time, Mel and Jerry came towards me, their presence a welcome diversion from the never-ending carousel of thoughts going round and round my head.

"This looks amazing!" Jerry wrapped me in a hug, before stepping back and examining my work, print by print, pride evident.

He stepped towards my photo of an older woman sitting on the bench outside a bright blue vintage clothing store, the sign reading "Courage My Love" visible behind her. Fearlessness in her eyes and a smirk on her lips, gold mannequins on the upper balcony were over her shoulders, seemingly whispering conflicting ideas in her ears.

"Thank you so much for coming," I said as I set down my wines and stepped into Mel's arms.

"Wouldn't miss it," Mel said. "Everything looks gorgeous!"

"Speaking of gorgeous..." Ryan's voice came from behind me. "You both look lovely tonight."

Mel tutted and rolled her eyes as we turned. He grinned before pulling me into a big hug. I peeked over his shoulder to wave at Lauren before scanning the crowd to see if Jake had arrived with them.

"Nice work, V, wow!" Ryan stepped closer to see my photos.

Lauren noticed my gaze before hugging me.

"He's not here yet, but he's heading over soon," she said before she pulled back. "How are you doing?"

"I've been better, but I've also been worse?" I said, attempting levity with an unconvincing half smile. I wasn't sleeping much, and there wasn't enough concealer in the world to hide the dark circles under my eyes. At least my hair was clean.

I wasn't sure how much Jake had told her about everything that had happened between us.

"Yeah," Lauren said, nodding. She paused, seeming to consider her next words. "I hope you guys can sort things out. I've never seen Jake happier than he is with you." She smiled sympathetically, then turned to join the others, who were laughing and reminiscing as they looked at the photo of all of us from Ward's Island.

I'd been avoiding looking at it all night, but now my eyes landed on the photo. Jake was on the left side, his face lit up, mid-laugh. He wasn't looking at the camera, or anyone else in the frame – he was looking at me. There was a softness in his expression, the kind that didn't usually show up in photos. I glanced away, shaken by how at home he looked. The irony wasn't lost on me. I could capture intimacy in others, but had no idea how to risk it for myself.

I blinked away the burning at the back of my eyes and rejoined my friends. For the next fifteen minutes, I met other patrons of the show, talked about my work, and pushed all thoughts of Jake to the back of my mind.

And then he walked in.

A bouquet in his hands, his gaze swept the room until it landed on me. Our connection punched through the crowd, leaving me breathless.

Ryan draped one arm over my shoulders and leaned toward my ear. "Put him out of his misery, V. He hasn't been this sad since Halladay went to Cooperstown without the Jays logo on his cap."

I huffed and squeezed him back.

"We'll give you guys some space and check out the competition," Jerry said. "But don't worry, we're staying for the big announcement."

The four of them wandered over to the artist next to me, stopping to greet Jake on the way. He looked drained, a stark contrast to his energy captured in the photo behind me.

"Hey, Em." His eyes washed over me as he approached. He held out the flowers, a beautiful autumn bouquet of pink and purple dahlias, orange roses, and one bright yellow sunflower. "Congratulations. This is amazing." He looked around, taking in my display and the busy room, then turning back to me.

I thanked him for the flowers and laid them on the table next to us, then stepped forward and reached my hands around his waist. He breathed deeply as I tugged him closer. He tucked his head down against mine, his hands splayed across my upper and lower back, anchoring me to him with an unwavering grip.

"It's good to see you," I said. "Thanks for coming." I lingered in the moment, reluctant to break our connection.

"Of course," he said, dropping his arms and stepping back. He moved closer to my work and read the captions in silence.

He'd been so excited about coming. And now we were here, like this.

Jake moved from photo to photo, sharing occasional words of admiration, a proud smile growing on his face. When he reached the one of us, his smile faded and he chewed on his bottom lip, reading the caption before turning to face me.

"I want to buy this one," he said. "Someone told me I need some art in my apartment for my plants to look at."

"Yeah, those pothos definitely need some culture," I said, my grin more genuine than it had been all night. I picked up a "sold" sticker and fixed it to the bottom right corner of the frame. "The show ends Sunday, so I can get it to you after that."

"Thanks."

I nodded.

"I miss you," he said.

"I miss you too." I wavered.

"It feels like you're a thousand miles away, and I hate it."

"Jake…" I shook my head. I owed it to him to try to explain. "Trust doesn't come easy for me – it hasn't for a long time. I don't even know if I'm capable of–" My voice cracked, and I pressed my hand to my eyes.

"I get it," he said softly, wrapping his arm around my shoulders and guiding me to a private corner, away from my display.

I turned into him, sniffing against his shirt.

He rubbed circles on my back. "But I'm not eighteen anymore. I need you to believe me when I say that I'm here." He hesitated for a moment. "I'm staying in Toronto. Lauren's dad isn't recovering as quickly as they'd hoped, and her parents have decided to retire. She's asked me to partner in the practice, and we finalized the paperwork this morning." He paused and took a deep breath. "It's almost too good to be true, getting to stay here with everyone I love. I wanted to tell you after the wedding, but…"

I stepped back and looked up. That must have been what was "too good to pass up." I'd assumed that he'd meant the opportunity in B.C.

"You're staying?" I said slowly.

Stability. Permanence. The things I secretly craved but never believed I could have. My chest tightened, longing and panic colliding in a dizzying rush.

"I'm staying," he confirmed. "Not for you. Not as some grand gesture, but because it's the best thing for me." His voice softened. "Let me make it very clear: I want to be with you. For real. For a long time. But I don't want to pressure you into something you're not ready for."

I nodded, a future with him coming into focus, then blurring again through the prism of fear. I'd spent years keeping everyone but Mel and Jerry at arm's length, convinced it was the only way to stay safe. Could I undo that? Could I risk giving Jake the power to hurt me again?

"I've trained myself not to need people. I don't know if I can let you all the way in."

Jake's hand slid down my arm, his fingers curling gently around mine. "Then let me help. Not all at once. No timeline. Just…please don't shut me out. I couldn't fight for you then, but I need to fight for us now."

I swallowed hard, blinking back the tears threatening to spill. His words pressed against the walls I'd built, but I couldn't tell if they were strong enough to break through.

All I knew was that I wanted them to be.

"Take some time to think about it," he said, running a hand through his hair with a long exhale. "I've got to head back to Waterloo tonight and pack the rest of my stuff. The new tenant gets the keys Sunday, so I'll be back tomorrow night."

"Okay," I murmured, still processing that he was choosing to stay. Choosing me. Us.

An older couple whispered to each other, then glanced at me with a smile as they nodded towards my work.

*Oh right, I was here to speak to patrons of the arts, not wallow in the mire of my emotions.*

I turned back to Jake, at a loss for what to say.

"I'll let you get back," he said with a wistful smile. "I'm so proud of you. I wish I could stay for the announcement." He reached out and tugged one of my curls, his fingers lingering while his eyes stayed on mine for a long moment, before he blinked, turned, and strode towards the door.

I stood, arrested, that simple gesture unlocking a memory I hadn't thought about in years. Sarah, the afternoon after rent-a-friend, confirming Jake had slipped her the money to rent me because he'd overheard that Murray was planning to. Jake, gently tugging on my hair in the auditorium, something in his eyes giving me hope that maybe it would be different someday.

That day had finally arrived, and I was about to miss it.

A silver-haired woman with thick candy-apple red glasses brushed past me, pausing at my photo of a Spadina Avenue fruit market with the 510 streetcar blurring by. I stepped back, silent reels of my past flickering behind my eyes.

He'd always been there – from picking me up off the ground at orientation to holding me while I'd cried about Sarah, from participating in every ridiculous idea I had for the SAC to defending me from Murray at the carnival.

And it wasn't just me. He was always there for everyone he loved.

Now that I knew the full truth, the past rearranged itself, puzzle pieces snapping into place. For years, I'd looked at the picture wrong. Sarah was the one who had betrayed me and shattered my trust in people, not Jake. High school bullies had shown me how cruel people could be, not him. The only reason Jake hadn't been there when I'd needed him was because he'd been supporting his mother, while carrying the weight of his father's abandonment.

*I'd give you everything. I just need you to let me prove it.*

His words from the other night echoed in my mind. But he didn't need to prove anything. The evidence was there: Jake more than deserved my trust – even if trusting terrified me.

But I was done letting fear make my choices.

The future I'd glimpsed earlier was coming into focus, a photograph emerging in the darkroom. And just like I knew when I'd nailed the perfect shot, I knew that this was right. That this future could make me happier than I'd ever dared hope – if I was brave enough to reach for it.

A desperate urgency seized my chest. I looked wildly around the gallery, frantic, searching, heart thudding like a drum in my ears.

But he was already gone.

## Thirty-Four

# I Want You Forever

I beelined across the gallery towards my friends, scanning the room as I went, hoping I'd missed Jake lurking behind a potted plant somewhere. But he was gone.

"Mel!" I hissed as I approached, keeping my voice down so I didn't make a scene. The judges were gathering near the dais at the front of the room, preparing to make their announcement, but I couldn't wait for it. Jake might be on the train to Waterloo by the time it was done, and if I didn't find him now, if I didn't tell him what he meant to me immediately, I had a terrible feeling that something else would go wrong and we'd spend another ten years apart.

"Almost time!" Lauren said, squeezing my arm.

I spared a quick glance for the judges, then turned back to my friends.

"I gotta go," I said.

Mel's eyes widened. "Wait, now? They're about to announce the winner."

"Jake's gone and I need to find him. If I miss the announcement…Jer, you're me." I yanked my lanyard from my neck and shoved it into his hands.

Jerry blinked. "What?"

"You're the best!" I slid past him, weaving through the crowd.

The gallery doors banged open as I sprinted into the night. A sharp breath caught in my throat as rain sheeted down, cool against my overheated skin. My heels skidded against the slick pavement as I spun left, then right. There was no sign of him. Adrenaline surged, propelling me toward his apartment.

"Jake!" My voice carried down Dundas, half-drowned in the roar of rain and traffic.

A tall figure stood at the end of the block, shoulders hunched in the downpour, waiting at the stoplight to cross. I ran toward him, my chest a cocktail of fear and hope.

The light flipped green and he started forward, splashing through puddles as he jogged across Dundas, picking up speed. I ran faster, cursing the heels that I rarely wore.

"Jake!" I called again, closing the distance, until – CRACK. My heel caught on an uneven slab of sidewalk, and I pitched forward.

Warm, murky water splashed over me as I slammed into a puddle, soaking my dress and washing away my pride. I lay there for a few seconds, gulping deep breaths, before looking up just in time to see him disappear around a corner. My hands and chest burned as I pushed myself into a sitting position, focusing on my breathing. A tear slipped down my cheek, lost in the rain.

Maybe it was a sign.

Maybe I had gotten it wrong.

Maybe it wasn't meant to be.

"Emma?"

I blinked up through the downpour. Jake stepped out of the convenience store, a bag dangling from his hand, hair plastered to his forehead, eyes wide with concern.

For a second, it was grade nine all over again. Me, on the ground, breathless from a combination of shock and anticipation. Him, stepping forward, hand outstretched, ready to save me from myself.

He hauled me up and tucked us under the narrow awning over the doorway. His hands slid down my arms, steadying me, then gently swept my dripping hair off my forehead and back behind my ears.

"What are you doing?"

"I don't want to lose you," I gasped, water streaming down my face. Rain, or tears, or both.

"You didn't." His thumb brushed against my wet cheek. One corner of his mouth lifted in his achingly familiar half-smile. "I told you – I'll be back tomorrow."

"Tomorrow's too far away." My chest heaved. Everything that I felt for him – all the love that had laid dormant for ten years before stirring back to life over the past month – was clamouring to be let out. And yes, there was fear there too, but my bone-deep certainty that my heart would always be safe with him was finally drowning it out.

"I don't want to wait for tomorrow. I want you now. I want you forever."

A swallow rippled through his throat as his eyes locked with mine. His whole heart was right there for me to see, and I had almost missed it, my own eyes squeezed shut in fear.

Before he could answer, I clutched his shirt and kissed him, fierce and desperate, as the rain whipped around us. For a brief moment, he stood frozen, but then he gathered me up in his arms and kissed me back until all I could feel was him.

"I love you," he said, resting his forehead against mine, our breath mingling. "I know it's too soon, but I don't care. I've loved you since we were kids. And if you let me, I'll love you every day."

The last bricks in the wall around my heart crumbled to dust, washed away with the rain and the flood of his words.

I was safe. I was loved. I was chosen. I'd reached the end of my timeline without realizing it.

"I love you, too, Jake Griffin." The truth tumbled out, terrifying and freeing all at once.

His eyes flickered all over my face, as a cheeky smile spread across his lips. "Say that one more time."

"I love you." I exhaled, relieved to finally let him all the way in.

He kissed me again, urgent and wild, rain pounding against us, as the world fell away. A flash of lightning and a thunderclap cracked so close it jolted us apart.

"We should get inside. Wait – what happened with the show?" Jake asked.

"Oh my god." I started laughing. "I've got to get back. They were just about to announce the winners, and I left Jerry in charge of my career."

"Then let's go." Jake seized my hand, fingers laced as we splashed through puddles, drenched and laughing like teenagers. By the time we burst back into the gallery, we looked like we'd just barely survived a shipwreck.

There was a crowd gathered around a small riser at the far end of the room, where Jerry stood between Rowan and the gallery curator. He gripped the microphone like it was a hostage, and awkwardly held an envelope and a bouquet of flowers in the other hand.

"Thank you," he began, shifting nervously. "I…love…art. Art is my favourite. Art is excellent." He cleared his throat. "Uh, I want to say thank you on behalf of Emma, whose photographs are incredible. They make you look at the world and think, 'wow, I've sure missed a lot of details.' Like that time I misread the expiry date on my milk, and–"

"Jerry!" I called out, giggling as I made my way to the riser, among some laughter from the crowd.

"Oh, thank god," he muttered as he hopped off and handed me the microphone, envelope and flowers, before slinking back into the crowd.

"Thank you, everyone. I'm truly honoured. I'd like to thank the gallery for hosting this incredible show, the judges for their time and consideration, Teo Castillo for the wonderful opportunity, and my friends and family for all their support."

I handed the microphone back to the curator, who wrapped up the evening, thanked everyone for attending, and reminded the crowd to tell their friends that there were two more days left in the exhibit. But my eyes were on Jake, standing with my favourite people, beaming back at me. My heart was impossibly full.

I hopped off the riser and headed straight to them. Jake pulled me flush against his body, his hands cupping my face.

"You're amazing," he said, before kissing me thoroughly.

Mel cleared her throat, grinning. "There are children present, people."

I turned and leaned back against Jake's chest, his arms wrapping around me, right where I belonged.

"Who wants to hit the Trinity to celebrate Emma's win?" Lauren asked.

"I'm in. It's karaoke night," Jerry said.

"Melanie?" Ryan asked, a mischievous glint in his eye. "I've been working on a routine to 'Pony' that I would appreciate your feedback on."

Mel laughed. "Only if the shirt comes off," she said, grinning.

"You two probably want to get out of those wet clothes," Lauren smirked, her eyes darting between Jake and me.

"Raincheck for us," he nodded. "We need a good night's sleep since we have to be up early to head to Waterloo."

"Well, great job with the show, Em." Mel pulled me in for a wet hug and kissed me on the cheek. "I am so proud of you."

We said goodbye to our friends, then Jake led me through the gallery door. We stepped outside, and he tilted his head toward the sky.

"Looks like the rain finally stopped. Perfect timing." He shook his head with a laugh.

The streets gleamed under the golden streetlights, stretching and shrinking our shadows as we walked. The last four days without him had stretched on forever, but now they were a fading memory.

I leaned into him and groaned. "Ugh…my feet are killing me in these shoes."

Jake bent down and hoisted me over his shoulder, making me squeal with laughter. I reached down to pinch his ass.

"Hands off, Anderson! Can't you wait until we get home?"

He carried me through the slick streets on the short walk to his place, the world around us blurred and beautiful in the reflections on the wet pavement.

"Home," I said, with a deep breath. "I like the sound of that."

## Epilogue
## Four months later

# Lucky to be Alive

The Trinity in late December was bustling and filled with people excited for the holidays. Christmas pop music poured through the speakers, and long strings of brightly coloured lights and lanterns were strung up around the bar. An overdone Christmas tree welcomed customers at the door. Hanukkah and Kwanzaa decorations covered the walls and any available surface. It was like Party City's winter holiday section had thrown up after a long, drunken night at The Six. It was fantastic, and there was no place I'd rather be.

I lip-synced to Mariah as I danced in front of Jake's chair at the Trinity. He shook his head at me as I nodded to him, preparing him for his cue. As Mariah belted out her last line, I wailed into my finger microphone.

"Make my wish come true…All I want for Christmas is you… Baby!" I pointed to Jake as Justin Bieber's verse kicked in, but he pinched his lips shut tight and shook his head again. I stuck out my bottom lip and gave him my best angry eyebrows as he threw his head back and laughed.

"Nope. My Bieber days are done. I couldn't handle the fame." He smiled as he grabbed my hand and tugged me down to sit sideways on his lap. He reached for my jaw and turned my head to kiss me, threading his hands in the hair behind my ear and holding me still.

Since we were in public and sitting at a table with our friends, I drew back and wrapped my arm over his shoulders. He breathed softly and nipped my neck. We'd been together for a few months now and still could not get enough of each other. I squeezed Jake's shoulder and kissed him, then slid into my own chair.

Mel, the last of the six of us to arrive, burst through the door, a large silver gift bag stuffed with blue tissue paper in her hand. She shifted it behind her back as she weaved her way to our table, trying and failing o keep her Secret Santa a secret.

"Thank you for finally joining us, Melanie," Ryan said. "Stuck in traffic?" He grinned, knowing our apartment was a ten minute walk from here.

"Gridlock," Mel said, giving him a challenging look before she turned to me. "Thanks for the drink. Sorry I'm late." She stuffed her gift under the table with the others, wrapped her coat around her chair, and sat down. She lifted her gin and tonic to her lips and chugged the entire thing.

"Happy Holidays," Mel toasted, raising her empty glass and wiping her mouth with the back of her other hand. "No school for two weeks, thank god. I've had an Axe-body-spray-induced migraine for the past week."

We laughed and clinked our glasses together. I took a sip and let my hand fall to Jake's thigh, half-listening to my friends chat about their holiday plans. The truth was, the last few months had been the best of my life.

Professionally, things were taking off. My show at the Worth Gallery had been a huge success – I'd sold every photo, including the one that Jake had bought. His pothos were thriving under it, growing greener and more full by the day. Another local gallery had signed me to a year-long contract, replenishing as pieces sold. Jake and I had finished hanging my first six photos there this afternoon.

And then there was Panama. Winning the internship meant I'd spent a month working with Teo Castillo, shooting in the kind of light and landscape I used to only dream about: capturing street portraits in Casco Viejo, filled with vibrant colours and salsa rhythms; sneaking through the jungle trails near Gamboa, surrounded by the scent of wet earth and blooming flowers; and racing to catch sunsets along the Amador Causeway, golden light spilling across Isla Taboga's sandy shores. Every moment had challenged me, shaped my eye, and reminded me why I had chosen this path in the first place.

Everything was finally lining up.

I'd already told Mel about my plans to move in with Jake in the new year; we were excited to take the next step, not wanting to waste another minute apart. Mel was thrilled for me, but she was worried about finding a roommate that she didn't want to punch in the balls.

"Em?"

I blinked out of my thoughts and turned to face Lauren, who had apparently asked me a question and was looking expectantly at me.

"Sorry, what?"

"When are you moving to Jake's? I want your room. Can't beat that commute to work, and my current roommates are driving me crazy. They're so needy."

"You live with mom and dad," Ryan said, laughing.

"Exactly! I can't take it anymore. It was fine for a while when I first moved back here and needed to save money, but now that they're retired, all they do is plan activities for the three of us. We're going to see the new Avatar movie this weekend, and my mom made us matching T-shirts. I had to draw a line in the sand when she suggested blue face paint. Living with them makes me feel like I'm six years old again." Lauren pressed her hands together, her lips parted in a strained smile. "Please, Mel?"

"I'm in as long as you don't plan to take pictures of my feet while I sleep." Mel grinned. "Someone asked me to consent to that when they answered my ad."

"They're great feet," Jerry said through a laugh, as Ryan nodded in agreement. She shot them both a death glare.

I glanced at Jake, who had been ready for me to move in since the night of my art show. Most of my clothes were already there. There wasn't much left to move.

"You know where I stand," he said, weaving his fingers with mine. "Happy to move the rest tomorrow."

"I'll help," Jerry said, looking up at me, still smiling after replying to a text on his phone, then turning it face down on the table. "I accept those candy-cane Oreo cookie balls you make as payment. But lots of them."

"The freezer is full of them for you." I reached into my purse for my keychain, unwound my apartment keys, and tossed them to Lauren. "Merry Christmas. And I'm not even your Secret Santa."

"Eeee!" she squealed. "Thank you! Slumber parties every night, and not with my mom!" She tossed the keys in her purse, then hopped up from her chair. "Next round's on me, and then we can do Secret Santa!" She bounced towards Anusha, who was wearing an elf hat and chatting with a couple of customers at the bar.

"Slumber parties every night, Mel. Sounds like a blast." Ryan flashed an innocent smile before tilting his beer to his lips.

Mel shook her head at him, still fighting that smile. "You're not invited." She held his gaze for a moment too long as she finished off her second gin and tonic.

Lauren and Anusha returned and set the drinks on the table. Jerry helped Anusha clear the empty glasses, then reached under our round table, where we'd shoved our gifts, and emerged with a square, flat package wrapped in red paper, tied with a thin brown burlap ribbon in a perfect bow.

"To Mel, love Santa," Jerry read, as he handed it to her.

As Mel slid the ribbon off and tore open the back of the package, her mouth dropped open and her cheeks flushed. She pressed the gift back under the paper, a laugh bubbling out as she stared daggers at Ryan.

"What?!" He panicked. "What did I do? I didn't have your name! I've been framed!"

Everyone clamored to see it, including Ryan, who lifted it out of her hands and finished tearing off the paper. A proud grin spread on his face as he realized it was the sexy firefighter calendar I had shot for his department. Ryan was featured in three months as one of the youngest, arguably the most attractive, and definitely the most willing participant.

Lauren snatched the calendar from him as he leaned back in his chair, hands clasped behind his head, a wide smile directed at Mel as if this was the greatest thing that had ever happened to him. Lauren flipped through, cringing at each of her brother's photos.

"God, Mel, if you hang this, I'll have to move back to my parents for February. And May…and July. Christ, Ry, do you ever wear a shirt?" Lauren rolled her eyes at her brother before flipping through the rest. "I'll come back for December, though. Dang, who's Mrs. Claus?"

She shut the calendar and fanned herself with it before passing it back to Mel, who finally noticed that I had also included a gift card to the Trinity, attached to the back.

"You." She turned to me, shaking her head, smiling. "Thank you, this is fantastic." She held the calendar open, bringing it closer to her face, murmuring, "It's so important to support the Humane Society…"

She looked up at Lauren. "Sorry, Lo, this is going in the kitchen."

"Since Melanie is preoccupied with her gift, I'll grab the next one." Ryan reached under the table and pulled out a small gift bag that read, "It's the most wonderful time for a beer" in cursive. He checked the tag and handed it to Jake.

Jake tugged out the tissue paper, and tucked within it was a baseball card in a thick plastic protective case. I tilted my head and squinted at it, trying to get a better look, before Jake pulled the tissue clean off and burst into laughter. He looked right at Jerry.

"Where did you get this? I've always wanted one! My brother is going to flip!" He held it up to Ryan, who broke out laughing too.

Jerry grinned. "Ebay – I've been keeping track of them since we talked about it. The most glorious error card of all time."

Jake handed me the card – Billy Ripkin, Second Base, Orioles, #7. I flipped it over. Fleer, card 616. "I don't get it," I said.

"Look," Jake said, still laughing as he pointed to the knob of the bat, where "FUCK FACE" was written.

"Yikes, how did that get printed?" I said, as I handed the card back to him.

"I don't know, but I'm glad it did. Thanks, Jer, that's the best." He cradled his new "FUCK FACE" card adoringly. I snickered as I pictured him rocking the card to sleep and placing it gently in a bassinet once it was ready to rest for the night.

I reached under the table for the next gift and pulled out a rectangular box wrapped in gold paper, a sparkly green bow fastened to the top. "To Lauren," I read.

She wiggled in her seat, peeled off the paper, then opened the box. Her eyes widened as she lifted a spiral-bound booklet from the box, turning it to show us an original script from the movie Titanic, autographed by the entire cast. She ran her hands over the plastic protective cover in awe and flipped through a few pages.

"This is unreal!" She carefully placed it on the table in front of her before pulling a T-shirt out of the box. The design showed a proud orange cat "Titanic-ing" a softer-looking grey one at the bow of the ship – chin tipped to the stars, eyes closed, the "Heart of the Ocean" glittering at its neck. She threw her head back in laughter and tugged it on.

"Best big brother ever," she said, hugging Ryan. "Next!" She pulled out the gift bag Mel had brought and handed it to him.

Ryan yanked the tissue from the bag and dropped it on the table, before peering inside. He threw his head back and belly-laughed.

"This might be the greatest gift I have ever received." He pulled out a black throw pillow, then flipped it for us to see. There she was, in all her glory: Celine Dion, cloaked in Jesus' burnt sienna robes, her open hands raised, her long hair framing her anguished face. Ryan hugged it to his chest like a relic, thanking Mel, before realizing there was more in the bag. Out came a pair of pink crew socks, patterned with Celine's face in varying expressions, followed by a black crewneck plastered with a collage of Celines.

"Melanie, you spoil me," he said, standing to wrap her in a hug. He pressed a kiss to her cheek, murmuring a soft "thank you" against her ear. The hug lingered just a beat longer than you'd expect of friends.

I arched a brow at Jake, who shrugged, clearly as clueless as I was. Fine. I'd investigate later. If Mel and Ryan got together, it would be the second greatest thing that had ever happened to me.

"You're next, Jer," Mel said, handing him a meticulously wrapped package.

Jerry eased the wrapping off and slid a box into his hands. He lifted the lid, and his eyes widened.

"Holy shit, these are amazing!" He reached in and pulled out a set of four personalized wine corks and bottle openers, each featuring a three-dimensional replica of his head on top. Also in the box was a new travel bartender kit.

"This is so thoughtful." He looked at Lauren, who grinned and stood up to hug him.

"Well, selfishly, I knew I would get a couple of perfectly prepared drinks out of it."

"I love it, thanks, Lo." He tucked the set back in its travel bag and marvelled at his likeness on the corks and bottle openers before closing them back in the box.

"Last but never least, this one's for you, Em." He pulled out a large gift bag and handed it over to me.

I sat it on my lap and peeked inside. I ran my hands over the red and green fur and turned to Jake with a cackle.

"As if!" I said, setting the bag on the floor. I stood up and pulled out a large, fuzzy, Grinch onesie, his miserable face smirking on the green hood. I flipped it around to show my friends and held it up against my body, bending to kiss Jake.

"I love it, and I'll never take it off," I said, smiling down at him.

"If you don't, I will." He grinned. "There's more." He nodded toward the bag.

I sat back down, setting the onesie on his lap, and reached into the bag to find a large frame wrapped in silver tissue paper. I lifted it onto my lap and pulled the tissue off. My breath caught in my throat as I realized what it was. I stared at him, tears building in my eyes.

"You kept this?" I murmured, pulling the rest of the tissue off and holding it closer, inspecting every last centimeter.

He nodded.

"What is it?" Mel asked.

I turned around the frame, tears starting to fall, as I showed them the "Vote for Emma or she'll give you a concussion" poster. On it, my drawing of young Jake, who lay dazed on the gym floor, little blue birdies circling his head, as young me stood over him with bared teeth and a crazed look in my eyes.

"That's psychotic," Mel said, laughing as she reached for it. "Jake, buddy, how did you not run when you saw that? You're lucky to be alive!"

The rest of my friends laughed and winced as the framed poster made its way around the table. They lingered over the details – my wild grade-nine curls, the Spice Girls baby tee, the single tear tracking down cartoon Jake's cheek, and, best of all, one of my tiny fists clenched tight like I'd just knocked him out cold.

"She's not wrong," I said as I looped my arms around Jake's neck.

He grinned up at me and wiped the tears from my cheeks.

"No, she's not." He gave me two short kisses on the lips. "I'm very lucky."

"It's going in our living room, right? That's where I always envisioned it."

"Me too," he said softly, his gaze locking onto mine with tender affection. He slid his hand behind my ear, his thumb tracing over my bottom lip. Drawing me closer, he kissed me again, deeper this time.

Forever.

# Acknowledgements

A heartfelt thank you to the incredible team whose talent and dedication brought this project to life and delivered it into your hands. To Lisa Rivers, thank you for teaching us about story structure. Hopefully our next novel will be easier to edit! To Lisa Jager, who brought our characters to life through another beautiful, bold cover. We can't wait to see it on our bookshelves. To Heili Paluoja, thank you for your typesetting magic.

To our advance readers, Annie, Carla, Cheryle, Laura, Julia, and Sarah, thank you for your invaluable feedback, which helped us deepen and strengthen the final story. We hope you love it. A whole host of people gave us hilarious one-liners, name inspiration, and insight into photography, D&D, teenagers, the high school experience, and art therapy: Kristina Laukkanen, Karen Owens, Jack Torres, Brandon Driscoll, Krista Green, Carmela Graham, Erin Kuri, Aimee Denov, Elise Denov, and Hunter Graham, thank you for your time and input.

Thank you to all the places that inspired and welcomed us as we wrote this book. Kensington Market - we fell in love with you, despite the smell of cheese and pot. The Moonbean Café and Trinity Common, where we imagined Jake and Emma falling in love, thank you for your hospitality. We can't wait to visit again soon. The Air B&Bs in Cobourg, Ontario, where we escaped our families to focus on Jake and Emma's love story, and the apartment in Paris, France, where we wrote one sentence just to say that we worked on our novel in Paris. Creek Coffee & Co. in Highland Creek and Black Cat in Cobourg, your lattés gave us non-coffee drinkers shaky hands and writing super powers.

Our beautiful writing soundtrack was the backdrop for almost every writing session, and we couldn't have done it without inspiration from the following artists: Celine Dion, for being a national treasure; brilliant ginger Ed Sheeran; Beyoncé, for the perfect first dance song;

The Beaches, for the 2023 song of the summer; Far East Movement, for "Like a G6," the most inexplicably danceable song; LMFAO, for giving us "Party Rock Anthem," Teddy Swims and Benson Boone; and of course, the Spice Girls - one of the original inspirations for this book and Emma's friendship with Mel and Jerry (Geri).

Thank you to all of our family and friends for their support. So many of Emma's experiences were inspired by our own lives and our relationships with all of you. The Vacationers, the Booers, and the Garage Beasties were always willing to bounce ideas around. The Ladies of the Rouge shared, followed, and encouraged us.

We have the best kids in the world. Sorry we'll never let you read what we've spent the last two years working on! Thanks for your good-natured eye rolls whenever we said "Go away! We're working!" as we covered our laptop screens from your curious eyes. We love you.

For all the times we were asked, "How's the book going?" Well, we can finally say, it's finished! We hope you love it!

Love,

*Mia*

# About the Author

Mia Denson is the pen name of two friends and rom-com writing partners from Scarborough, Ontario, Canada. What started as a wine-fuelled joke has somehow, against all odds, become a real novel. They drink a lot of tea, eat a lot of snacks, and try to cut down the use of "eyes" in their manuscripts.

*You can find us at:*

Instagram: @miadensonwrites
TikTok: @mia.denson

Manufactured by Amazon.ca
Bolton, ON

54808587R00139